Captain Henry

2½ Insurrections, 2 Wars, 1¼ Centuries, and a Story of Love

A Trowbridge Vermont Novel

A Novel by
I. M. AIKEN

Historical Fiction
Literary Fiction

Published by Flare Books,
an imprint of Catalyst Press, El Paso, Texas

978-1-963511-70-3 paperback
978-1-963511-79-6 ebook
978-1-963511-80-2 audiobook

For further information, write info@catalystpress.org
In North America, this book is distributed by
Consortium Book Sales & Distribution, a division of Ingram.
Phone: 612/746-2600
cbsdinfo@ingramcontent.com
www.cbsd.com

In South Africa, Namibia, and Botswana,
this book is distributed by Protea Distribution.
For information, email orders@proteadistribution.co.za.

LCCN number: 2026942322

CAPTAIN HENRY

HENRY McDONALD

Deputy Sheriff.

Captain Henry

2½ Insurrections, 2 Wars, 1¼ Centuries, and a Story of Love

A Trowbridge Vermont Novel

A Novel by
I. M. AIKEN

Historical Fiction
Literary Fiction

AUTHOR'S NOTE

This novel blends historical events and real people with a story. Captain Henry McDonald was an actual guy and my ancestor. The obituary and several of the military documents are factual and can be recalled from government archives, which is where I found them. Much of the narrative follows my experience researching Henry, therefore many of the citations within the text are also well-founded. But I have no interest in writing an academic or nonfiction version of this story. Too many gaping holes in the service of my Henry in 1871. I provide Captain McDonald's obituary in full. The language is archaic. The entry is very, very, very long. And like a long movie, it also has a credits section (everyone loves seeing their name in the paper). As the author, I feel strongly that the entire obituary belongs in this book. It foreshadows the story. There are also lies in the obituary which the narrative refutes. That said, it is dense and filled with names and dates, some of which do not relate to the novel. I give you, my reader, permission to skim. But I urge you to read it again after the novel.

Captain McDonald's grave remains one of the largest in the Springfield, Massachusetts Catholic cemetery. The city made a bronze plaque to my ancestor and hung in it the city armory, which was built under his command. Sadly, the city then melted that bronze to make weapons during WWI or WWII. A photo of this plaque is presented in the novel.

A significant portion of *Captain Henry* incorporates my own journals and experiences from Iraq. I was in Iraq from December 2005 through November 2006, primarily in metro-Baghdad, although I traveled extensively for our missions. I maintained a journal during this period. Each month, I'd edit them and send them to a small group of family and friends. You'll find references to "*The New York Times* rule" within the novel. This was the rule I used when I wrote and sent my journals; I would only write information that I could verify with *The New York Times* (or another reputable news outlet). The corollary to this rule is that anything I wrote could be published in *The New York Times* without violating federal law or my oath. These are the same rules that our Sam, one of our main characters, attempts to follow. As such, the Iraq chapters read analytically and within an historical context. This is because the energetic activities of my life—and of Sam's life—would have been classified and likely still are classified.

Many contemporary war novels vet the work with the Department of Defense or a related agency. I remained clear of "secrets" by writing strictly about Sam's thoughts as she communicates home.

DEDICATION

I am writing this dedication on the sixth of January 2022, one year after a violent insurrection at the United States Capital. Those in public service, including the military, swear to uphold the Constitution against all enemies, foreign and domestic. This novel is dedicated to all of those who have taken, then upheld, this oath.

- Brian D. Sicknick, Capitol Police
- F Jeffery Smith, Metropolitan Police
- F Howard S Liebengood, Capitol Police
- F Gunther Hashida, Metropolitan Police
- F Kyle DeFreytag, Metropolitan Police

The insurrectionists wounded about one hundred and fifty police officers on that January day, fourteen days prior to the inauguration of the next president.

Also, I'd like to honor Elizabeth C. MacDonough. She has been serving our nation as the Senate's parliamentarian since 2012. I carry a mental picture of this woman wearing the white-and-black striped jersey of a referee. From her office, she makes difficult calls about the rules that govern our Senate. On that day, Elizabeth's office was ransacked, and her personal phone and possessions were stolen.

I do not know Elizabeth personally, but we share community and lifelong friends. She and her staff represent the important legacy of our established rules of law and order, and the value of nonpartisan judgment. Like the Capitol police and hundreds of others working in that building, they continue to honor their oath. They serve us without political affiliation whilst striving to ignore personal bias. Their work embodies the best of what we want from Americans and those who defend our Constitution.

Bronze plaque that once hung in the Springfield City Armory

1 | William Tecumseh Sherman McDonald

BRIGHID, DECEMBER 2005

I did it. What it is I did hasn't come clear—yet.

I spent time in Killeen, Texas, at a hotel outside the Army post. I took one room. Sam had a separate room on the same floor. And for two weeks prior to her official deployment to Baghdad—alongside 19,999 other soldiers in the U.S. Army's Fourth Infantry Division—she shuffled between the post and the hotel. Me, I shuffled around the hotel and the shopping mall across the street. Please don't think I spent my time inside the mall. No, I walked the pavement of the parking lot. Each predawn, Sam got up to do physical training. I walked the perimeter of the mall. We then met at the hotel for their buffet breakfast.

One hundred percent of the people there were linked with the Iraq deployment. The line for eggs included a dozen uniformed personnel casually stepping forward. There were other civilians at the hotel. Some wore their civilian-ness uncomfortably like an ill-fitting suit, brown t-shirt over light-colored trousers that looked just like an Army uniform but plain. Same make, same pockets, different color. Not very civilian-y. Likely not really civilians, I came to think. They were not the secret lovers of young soldiers. Though I was not the only lover secreted at this off-post hotel—there was another marine lieutenant staying there, too, a female officer with a female guest. We made eye contact a few times.

Nobody asked. Nobody stared. Folks left us to eat our breakfast alone. You know the mantra, "Don't ask...blah, blah." Silence is the same as not asking, isn't it?

What I did was move into Sam's empty house in Trowbridge, Vermont. I'd visited her there and such. In my mind's eye, I had the place looking like an English Victorian manse, neatly draped with white linens over the furniture and shades drawn tightly against the sun. When I let myself in, the truth followed. The home looked homey, with sunshine and eclectic furniture spanning at least a century and a half. It had been home to the same family for longer than that. There were photos, some black-and-white with scalloped edges, some the bright colors of the post-World War color snaps. There is one official picture of Sam graduating from boot camp.

I am a noob.

I am the not-a-wife of an American soldier.

I am a foreigner in a tiny town in Southern Vermont that looks at foreigners as, well, foreigners. Strangers.

I asked myself, Do I belong here? I am underemployed and clinging to the edge of a map, living in a house that still hosts Sam's Aunts' stuff. They've been dead since our university days.

There is a long-standing argument about who qualifies as a Vermonter. To many, being born in Vermont is not sufficient. Moving here and living most of a lifetime doesn't qualify, either. It is a funny sentiment in a tiny state with a tiny, aging population. To those people sporting the bumper sticker "Keep Vermont for Vermonters," you need to be squeezed out from a mommy and daddy who has each been born in the state. According to these folks, becoming a Vermonter requires heritage and lineage of Vermonters begetting Vermonters.

I don't think I am a Vermonter. My Sam is regarded as an outsider even though her family settled here after the American Revolution and built this house during the War of 1812, or something.

But I think those bumper stickers are the sort of nonsense that masks bigotry of all sorts.

Time to ask the question, isn't it? No, not that one; she does love me. I don't even need to pick petals from a June daisy. Check! The question is, where are my people in this story? In my story?

Thus, I am sitting in a small wooden room in Springfield, Massachusetts, an easy drive from Sam's house. I am flipping through paper index cards reporting vital statics. The name "William Tecumseh Sherman McDonald" stands out. First, it is the longest name that I have yet seen in the City of Springfield records. Second, who would name a child "William Tecumseh Sherman" anything? Behind this name hides a very American story. Third, the little index card shows that William Tecumseh Sherman McDonald lived for four months and sixteen days. Born on the sixth of August 1892, dead on the twenty-second of December 1892.

McDonald? You want to tell me that my name is Brighid Doran. That's true, it is, but only because I kept my mother's name. McDonald? That's my father's family.

The typed index cards provide me references to handwritten vital statistics books on the shelves around me. I lift down the birth registry. I find the baby boy on page 695.

Have you smelled old style card catalogues recently? And the smell of old books on old shelves? The wood used is quarter-sawn oak. It is a right and proper smell. It is the smell of research.

On Page 695, I see that the clerk wrote his entire name, "William Tecumseh Sherman McDonald," in the small rectangular space. His neighbors on the page are Caroline Ryan Green and Helen Clare Gardner. "William Tecumseh Sherman McDonald" is the longest name on the page, thus is written in the smallest letters.

Eugene Napoleon Boueguet earned second place for both length of name and historical gravitas. Placing Napoleon in a name implies expectations that no infant should really face and a character no child should try to embody as they grow through the American school system.

Adelaide Louise Whitehouse and Maria Anna La DeForge came close in length.

One "Prince" had been born in Springfield on the twenty- seventh of August; little Howard Prince Grover.

The fifth column of the register reads: sex & condition. Number 909 and number 910 in the book are recorded as "M Twin" and "F Twin."

Number 924 had no last name. The clerk left a careful space on the left of "Daniele," as in "Daniele no-last-name." Then under sex and condition, it read: "F Illegitimate."

Page 695 of the registry of births, which started with 901 and ended with 945, recorded three illegitimate births and one pair of twins.

The death registry for that same year recorded William on page 633. He sat on the top line of the page. He was the 1,924th person to die in the year 1892 in Springfield, Massachusetts. Date of death read as "Dec. 22." In the column titled "Name and Surname of Deceased," the clerk wrote an abbreviated form of the infant's name with "William T. S. McDonald." He died of "respiratory paralysis."

There is so much for the modern eye to see about our culture a century ago. In the name column, it reads: "In case of wife or widow, maiden name and name and surname of husband." In these records, women belonged to fathers (if legitimate), then to husbands. If born out of wedlock, her papers are stamped "illegitimate." In the next column, the title is: sex. Then, in parentheses, the instructions read: "and color if other than white." William T. S. McDonald had been recorded as male, single, and aged four months and sixteen days. Furthermore, there was no tick mark in the column labeled "and color if other than white." He was born in Springfield to Henry McDonald and Catherine A. Burke, his mother's maiden name catalogued as per the registry's instructions. Henry had been born in New York City and Catherine in Enfield, Connecticut.

Catherine. Who was she? What did Henry call her when they stood together in the kitchen? Cathy? Katie?

Imagine the pain of losing a child at the age of four months. Born after nine months of hope, of anticipation, another four months of care, then gut-screaming heartache for Henry and Catherine as they watched their baby boy slip away from them. She carried him. He named him. A young woman, from an Irish family, would have stuck with the favorites of the day: Daniel, Patrick, Francis, or John. Maybe she asked for her boy to be named Francis Xavier McDonald. Little Frank, loved by his mother, baptized by the parish priest. Instead, her baby boy was named William Tecumseh Sherman McDonald. In my imagination, Katie called her son Billy. Katie held Billy as he struggled through his last breaths. Maybe she tried to help with steam and mint. Maybe Henry McDonald ran down a Springfield street for a doctor to save his boy. Maybe the boy had been sick for days, or weeks, or maybe he had troubles since birth? Details without data.

Billy's biography exists only on typed index cards and on two pages of a municipal registry of vital statistics.

Of course, his name, once lost, has been rediscovered by me.

Who names their baby William Tecumseh Sherman McDonald? In August of 1892, Henry McDonald made that decision.

The original William Tecumseh Sherman laid a path of scorched earth as an Army general during the American Civil War. He captured Atlanta, then burned his way through Georgia and the Carolinas. He set plantations ablaze and destroyed food, barns, warehouses, wagons, and train depots. He destroyed the support that the Confederate States required to continue fighting their war against the national government and the northern states. After the war, William Tecumseh Sherman served as the commanding general of the United States Army.

He died in February of 1891. In 1892, Henry McDonald memorialized and honored the controversial general with the birth of a son. Henry's hand gently supported Katie's shoulders while both parents adored their new son, swaddled in soft cloth and warm wool. You, my child, shall be named for an Indian Chief and a Civil War General by my great-great-grandfather.

"And a son shall be delivered unto them, and he shall be named..."

William Tecumseh Sherman represents only part of Henry and Catherine's decision, given their son was also named after Tecumseh. Shawnee Chief Tecumseh campaigned against the United States Government. He promoted unification of the native peoples in North America. Chief Tecumseh died during the War of 1812, allied with our enemies, the United Kingdom, in a brief war against the United States.

Eight years after Chief Tecumseh's death, Mister and Mrs. Sherman of Lancaster, Ohio named their infant boy Tecumseh Sherman. The local priest nixed the idea of baptizing a child with such an unholy and pagan name. Instead, the boy got slapped with a new first name, William. Why William? It was Saint William's day that day, and the boy needed a proper Christian name.

General Sherman's legacy remains contradictory. Following the

Civil War, the general waged war against the descendants of Tecumseh and nearly all other native peoples. General Sherman occasionally sympathized with southern white racial opinions, yet was seen as a liberator and as second Moses for enslaved peoples. General Sherman conquered lands and people. Hated by millions; revered by millions.

A year after General Sherman's death, and eighty years after Chief Tecumseh's death, an infant boy lived for a few months carrying the names of two warriors: a Native American warrior and a U.S. Army warrior. A child born in the final decade of the 19th century had been expected to carry, in his name, his father's expectations. The name exemplifies the U.S. government's contradictory history with—and belligerence toward—the native peoples of North America.

One long, four-barreled name echoes four centuries of colonization, exploitation, and warfare in North America. A heavy burden for a baby struggling to breathe.

Like looking through a glass-bottomed boat over a reef or through the Hubble telescope into deep space—I may have just discovered the other reason I moved to New England. I sit with stacks of municipal records informing me that for four and one-half months, I had a great-uncle named William Tecumseh Sherman McDonald. He lived here in Springfield, Massachusetts. Springfield is ninety minutes from both sides of my unsettled life. It is ninety minutes from a several hundred-acre estate in Trowbridge, Vermont. It is also ninety minutes from a tiny, dark apartment near a sprawling set of business campuses dedicated to the computer and internet industry. Both of those locations remain empty until I walk through the door. Then I am alone.

Is this my relative? The last name and the city match. Who is my Henry?

Why do I feel homeless? I am at home surrounded by these oak bookshelves and oak paneling. I am at home on this stout oak chair at this firm oak table. I found something on these shelves that may be a part of me. I breathe in the air, feeling at home in these stacks, looking at ancestors.

Sarah Ann Musgrave, my Sam, dropped out of school after her

first year enlisted in the U.S. Army. She finished boot camp weeks before the terrorist attacks of September 11th, 2001. We met at university when I stepped into the road in front of her bicycle. I said, "Hello, my name is Brighid." Sam wore a helmet and a tweed blazer with suede patches on the elbows and classic Levi's. I never once thought of a woman in that sort of way, but I could not keep my eyes off Sam. I had to know who and what she was. We're all given such freedoms during university days. I smile, thinking, *Yes, I dated a woman at school.* That was supposed to have ended. She went to the Army. I continued with courses until graduating in 2002.

In 2005, as Sam prepared for a one-year tour to Iraq as a lieutenant in a military intelligence unit, I was in New England living in a crappy apartment near a crappy job. When she gave me keys to her house, I looked down at them and said, "Yes." Now I have no idea what I said yes to. I said yes because I hated San José and the job there. I said yes because I like Sam.

"Do you mind looking after my place while I'm gone?" she asked me, sitting in the Plaza Hotel in Killeen, Texas. I lived in California. Her place was in southern Vermont. We formed a very large triangle over the United States.

Do you mind looking after my place while I am gone? The sentence played over and over in my head. Sometimes, I wonder if she meant: *Do you mind looking after my place when I am gone?* What goes through a soldier's mind when preparing for an extended combat tour? Am I supposed to live in this house, stuck on a hilltop in a remote mountain town? Or am I supposed to check it monthly? Do I mow the lawn weekly? I failed to ask any follow-up questions.

So I moved. I trimmed a leg from the distance triangle, except Sam deployed to Iraq.

Now I sat in the Springfield City Hall researching paper documents related to the McDonald family. I have a hunch that this bunch of McDonalds are my McDonalds. If they are not, I should lay claim to them if no one else has. I think Henry and Catherine are amazing. I don't find many others of that name here. Today, one can find a McDonalds at millions of street corners where billions of hamburgers have been served. Those are not my McDonalds; that business was kicked into life by a fellow named Ray Kroc. To listen to my mother, our McDonalds were of the old clan days, running around in woolen plaid getting the snot kicked out of them by the English and other Scottish clans. My mother would say, "The McDonalds have lost more battles and been kicked out of more countries than most people, except the Jews."

Here in this city hall, I use paper and pen to take notes, unusual for me given I spend fifty plus hours a week on computers. The city provides scraps of recycled paper for notes by cutting copier paper into rough quarters. I write with my awkward loopy letters, "Records to Print," followed with instructions: "Births, Irving T. McDonald, 14 April 1894, page 103; William T. S. McDonald, 1892, page 49; Marriage, Henry McDonald, Katie A. Burke, August 27, 1884, page 74; Death, Katherine B. McDonald, December 7 1922, page 119; Henry McDonald, May 25, 1900, page 29."

On my own full-sized sheet of paper, I construct a diagram of this family. Henry and Katie lost two children in infancy. In the year before young Billie—William T.S.—Alice was born. She lived for one year, one month, and twelve days, dying of "membranous croup," another dreadful respiratory disease. Katie and Henry would have been helpless whilst listening to the last wheezing, labored breaths of Alice. Harry C. was born the year before Alice in 1889. Edna Rose two years prior. Charles B. was born in 1886, Irving T. in 1894. Katie and Henry had six children in nine years, and two died as infants.

Tragedy and mystery are different. Tragedy involves watching children die for the want of air. My family, every family, faced tragedy every generation: children lost too young, separation, forced migration, violence, and war. In exploring the mystery, I ask why.

Reading the death entry, then holding a new reprint of Henry's death certificate, I read that Henry had been a white male who died at the age of forty-five years and five days of an "atomic condition of the central nervous system superinducing cardiac paralysis." Henry served as the city marshal for Springfield. His father, Charles P. McDonald, and his mother, Sarah Madden, were born in Ireland.

My great-great-something was a city marshal in this same city where I found his records.

I open my laptop and search for Henry McDonald of Springfield, Massachusetts. Instead, I find a McDonalds restaurant on Main St. and a living Henry McDonald in Springfield, Ohio. I have to buy a subscription to a newspaper archive service to discover my Henry's obituary, published in *The Springfield Weekly Republican* on Friday, June 1, 1900.

MARSHAL M'DONALD FALLS DEAD
COMPLETE NERVOUS COLLAPSE
His active and Valuable Life in Military and Civic Duties

Major Henry McDonald, city marshal, died suddenly at 7:10 Friday morning at his home on Park Avenue, as a result of a complete nervous collapse. He had arisen at 6:45 and was apparently in his usual health. He stepped into the bathroom and returning a moment later was preparing to dress himself, when he fell to the floor. His wife and children were attracted by a groan, and rushing to his side found him lying on his face, apparently unconscious. He was turned over, but showed no signs of consciousness except in opening his eyes in response to an entreaty from Mrs. McDonald, and died three minutes after the arrival of Dr. E. C. Collins, who had been hastily summoned. An autopsy held in the afternoon showed that death was due to a complete nervous collapse, as every organ of the body was perfectly sound.

The death of Marshal McDonald removes from the midst of the city's activity a man who had long been identified with its interests, particularly in civic and military lines. As deputy sheriff for 10 years, and city marshal for over three years, he came in contact with the people in every walk of life and was called upon to exercise judgment and tact to an extent required only of servants and guardians of the public. He was a man of sterling character, tireless in his efforts to do his duty, and ambitious to make the police department of this city the cleanest and most efficient possible. That he had been successful is the testimony of everyone familiar with affairs as they exist today. From the time Major McDonald became marshal, January 1, 1897, until his death, he worked early and late to improve the facilities for preventing and discovering crime and to make the appearance of the force a credit to any city. His interest in his official duties is shown in the fact that although he was entitled to a vacation of two weeks with regular pay each year, he never took advantage of the privilege, and only left his post to join in the Cuban campaign with his company in the 2d Regiment. The marshal had a rather brusque manner, and his inclination to be uncommunicative with strangers kept many people from knowing him intimately, but to gain his confidence meant a pleasant surprise. It was then found that he was a man of entertaining ways, sympathetic and cordial in act and word, and unchanging in his views of honesty and sobriety. He did much to lighten the burdens of those employed under his supervision, and the same sympathy was quickly shown to those who came to him in trouble.

Major McDonald's methods have borne fruit in many improvements that have been introduced in the police department. Being a military man, he natural sought to inspire something of that spirit in his officers. They have been required to march properly, to be punctual and courteous in the performance of duty, and orderly and neat in appearance. Rules have been laid down covering service when on duty and the method of ringing in reports from different points of the beats has been changed and improved. The marshal was not slow in accepting the opportunity to give the officers gymnastic training at the Young Men's Christian Association building, and the regular work now done there is keeping the men in excellent training. It is scarcely realized by those who see the results of these improvements, that such matters have been the subject of continual consideration by the marshal. It was no uncommon thing for him to spend many sleepless hours in bed or walking the floor of his room thinking over the work of the department or some vexing problem that had arisen during the day.

The military experience of Major McDonald can hardly be considered apart from his activity in public life, for the former began with his boyhood and continued actively until about a year ago. His first experience was in the navy, where he was influenced by the work of brave men, and where he served on the Hartford, at one time Admiral Farragut's flagship. This was followed by five years' service in the regular army. He was first stationed in the South during the reconstruction days and was frequently called into service to aid in quelling disturbances. He was also in service in the West and had heard the dreaded Indian yell. In this city, he was identified with Company B of the 2d Regiment and did more than anyone else to bring that company to the standard of efficiency which made it the envy of other organizations. He made application for retirement in 1897, but Colonel Clark refused to endorse it, on the ground of the captain's efficiency and that his continuance was necessary for the welfare of the regiment. Had Major McDonald retired at that time, it is possible he might still be alive. He went with his company into the war in Cuba. The great battle of El Caney had been fought, Company B had distinguished itself, and the troops were waiting outside Santiago. When danger was practically passed, Major McDonald, then captain, sustained permanent injuries as the result of a fall in the slippery mud about the camp ground. Thus after a long service, filled with every conceivable danger, the brave man was cut off from further service with his company by a mere accident. The company commander had shown especial bravery in the battle of El Caney. His company with Company K were joined with the 22nd Infantry of regulars and were submitted to a galling fire. Captain Warriner of Company K was shot and carried to the rear, leaving both companies under the care of Captain McDonald. He was on the alert of their interests, and frequently exposed himself to give men directions and to warn them to keep under cover wherever possible. This heartfelt interest in his men that made the captain forget himself in time of danger, showed itself in the organization and efficiency of his company. He made the men take the same interest and pride in their organization. They came to feel it a duty to be at drill, and to fail to qualify as a marksman was a disgrace. Company B was the first company to qualify every man as a marksman and the rifle team won the world's record at 200 yards in 1899.

Road racing on bicycles was introduced by the company in the early '90's and Major McDonald was proud of the results obtained. His work in the militia was based on experience, and he made it count. The men respect him and those who came in contact with his personality loved him. The rough manner really attracted many of the militiamen. It was greatly regretted when he left the company and regiment in July of last year. He had been in the militia 23 years, and his absence from the regular Monday night drill made a vacancy which was deeply felt.

Major McDonald's home life was peculiarly pleasing. His home was, as he often termed it, "a haven of rest." It was there that he endeavored to throw off the perplexities of daily work and entered into the life of his family. There are four children in the family. The oldest a boy of fourteen, and the youngest a boy of six years, and the father was always ready to discuss with friends the differences in the children's traits and comment on how they might grow up. Since his return from the Cuban campaign he had found it necessary to remain at home more than usual, and the care given him during his illness occupied much of Mrs. McDonald's attention. He was always uncomplaining, and even in his home refrained from mentioning his ill-health. Mrs. McDonald had feared that he might succumb to one of his nervous attacks, and continually urged him to consult a physician. Last Sunday evening he walked home from the police station and on entering the house sank into a chair exhausted. After a short rest, he went to his room, retiring at an unusually early hour. He had been very nervous since his injury in Cuba. For a time after his return, there was no feeling in his legs. This was gradually restored but his nervous system was completely shattered. He was disturbed by the rattling of a window-shade, the dripping of water from a faucet, or even the noise of the wind outside of the house. He would make little comment at such times, however, endeavoring to remain quiet. When this was no longer possible, he would pace the floor. The family was prostrated by the sudden death. He leaves, besides the widow and children, his mother and two sisters, Mrs. George Davis, and Mrs. John J. Crowley, all of this city.

Major McDonald was born in New York city in 1852 and was therefore 48 years old. In 1865, he began a period of severe schooling on the naval training ship St. Mary's, and was later transferred to the Hartford, famous as Admiral Farragut's flagship. He sailed in the South Atlantic squadron on this ship, and after a brief experience returned to New York city. After a year and 11 months respite, he enlisted in the 2d United States infantry, then in the South. During the next five years he went through all of the phases of the period of reconstruction and traveled through 38 states and territories. At times state affairs were a jumbled mess, and he frequently saw two or three governors contending for the same seat. The Ku-Klux clans, moonshiners, and other features of the period gave him ample entertainment as a soldier. These experiences and his life as one of the guards for surveyors on the Union Pacific railroad, made the basis for his future success in the state militia. He was a fine disciplinarian, brave, resolute, and orderly in everything, and as a result left the army with a fine record. He was discharged with the rank of sergeant October 23, 1874, and began life in this city as a mechanic at Smith & Wesson's. He was employed later in the United States armory, being in both institutions about seven years. He was later employed for five years with the Bullard arms company and was appointed deputy sheriff by Simon Brooks January 1, 1887. During this time, he was court crier. He was appointed marshal by Mayor Dickinson January 1, 1897, reappointed in 1898, and continued by Mayors Gilmore and Hayes.

Major McDonald joined Company B of the 2d Regiment in the fall of 1876. George Holbrook was then captain, F. G. Southmayd first lieutenant, and James A. Turnbull, second lieutenant. He was passed to the rank of first sergeant without holding the intervening offices, and was chosen first lieutenant April 2, 1877. In 1882, in company with all other commissioned officers, he made application for retirement, but was re-elected in May of that year, holding the office until Captain Southmayd was elected major in February, 1889, when he chosen captain. He continued in this capacity until July, 1899 when he was retired, at his own request, with the rank of Major. Major McDonald was an excellent marksman, and took part with the regimental team in contests at Walnut Hill and Creedmoor.

Major McDonald's death was caused by what is known to physicians as an atomic condition of the central nervous system superinducing cardiacal paralysis. The autopsy yesterday afternoon was conducted by Dr. Herbert Emerson, in the presence of Drs. T. F. Breck, D. J. Brown, Philip Kilroy, and E. C. Collins. It was found that lungs, brain, heart, in fact all organs of the body were in perfect condition. The injury which Major McDonald sustained by his fall in the Cuban camp resulted in spinal hemorrhage, followed by paralysis of the lower extremities. He recovered from this paralysis, but there was a lack of tone in the nervous system. It is frequently the case that when injuries to the spine are sustained the sufferer apparently recovers but the nervous system undergoes a change, which can only be discovered with a microscope, but which later causes death.

The funeral of Major McDonald will be held tomorrow afternoon and will probably be one of the most largely attended of any held here in some years. A brief service will be held at the home on Park Avenue at 2, followed by services at the

Cathedral at 2:45. Companies B, K, and G of the 2d Regiment will assemble at the state armory at 1, and Company H of the naval brigade will assemble at 12:15 and, headed by the 2d Regimental Band, will march to the home. The present members of the headquarters staff and those who have served on the staff in past years will also attend the funeral in a body. The entire police department will attend in a body, and the arrangements for their gathering are being made by Assistant Marshal Wright and Captain Boecklin. The patrolmen will also wear crepe upon their uniforms for 30 days in honor of the dead marshal. The mayor and representatives of the city government will hold an informal meeting in City hall this evening to perfect arrangements for attending the funeral. The mayor will this morning send requests to all members of the city government to attend the funeral, and carriages will be furnished. The police department committee will probably introduce resolutions respecting the death of the marshal for adoption at the city government meeting Monday evening. The board of directors of the veteran fireman's association, the only organization outside the militia to which Major McDonald belonged, arranged last evening for the attendance in a body of the association at the funeral of Marshal McDonald tomorrow afternoon. The men will march in citizens' clothes.

The active bearers for the funeral will be the following members and veterans from Company B: Sergeant Robert D. Draper, Corporal Henry P. Roberts, Corporal Michael F. Kelleher, Privates Edwin W. Wright, John Bryson, and John F. Hurley. The firing squad, also from Company B, will be in charge of Lieutenant J. J. O'Connell and is as follows: First Sergeant F. A. Wakefield, Sergeant H. C. Wakefield, Corporal Henry P. Roberts, Corporal M. P. Ryan, Privates Morris Grinowetz, Eugene E. Grenier, John A. Hamburg, A. W. Waters, Robert E. Oliver, E. R Burger, B. J. F. Berggren, Star Folsom, F. W. Knox, A. J. Weeks, T. W. House, Henry Pannier, E. A. Robertson, and E. Shakleton. The burial will be in Saint Michael's cemetery. Mayor Hayes sent the following communication to Assistant Marshal C. M. Wright yesterday morning: –

Until further ordered, you will perform all the duties of city marshal in accordance with the ordinances and laws pertaining to the office in place of Major Henry McDonald, city marshal, deceased.

Estimate of Marshal McDonald

Given by one of his close friends—His Manly and courageous character.

A prominent citizen, who was very close to Marshal McDonald, gives the following estimate of him: Major McDonald was a generous, open, manly man, sincere in what he thought and did, sincere in his friendships, sincere in the performance of every duty. It is not what we believe, so much as the force and intensity with which we believe, that affects our character, and it was the intensity and force of his belief in the performance of duty, and his courageous doing of it, that made him what he was, a strong and determined man. Such men always make enemies, but they make friends as well, friends of right and truth, friends who are real friends, who admire the brave and courageous, in peace as well in war, and Henry McDonald was a brave man, on the field of battle, equally brave in striving to rid this city of vice, and make it a clean city. He was often misunderstood, but the ones who misunderstood him were superficial observers. Those who knew him, knew him to be without fear and always to be depended upon. It is true that Captain McDonald was exacting in demanding full performance of duty from his men, but he set the example in doing, and never asked of others what he was unwilling to do himself. Behind his commanding exterior there was a man of tender affections and wide sympathies, loyal to every cause he espoused, firm and lasting in friendship with little or no enmity, whose many quiet acts of kindness were little known, but will be long remembered.

The men under him, in his company and on the police force, all knew that in their captain and chief they had a true friend who was prompt in his appreciation and steadfast in demanding for them full recognition of their services.

Marshal McDonald had unusual opportunities for observing men. In the fire department, in the militia, in the army and navy, he was thrown in contact with them under varying circumstances and he profited by his experience. He had a keen insight of their motives and it may be truly said that he knew men and he was rarely mistaken in his estimate of them. He disliked display, hated sham, and had a supreme contempt for the military or civic coward. In the war with Spain no one ever questioned his bravery, and the soldiers under him to a man were loud in their praise of his leadership and courage, but especially of his untiring zeal for their comfort and his insistence upon their rights as his first duty. He was wont to say, "The first care of a captain is to see to the comfort of his men." His men knew that he felt they were in his charge and keeping, and so far as he could, he would protect them. On his return from the war he calmly took up the duties of his office and with the greatest patience, without complaint, bore the pains of a fatal ailment that finally brought him to his death.

As city marshal, it was his constant effort to make the police force a company to be proud of, to have it composed of men, brave, honest, and diligent, who realized the responsibilities entrusted to them, and in return, therefore, should render full value by constant and determined vigilance. He succeeded as far as existing conditions allowed, and he achieved marked results in the appearance and faithfulness of the men; but he was not satisfied and was still working for better things, and the best officers were his best friends, and the lazy and worthless his sharpest critics. He was ambitious to make Springfield a model city so far as police protection could make it such: he believed that it was not enough to make property safe by ridding it of the thief and burglar, but that he had a higher duty to perform to rid it of the den and joint: to remove the snares of unchastity, to drive every vestige of indecency from the town and make this city a model moral city. This was no easy task, but he undertook it, knowing well the consequences and criticisms of the uninformed and unthinking. It will be a long while before his place is filled, and a man be found who will sacrifice himself in the discharge of an honorable but thankless duty. Marshal McDonald was a loyal friend, a brave soldier, a good citizen, an untiring, faithful public servant.

Having read and re-read the longest obituary I have ever seen, I can still barely wrap my head around the various jobs and honorifics given to Henry McDonald. He had been educated by the navy, enlisted in the Army immediately after the Civil War, and served in the Massachusetts Militia, the forerunner to the National Guard. He had held every rank from private to major. He served the community as a cop and a firefighter. This is the man who named his child William Tecumseh Sherman McDonald.

Eight years after the death of his infant boy, Sergeant-Captain-Major-Marshal Henry McDonald died of an injury sustained during the Spanish American War. This obituary was published during the summer of 1900. Teddy Roosevelt served as the 26th president the year following, from September 1901 until March 1909. Prior to his presidency, the people of Massachusetts told of their own Second Regiment at the Battle of San Juan Hill, a battle better remembered for Teddy Roosevelt and the Rough Riders.

The *Wikipedia* page tells me that on the first of July 1898, a combined force of 15,000 American troops—including all four of the Army's "Colored" Buffalo soldiers, Roosevelt and his "Rough Riders," the 71st New York, the 2nd Massachusetts Infantry, and the 1st North Carolina—attacked nearly 1,300 entrenched Spaniards in a dangerous Civil War-style frontal assault at the Battle of El Caney and the Battle of San Juan Hill outside of Santiago, Cuba.

These battles on the island of Cuba resulted in the United States possessing a military base in Cuba named Guantánamo. A base, sometimes called Gitmo, now famous for housing enemy combatants and terrorists. Gitmo featured as a key plot thread in the movie *A Few Good Men*.

This is my Captain Henry. He thumped KKK-ers on the head, rode west in a blue Army uniform through the setting of every cowboy movie made, fought crime as a cop, stomped fires as a firefighter, and then walked into combat next to Buffalo soldiers and Rough Riders and Teddy Roosevelt. He peddled bicycles and shot straight.

Later, alone in Sam's bed, I write an email about Captain Henry to Lieutenant Sarah Ann Musgrave. I attach the obituary then hit send. But, of course, it's Trowbridge. I have no internet.

2 | Enroute

SAM'S JOURNAL, DECEMBER 2005

B:

Each of us peeked.

Unmarked white buses, curtains drawn closed over each window, with orders to not open the curtains. What did they expect? How do you not peek? Kuwait greeted us with the stink of burning petroleum, hot tarmac, and darkness.

At dawn, my nose rested on the nose print of the last soldier to take this ride. I folded myself over the folding tray table with my head on my hands, my nose against the glass, and the curtain mostly closed.

The desert expands to all of the horizons, once we broke free of the city lights. Just like last time, I saw the desert people. People who move through this terrain. A few camels. A few camels with people. A few goats. A few goats with people. People walking. People traveling in tiny, urban cars. One small white car with no people, abandoned to the desert.

Eventually, sand.

As a kid, I thought that the desert would look like Crane's Beach, north of Boston, with rolling dunes of luxurious sand and hillocks marked by coarse grasses that scribe circles around their territory. As a kid, Crane's Beach felt huge and foreign to my native hills of Vermont. Miles of yellow sand, bordered by water. Water, water, and then—in a perfect backdrop—the lush green of New England forests. That's not what a desert is! It took the U.S. Army to teach me that.

This is the real desert. No surf. No green tapestry hanging against the back wall. There is no back wall. No front wall. No side walls. Horizons. Or is it just one horizon spinning around, there just when you look? The veterans on this bus knew we vectored towards Camp Buehring, in the middle of this place that is devoid of landmarks. Camp Buehring: the Gateway to Iraq. They knew this path, this bus, this destination with the familiarity of a commuter.

I might have been here before. Who knows? My first time through here, these places didn't have American names. If they had local names, we didn't know those either. I was a junior NCO looking at a grid map devised by the U.S. Army. My memory identifies this place as 38R-QU-*blah-blah*.

My first time through involved heavy vehicles and the fears of any soldier looking at a new frontier. America had pointed the spear at the belly of Iraq. I held that spear and pushed it forward. That was then, when we moved north from 38R-QU-*blah-blah* to grid coordinates that started with 39R-PV, and eventually into 39R-MB, lovely Baghdad. I didn't know why I was there then. I still don't. CNN says we have a job to do.

Since that first tour, the United States built a human pipeline that transports warriors into and out of the region. The pipeline starts at parade grounds and gymnasiums on large U.S. posts. For me, Killeen, Texas and Fort Hood. We stood while our national and divisional colors got rolled into tubes for the gradual transfer of authority from Texas to Iraq. Twenty thousand soldiers will be part of this division, our division. Whomever you were before, you are now a member of the Fourth Infantry Division.

Each leader tried their best to echo the words of an ancient Saint Crispin's Day speech: "For he today that sheds his blood with me shall be my brother."

Our families watched. We said our loving goodbyes. Got our last hugs. Snuck in small gifts from WAGs, kids, parents. You came down for that.

With a performative flare, we stood at attention again, then disappeared down the road on an unmarked white bus. We'd gone to war. We had had our last kisses and canoodles. Where did that bus go? Around the corner to another gymnasium. There we laid on the wooden basketball court on our way to combat operations in Iraq for the year 2005-2006. No promises of "over by Christmas."

Plain white buses to plain white planes.

Plain white planes to plain white buses.

Plain white buses into a desert that looks familiar to me.

Now to plain white tents in Roman-neat rows.

Camp Buehring emerged out of the Kuwaiti desert two months after we declared victory. I think I was patrolling on that day. Which day? The day we were told "Mission Accomplished" or the day that Camp Buehring got its name. Both?

At three forty-five, I stood in line outside the communications tent for my first call home. My entire military intelligence company had been granted the same time slot. We're a pretty light company, with a few platoons and maybe one hundred soldiers. I thought about my email to you. Did you get it? Will you be waiting by the phone? What do we say to each other? What can we say to each other? Who will be listening?

While most people in my position can play by *The New York Times* rules, you and I have an extra layer of complexity. The rule has two parts. Part one: if you can read about it in the *Times*, then the information is public and you can discuss it. Part two: whatever you say or write must be okay to print on the cover of *The New York Times* or to report on *CNN*. Then there is you and me: "outed is out."

Forbidden topics include: location, activities, dates, mission, home, and love.

I can either call you from this tent at this horrible hour, or I can lay down in my sixty-man tent that is stuffed with seventy-five female soldiers.

You answered on the first ring. We halloo-ed at each other until we found a rhythm that worked over the crappy telephone system.

"Yes, I am well."

"Yes, I am safe."

"I am hot."

"I am eating."

"I am sleeping."

Mostly true, I think. I thought that with my commission, I would no longer live in barracks with snoring, farting, and masturbating girls. I'd live in *officer's country*. Well, let's admit that Camp Buehring was not prepared for a division that was thirty percent larger than normal. Oh, and has actual female soldiers who serve as privates, senior NCOs, company grade officers, and field grade officers. The lady-soldier tent appears to have been an afterthought for this poor Army, just like their decision to change uniform standards mid-war.

B, you carefully asked me about buying a satellite internet system. You don't need my permission. I was surprised that you moved into that big empty house in the middle of a nowhere forest. You packed your life and moved. That's an old joke, an insider's joke, isn't it?

What am I supposed to say to you? Please be my house sitter while I deploy to Iraq for a year. No. I must say: B, live your best life and we'll figure it out when I am home (and whole).

I asked you to describe the trail that goes west from the house. I asked about the barred owl that often visits through the winter. She hunts the fields that surround the house, mice scampering under the Vermont snow. Sometimes, she perches on a fence near the house.

We found a pleasurable rhythm that followed all of the rules. Then, commanding voices started yelling again. Just like in the D-Fac, the dining facility, they told us to move on.

"Time to wrap it up!"

"Time to say, 'I love you.' Two-minute warning. Two minutes."

"Give 'em a smooch from me. I love you, goodbye." Those were the words sung by the sergeants. They mocked and pushed us along their daily assembly line of lonely soldiers.

To you, I said: "One-Four-Three."

You replied: "Two."

I am thrilled that you also knew the story of the Minot's Ledge Light in Cohasset, Massachusetts. It flashes its pattern of 1-4-3. I and LOVE and YOU. Not great cryptography. I needed to hear you. You heard me and I heard you.

As mid-December approaches, I think of the Winter Solstice back home with the Aunts. Darkest and longest night of the calendar, up there north of the fortieth parallel. Not here in Kuwaitistan, where every day begins and ends at the same time, or so nearly so. From sunrise to sunset, the day length remains the same. The temperatures remain the same. The skies remain the same.

Two platoons—including my diminished platoon of fifteen—stood in formation to fly. To get our complement to fill the C-130 Hercules, command added random staff officers. Several of us had been on the same plain white buses and plain white planes. Now, fifty-five soldiers and officers stood ready to fly into Iraq. In this formation, we are pax again, being yelled at by sergeants who spend their days yelling at pax.

"Soldier, where is your rifle? Oh, sorry, padre. You're good." Military cleric don't carry weapons.

Yell first, understand later.

We were limited to our rucksacks, small pack, and weapons. We stood in the full dark of a hot desert night. Unlike traveling on the white buses and white planes, we were kitted out in our full battle-rattle. Our flak vests now included the heavy SAPI plates, ceramic inserts that weighed an additional two kilos. My flak vest was the dark woodland camo pattern. My helmet cover used the three-color desert camo of my first deployment. I wore my new green digital camo uniform. Nothing matched; my kit straddled multiple uniform "standards." Like the colorations of our uniforms, we carried a mixed bag of weapons. Some officers carried the full-length M-16 that first came to the Army with Vietnam. I held the shorter and more modern M-4 carbine.

Before the engines of the Herc came to their full roar, the Air Force sergeant yelled at all of us: "Buckle up. Keep it tight. If you need to vomit, do it in your own fucking helmet, then carry it with you. I am not fucking mopping your puke from my deck."

Often, when a sergeant does this, they look around and add, "Oh, sorry, padre," or beg the forgiveness of some colonel. To a seasoned sergeant, a young lieutenant has the same prestige level as a slick-sleeved private. Any captain in this scenario eats the same shit as every other pax. We're just pax, packed in as cargo to this sergeant's cargo hold. Until we land, he's the boss, regardless of his rank or ours.

"Grab your shit. Hold it tight."

The load master returned to his throne, strapping in with the multiple-point straps that pilots use.

CHAPTER 2

Over Baghdad, we dropped. Or, the plane dropped from below our asses. It dropped so quickly, I would have floated upward had it not been for the seatbelt cinched tight across my hips. We were each weightless, except for the belts tethering us. The plane had rolled to a forty-five-degree angle as we fell from the sky down to a runway at Baghdad International Airport. It hit the runway at full speed, then decelerated such that we all tumbled forward, leaning on the person next to us.

As instructed, all of my gear had been strapped or tied to me. My helmet straps snugged under my chin. My flak vest cinched. My small pack clipped to my vest with a carabiner. I had placed my legs through the shoulder straps of my pack.

The tail started opening. The color of dark changed. The loading ramp got held horizontal and we turned. Spun? It was then that the load master stood.

"Unbuckle. Check your shit. Stand when I tell you."

We were still moving. This is the point when civilian flight attendants grab their mics to tell people to remain seated with their seatbelts fastened.

"Rucks on. Helmets tights. Form two lines." The sergeant walked aft and looked at the still-moving ground. The tail ramp dropped a few more degrees. We could barely hear the load master for the roar of the engines.

"Welcome to Baghdad International Airport, we sincerely don't give a fuck if you enjoyed flying with us tonight. Stand up, rucks on. Face aft—face the rear door. Get off my fucking plane. Bye-bye now."

The rear door dropped a bit more as we finished taxiing. And when the plane did stop, the tail door never touched the ground. We humped down the ramp, then jumped to the asphalt. Fifty-five U.S. soldiers from the Third Infantry Division stood in two files ready to board. As we passed each other, we tapped palms silently. The C-130 spun up to full power before we entered the nearest airport building. Fifty-five soldiers in, fifty-five soldiers out. A process that will continue until 20,000 soldiers associated with the Fourth Infantry Division have rolled into metropolitan Baghdad, each soldier replacing a soldier attached to the Third Infantry Division.

That was my first experience with weightlessness. I loved it. I have one more thing to say about G-forces: Blackhawk helicopters!

Someone set up a city bus service using Blackhawks. If your unit is too small or you need to skip over a territory to get to your mission, you can take a Blackhawk from one forward operating base to another. The pilots that were finishing their year flew with the craft of racecar drivers. Thankfully, we had proper multipoint harnesses. There's nothing funnier than having your backside accelerate like that. My spine crushed a bit when the bird accelerated my seat before my shoulders. It is like being in the back of a sports car.

You can tell the veteran pilots from the noobs. The noobs drive like my Aunts did in their Chevy farm truck.

3 | Kitchen

BRIGHID, JANUARY 2006

Something about Chief Alex Flynn intrigues me. Here we sit in Sam's kitchen at Sam's kitchen table. I have not yet fully embraced this home as my own. In the eyes of the Army, I am Sam's roommate, her chosen sister, her legal representative, her power of attorney, the executrix of her will, and the one who wields the medical power of attorney. At the point when I pull out those papers, no shits are given about her tenuous legal status under military law.

It isn't a tenuous legal position, I tell myself. Sam serves honorably and lawfully as a soldier in the United States Army. The Army was held (is still held?) in the grip of the lavender politics of past decades. Fuck 'em.

"Odd, huh?"

"Odd! I had my own room at the Park Plaza Hotel. Had to! The Army paid for Sam's, and I paid for mine. Can't have Uncle Sam pay for a female soldier to canoodle with her girlfriend. We rumpled sheets in both rooms and did what we wanted. We weren't the only couple. There were a pair of female marine officers who were racked together. That must have been allowed so that the Marine Corps could save money."

"Just no touching!"

"No touching." I nod.

"You do love her though, don't you."

"Since the first time I saw her on campus. It about broke me when she decided to enlist and skip her degree."

"I thought she is an officer."

"Oh, she is. The Army paid for the rest of her schooling with the Green-to-Gold program."

"That's cool. No debts."

"One big one. She must serve and deploy and remain with the

Army until that debt is fully paid."

"Year for year?"

"Something like that. Now, she is in Iraq for a year." I continue, "The year kinda started when they deployed to Kuwait in the late fall. She flew into Baghdad in late December. My best guess is that she will be home in Vermont around winter solstice." *Fine,* I say to myself, *that is eleven months, not twelve, but she's already spent a month-ish in Kuwait in a miserable base there.*

"Do you guys talk?"

"Sort of. She gets a time slot on a telephone in a room full of telephones where everyone in the tent is calling home. We get a few minutes before someone yells, 'Time to hang up.' And given she's in a room with her own unit, we have to be circumspect."

"And the phone are tapped?"

"By someone, likely, yes. The Army probably thinks it is not spying on its soldier's private phone call, but I'll bet that some three-letter agency doesn't miss the chance to listen in."

"What is that buzzword? I forgot," Alex asks.

"What?"

"The one about keeping their daily secret stuff secret."

"Oh, *OpSec* or Operational Security," I reply. "Nobody can talk about troop movements, personal activities, future dates, recent dates, or operational activities past or planned."

"You can't talk about the war, and you can't talk about your relationship."

"We still talk."

"I'll bet you do. I'll bet you do." Alex smiles at me, holding a steaming mug of generic American tea that almost smells like tea. We have a planned agenda for this meeting, but we ignore it.

"We email almost daily. Little nothings. Things like, 'Saw ice today in Baghdad. Heading to bed. S.'"

"Ice in Baghdad?"

"Apparently, one night in late December, it was cold enough to freeze water."

"Soon, it will be hot enough to cook an egg on a sunny rock."

"Probably. We do share stories, journals and such. We have a small server that we rent. It's a website that always reads: 'Under Construction' with a little guy in a hard hat swinging a shovel. She logs in and writes journals on hidden pages. I log in and write similar stuff. She figures that while email and phones are monitored, these entries are harder to track since they are never public. The writing is encrypted from her laptop to the server. She writes. I write."

"Are they letters?"

"Sort of? Journals. She is still paranoid about people reading in on her thoughts. She is incredibly guarded."

"That's not paranoid, though!"

"Yes, she is. She takes this OpSec shit so seriously."

"I am not saying she isn't guarded," Alex clarifies. "I am just saying that Sam isn't paranoid. To be paranoid, you must possess a delusion that someone is out to get you. Sam isn't paranoid because they actually are out to get her. She is in a combat zone as a military intelligence officer. She is a lesbian in the U.S. Army."

"That's two strikes," I agree.

"Yup."

"Wanna see one of her journals? I've only got one so far."

"Sure, if you are willing to share."

"When you read this one, you have to keep in mind the rules. First, no doubt she's thinking I don't want to hear stories about bustin' down doors and gunfire and risks and the messy shit that war really is. Second, she's got the OpSec rules. Only information that is already public is fair game."

"And I'll guess, no lovey-dovey nonsense either."

"Don't get me wrong. She loves me deeply. But for shit's sake, she is a stoic Vermonter who got dumped on her aunts by a mother who hugged her like five times. She had to learn to shake hands as an adult."

"I'm sure you've noticed, the folks here don't shake hands."

"Like, ever. She wasn't a hugger and a shaker before the Army got a hold of her. She was trained as a cop, then in intelligence. She comes across with the chilliness of Vermont granite."

"I have met her a few times and seen her around."

"Yeah, you want to say she walks around with a stick up her ass." I smile at Alex.

"I'd never say that. She does carry herself with formal posture, that's a truthful and positive statement. She looks every bit of a soldier."

"My soldier." I spin my laptop. It has a page up called *Enroute.* I continue, "This entry seems to be about her traveling. I'd guess it starts just as we said goodbye in Killeen."

Alex silently reads.

I attempt to sit still. But I am Fidget Brighid. I reheat water in the electric kettle and open the tea drawer looking for something. I don't know what it is. I move around the countertop looking for that not-something. Maybe I am thinking that Sam never actually took over her own house. She inherited it from the Aunts. Technically, it was hers before they died. But after they passed, it seems Sam just left it as the Aunts' house. It never became Sam's house. She has told me stories about her Aunts and Uncle Douglas, but I only started to understand while living here amongst their things. The Aunts were not chintzy, dolly folks. They wore denim and muck boots. I think some of their boots are still here.

I never did ask why Alex stopped by. I offered tea and a chat.

"Who is she writing for?" Alex asks me, while turning the laptop away.

"I dunno, I guess. Just writing."

"I suppose. What does she do between this shitty day and the next shitty day?"

"Watch movies? Read books?"

"But where do they get books and movies?"

"I have no idea, actually. I do know about 'General Order Number One.' It is the multi-page document she showed me in Texas. It is like Moses's ten commandments, except a hundred times longer. No sex. No pregnancies. No personal weapons. No crossing the threshold of a door to private quarters unless all members are the same gender. No booze. No drugs. No this and no that. Fuck up and get court martialed."

"Tough but necessary?"

"Probably, huh?" I pause. "You stopped by and I've given you tea and bored you with my girlfriend's totally-not-private journal entry. What can I do for you?"

"Maybe nothing. I'd seen you around town. People talk. I thought I'd introduce myself."

I look at Alex Flynn and there is so, so much I do not know about Alex Flynn. If I think that my Sam is enigmatic, Sam ain't got nothin' on Alex Flynn.

"I am glad you stopped by. Trowbridge isn't really a welcome-wagon town. No cakes and pies for the new girl."

"No, sorry. You married an ancient house. You came to town as a new feature in an old landscape."

"We're not married!" I say, a bit too quickly.

"You know what I am saying. Your Sarah has been paying townspeople for years to mow lawns and clean house and to check heating and such. She's become just-another-absent landowner in a town where most lands are owned by folks who don't live here."

"I am not changing anything." I suddenly feel on the defensive.

Alex raises a hand. "I'm fucking up here. Sorry. I wanted to say hello, welcome, and ask if you want to come over and play."

I am feeling raw. Vermont has permitted marriage between same-sex couples for years now. But, no; I have a stack of legal documents that gives me all the responsibilities of a marriage without the benefits and protection of a marriage. I have access to Sam's bank account. I have one of her credit cards with my name on it. I am now jointly registered on all of her vehicles. I took a firearms safety course and have keys for the safe and her rifles, shotguns, and a few pistols. I am living in this house, now held in a trust such that if something goes wrong with Lieutenant Sarah Ann Musgrave, I can continue to live here and inherit this pile of timber from her. Like I fucking want it without her. And here's Alex making a joke of marriage.

How's Alex to know?

Fuck, if Sam got hurt, I don't even know how'd I get on base. I don't have a military or spousal card. I can give all the instructions in the world to the doctors and nurses because of the paperwork we signed, but I can't get to the hospital's front door because it will be on a military post with armed guards who require military ID to enter. But Alex doesn't know that.

"My fault, Alex! You can't know the complexities we live with."

"No, all me. I am trying to ask if you want to join the squad?"

"Really? What would I need to do? What does it take?"

"Takes someone dumb enough to wake up after midnight to run towards someone else's shit."

"And I am that dumb one?"

"Brighid, I don't know you. I am. I do it. So does Harry, my assistant chief. But I think you are badass and tough enough."

"What the fuck, why not? What else am I doing at night?"

"Calls come during the day too, and that is when we have the fewest people around."

"I am normally here during the days."

"I know, I've watched Sam's truck."

Small towns.

I grin. "Well, I'll say yes, then maybe you'll think I am just dumb enough."

"Just dumb enough to be wicked good at this, maybe."

"What's next?"

"Come to a meeting. Come to calls. And we'll get you enrolled in an EMT class next semester."

"Why not?"

That's how it starts, isn't it? Well, not always. I think Sam answered a calling. A calling so strong that regardless of the hurdles and laws, she went forward.

Alex stands. "I'll drop by with a pager and such tomorrow. Going to be here?"

"Yup." I try for the TV-show version of the Vermont, "Yup."

I am not going to draw parallels with Sam.

4 | Rising Fawn

HENRY, DECEMBER 1871

Headquarters Post of Chattanooga, Tenn.
U.S. Barracks, December 12, 1871
Special Orders No. 92

In obedience to authority contained in instructions from Headquarters Department of the South, dated April 3d 1871, and, upon application from James Skiles, Deputy United States Marshal, for the Northern District of Georgia—Sergeant Wm. Porter with five (5) men from this command, will accompany him to Rising Farm, Ga., a station on the Alabama and Chattanooga Rail Road, and protect him in the performance of his duties, viz.—that of serving warrants, and arresting members of the Ku Klux organization.

The detachment will be supplied with one (1) days cooked rations, and forty (40) rounds of ammunitions per man.

Sergeant Porter, in the discharge of his duty, will act only as an auxiliary to the civil Office with whom he will be associated, and will bear in mind that he has no original authority, and has no right to use force, except when specially directed by civil authorities, or in the last extremity, for self preservation.

Upon completion of this duty, Sergeant Porter, will return to his proper station, and render a detailed report of the performance thereof to these Headquarters.

The Quartermasters Department will furnish the necessary transportation.

C. A. Dempsey
1st Lieutenant 2d U.S. Infantry
Commanding Post

Private Paul Abrams approaches the post's blacksmith shop with the hesitancy of a young pup, uncertain of his welcome. He slows his pace near the door. He had traveled across the post at a rate that demonstrated hustle, but at a speed less than a run. Not hustling earns a dressing down. Running earns a different dressing down from a different sergeant. As does the failure to offer military courtesy to ranking sergeants and officers. Tugging at his tunic and straightening his uniform, Abrams regulates his breathing. He adjusts his voice with a quiet cough, avoiding the dreaded teenage squeak.

Private Henry McDonald sits casually on a log stump. His left foot pumps bellows. In his hands, he holds a newspaper. Henry's blue woolen tunic hangs on a peg, and his shirtsleeves are rolled to his elbows as he rests comfortably next to the blacksmith, next to the forge, next to the heat.

"Henry?"

"Yes?" Henry drops the newspaper slightly to make eye contact with his fellow private. Henry stops reading aloud. His breathing remains steady as he pumps up and down with his foot.

"Sergeant Porter is looking for you."

"Alright. I'll be there directly."

"The sergeant said to tell you that he was in his office."

Henry had found his cadence reading aloud, speaking clearly, while casually pumping the blacksmith's bellows with one leg. Henry returns to the paper, finishing the last sentence of the article. The men in the shop each turn their faces, nodding in appreciation of his efforts to read the news.

"Well, Mose, thank you for the warm fire, my friend." Henry folds the newspaper, then tucks it into a clean corner. He gives a quick splash of water on his hands, unfurls his sleeves, then eases into his tunic. He places his hand on the blacksmith's shoulder as he passes.

The two privates walk together a few steps, Paul matching Henry's long, confident stride. Henry veers left, saying, "I'll see you in the barracks after, okay?"

"Okay," Paul responds, accepting that he is not to tag along. The sergeant did not say, "Return with McDonald," or "Bring McDonald to me," did he? With a slower pace and head down, Paul ambles back to the barracks, only to be called out by a sergeant for walking with his eyes down and his hands in his pockets.

Henry enters the stable block that houses the officer's horses. It is the neatest and cleanest of the stables on the post; better built, too. The horses stand behind neat, clean oak gates and oak walls. The cobbled floor clicks beneath his boots. In a movement similar to Private Abrams but executed with confidence, Henry tugs the wrinkles from his tunic then smooths his hair before knocking on the tack room door.

"Come."

Henry opens the door to the warm embrace of clean leather and tobacco smoke, blended with the smell of manure and hay. The post's sergeants had turned this tack room into a club room for themselves. A few chairs and a table lends to the status. As Henry presents himself at the door, a bottle of bourbon disappears behind a saddle.

"Mac, good, walk with me," Sergeant William Porter steps to the door, closing it behind him. "Lieutenant Dempsey is sending us out tomorrow on another of these Ku Klux missions with Marshal Skyles. We're out at dawn on the first Alabama train. Forty rounds of ammo, food for the day—you know the drill. Have one of the privates pack a few sets of shackles. Let's say four."

Sergeant Porter walks Henry down the center aisle of the stables. While not as warm as the tack room with its small stove heater, the horses kept the chill of the Tennessee winter out of the building. "We'll need four more men. You can have your adjutant, Abrams. Let's pull in Sturtevant, Belville, Donovan, and Mueller."

Private Henry McDonald holds the lowest rank in the United States Army. Private Paul Abrams holds the same rank, born in the same city, and likely two years older than Henry. Paul is often found helping Henry organize a small band of soldiers and their equipment at the vestigial Civil War post.

Henry reaches for the door.

"Mac, one more thing. There will be a civilian attached to our party. His name is Asa Boydston. He was a spy on our side during the war and fought with one of these local guerilla groups. Tell the squad to avoid him, don't talk to him, or interact with him. Got it?"

"Yes, Sergeant. I'll pass that on."

The squad of six leaves Chattanooga before dawn, marching westerly towards the depot located on the banks of the Tennessee River. The eastern sky offers hints of a future sunrise. Private Henry McDonald stands with the other soldiers, observing the distance between Sergeant Porter's detail and the civilians at the depot. As the train pulls toward the platform for its first run of the day, the local civilians and military split as if directed by an unspoken arrangement. The soldiers load into the rear carriage. The civilians climb into the forward carriage.

Chattanooga occupied an oversized role before, during, and after the Civil War. The people of the Chattanooga region held mixed political beliefs. Many supported the federal government; others supported the insurrectionists and plantation owners. The people of eastern Tennessee—holding views similar to those found in northern states—formed independent bands of armed men who allied with the United States Army. These guerilla fighters coordinated efforts to burn bridges within rebel territory as a means of aiding the advance of government troops. Southern soldiers and guerillas then hunted and hanged the people they believed responsible for burning those bridges.

Henry and his father had read descriptions of the federal forces bombarding the city with long-range artillery in 1862, when Henry was ten years old. The following year, during the summer of 1863, the federal forces engaged confederate general Bragg in a lengthy battle. The lad Henry cheered on the U.S. Army, tracking their movements on maps in the New York newspapers. Bragg yielded the city and retreated to Georgia Later that year, the city hosted Ulysses Grant and William Tecumseh Sherman. With Grant and Sherman in Chattanooga, readers in the north knew that Chattanooga formed the foundation of the fight against the rebel forces.

Of course, those newspapers read at home in New York were likely biased. Locally, most described Chattanooga as an occupied city;

occupied by a foreign invader, the U.S. government and its military.

In 1864, General Sherman launched the Atlanta Campaign from Chattanooga. Sherman and his soldiers marched out of Chattanooga and followed the Chickamauga Creek, flowing south into Georgia. Chattanooga possessed rail connections north to New York, Washington, and Richmond, Virginia, west to Nashville and Memphis., southeast to Atlanta, Charleston, and Savannah, and southwest to Meridian, Mississippi. This earned Chattanooga the nickname: the Gateway to the South.

As a boy, Henry begged his father to let him join the Army in any capacity, such as drummer boy, orderly, or trainee. The war ended just as Henry turned thirteen. It had been the dominant topic of his life. He knew the names of the battles. He could point to each major battle location.

Henry enlisted in a peace-time army in March of 1870, and then was promptly sent south into the battlefields he knew so well in his mind's eye.

Now, in 1871, the United States Army continues to operate the Department of the South from this city, six years after the surrender of southern generals. With the new decade, and fresh troops, the Army strives to control southern conservatives. These southern conservatives desire a return to pre-war conditions, a phrase embraced with the Latinate term antebellum.

One of the U.S. government's measures included the establishment of an agency called the Freedmen's Bureau. In formal writing, the title had been written as Bureau of Refugees, Freedmen, and Abandoned Lands. The agency's mission instructed the U.S. Army to direct provisions, clothing, and fuel for the destitute and suffering refugees and freedmen. The Freedmen's Bureau then became part of the Department of War. Yet, Congress never funded the fledgling agency.

By 1870, the Freedmen's Bureau suffered attacks from the Ku Klux Klan and other terrorist organizations across the south. The KKK and others used violence against the same people the Freedmen's Bureau had been established to protect: emancipated peoples, poor people, refugees, and those removed from their lands by war. The KKK attacked formerly enslaved people, those people who taught them, and sympathetic white republicans (the liberals of the day). The KKK was, then, supported and funded by southern Democrats. Northern Democrats obstructed efforts to fund the Freedmen's Bureau, fearing that the program would encourage slothfulness amongst those recently released from bondage.

The Civil War ended in May of 1865. But Henry found that war continued in Georgia and Mississippi in 1871.

In 1866, the government passed a series of laws, including the Civil Rights Bill of 1866. This bill provided citizenship, the right to vote, and the right to own property to anyone born in the United States, except Native Americans. Due to objections to the bill in Congress and a veto from President Andrew Johnson, Congress proceeded to pass the 14th Amendment to the U.S. Constitution. Section I of the 1868 amendment read:

> All persons born or naturalized in the United States, and subject to the jurisdiction thereof, are citizens of the United States and of the State wherein they reside. No State shall make or enforce any law which shall abridge the privileges or immunities of citizens of the United States; nor shall any State deprive any person of life, liberty, or property, without due process of law; nor deny to any person within its jurisdiction the equal protection of the laws.

Under these expanded civil rights laws, southern states elected and appointed black men to public offices such as senators, congressional representatives, state houses, city councils, and mayors. Hiram Revels served Mississippi as a U.S. Senator in 1870. Some evidence points to two thousand black men holding or being elected to public offices during the years following the 14th Amendment. Then, from south-central Tennessee, near Nashville, rose a small band of people supporting further insurrection against the federal government. They actively fought against the new civil rights laws by forming groups like the Ku Klux Klan, the Red Shirts, and the Knights of the White

Camelia. Congress responded to the violence and disobedience with another series of laws, then another. For a number of years, one could observe this volley between Congress and southern rebels. New violence triggered new laws. New laws begat new violence.

Thus, in December 1871, Private Henry McDonald sits on a train watching the Chickamauga outside of his window as his squad heads south into Georgia to arrest members of the Ku Klux Klan. Six and a half years prior, the Chickamauga and Lookout Mountain became famous as battlefields when nearly 100,000 Americans fought to control these very rail lines. Henry, a well-armed and well-fed soldier of the United States Army, is now advancing through these historic battlefields into a new battle—this time against small bands of guerillas.

Sergeant Porter and Deputy United States Marshal James Skyles sit in front of him. The marshal carries a satchel over his shoulder with the leather pouch resting on his left hip. All of the soldiers carry loaded Colt revolvers and Spencer repeating rifles. Soldiers also carry field provisions including bedding, small clothing, and food. These soldiers acknowledge that they fight in an undeclared war against a shifting enemy and no sense of battlelines.

The train follows the Tennessee River turning south. The terrain shows the unhealed scars of battles: redouts, trenches, trees shattered by artillery, strewn and destroyed fences, and impromptu battlefield graves with fading markers. Men buried where they had been felled. Henry once paraded tin soldiers on the floor in mock battles following the maps and arrows displayed in the newspapers. The imagined artillery and gun fire simulated with mouth noises failed to represent this haunted land of ghosts.

War robs men and land of life, leaving only debris.

Henry's toy battles started lifeless, remained lifeless, and when the toys got picked from the floor, sterility returned as if Henry had never lain on the red oak planks pushing soldiers with his fingertips.

But here, every whistling bullet, every shouted scream, every exploding shell left an indelible mark on the land and in the souls of all who experienced the years of battles on this hallowed ground. Years from now, the ground may heal; the fence posts set right. People may yet read a few sentences embossed on a votive stone or a commemorative plaque. These ghosts will eventually die and fade over decades, as people forget the men who had once lived here, once fought here, once died here. A youth may wish to hold his breath or whistle whilst passing a graveyard, but given the size of this conflict, the graveyard of souls started in Chattanooga and likely never ended, reaching deep into the communities where these young soldiers are now headed.

Crossing the imaginary line into Georgia, Henry unholsters his revolver to examine that it is loaded and runs smoothly. Having qualified as a marksman, Henry carries the shorter Spencer carbine rifle. The other privates carry longer rifles, which snag on doors and bang along corridors and benches within the train carriage. The longer rifle helps with accuracy but hinders the soldier within close quarters. When used well from a protected firing position, a soldier with the longer rifle could lay fire on a target at a rate of twenty rounds per minute. The shorter carbine permitted greater agility. It weighed less, banged on fewer obstacles, and the barrel came up to a target with greater ease and speed, but was less accurate at longer distances. Henry's carbine offered a skilled marksman a tactical advantage with the freedom to move quickly and bring the weapon to bear faster.

The rifle's magazine holds seven rounds. Each member of the squad has been issued five cartridge boxes. Thus, each soldier possesses forty-two rounds for their rifles—roughly two minutes of a sustained gun fight. The soldiers each have a few rounds for their revolvers as well. But in a gun fight against a well-armed force, the squad would have to retreat. They would be outgunned by former rebel soldiers, farmers, and those committed to the southern cause.

When Henry is done taking inventory of his own kit, he inspects the kit of each of the privates. While the sergeant and marshal smoke and talk quietly, Henry moves about the train, sitting next to the men, offering a hand, a joking word, a quick story. Calming and preparing his fellow soldiers provides Henry with an outlet for the anxiety he refuses to acknowledge.

The train steams on through the valley south of Lookout

Mountain, to Morrison's Station, to Trenton Station.

Henry guides Private Abrams, suggesting that he position his ammo so that it can be reached easily.

"Paul, you're not going to need your smalls or shaving kit." Henry attempts to mask the sense that Paul packed as if going to his grandmother's for the weekend, where a clean chin and clean knickers stand at the pinnacle of civilization. "Here, put your ammo on top, right here. When one of these KK-crackers start banging away at us from the second story of a barn, you're going to want to reach in here and grab bullets, not soap, my friend."

They travel thirty miles, transporting the soldiers from the relatively familiar and safe city of Chattanooga to the hilly and rural Dade County, Georgia. Stepping from the train, the soldiers settle their packs on their backs, shoulder their rifles, then form two files.

"Private McDonald and Belville, go with the marshal to the post office. The rest on me," says Sergeant Porter.

James Skyles leads the two privates to the front door of the post office. The locked door hosts a sign that read: "Closed Until Mail Sorted." Skyles bangs on the door once, then again. On the third attempt, he announces: "United States Marshal, open up." He rattles the door again then pounds on the door. "Marshals! Open up!"

Paul Abrams comes running around the front of the building. "We got him! We got him!"

Skyles addresses the two at the front door, Belville and McDonald. "Stay here. Detain anyone who comes out."

Skyles walks around to the back of the building, which shares a platform with the train depot, simplifying the effort required to hand off parcels and mail bags to passing trains. He approaches the man, who is immersed in his task of sorting post and appears not to have noticed their arrival.

"Mister J. G. Hale," Skyles says, commanding his attention. "I have a federal arrest warrant made out in your name. You are charged with violations of the Ku-Klux Acts passed by Congress."

The man looks poised to bolt. The soldiers step nearer. "What have I done? I've done nothing. I am just sorting the mail, as I do most mornings. You can't arrest me. I haven't broken any laws. I signed my loyalty oath."

"Private Donovan, place Mister Hale in shackles, please."

"Yes, Sergeant." Donovan drops his ruck, opening it. He retrieves a set of steel wrist shackles and restrains their prisoner, binding his hands at the front.

Private Sturtevant tosses the mail bag onto the post office floor then shuts the back door.

"Donovan and Sturtevant, you are to remain here at the depot with Mr. Hale. Place him on the bench over there. And don't let any northbound train pass. Understand? Hold the next train for us. We will be returning shortly."

"Very good, Sergeant."

Sergeant Porter leads the remaining four soldiers of the Second Infantry Regiment south along the main road, keeping the rail to their left. They march along a broad, rural road between treed fields. Six black men work at a roadside ditch with picks and shovels, their ankles bound by iron shackles. There is no white boss in sight. On the left side of the road, another half-dozen black men are bound by ankle shackles.

Asa Boydston, the former (or current) spy, appears from the shadows astride a chestnut-colored Morgan. He asks the chained laborers: "Where's the boss at?"

One of the laborers answers. "He lit out of here on his horse when he saw you."

"Was it Mister Blevins that ran off?"

"Nah, sir, he went to warn Mister Blevins that you all were coming."

Boydston addresses the marshal. "Let's just keep going."

The squad accelerates to a rapid march proceeding south. At the next building, they turn left into an active work yard. Another six shackled black men are lifting and carrying stone from the ground to a freight wagon hitched to a team of tired mules.

The marshal and Sergeant Porter approach the office. McDonald uses his elbow to tap Abrams in the ribs, and they run around to the back of the building in case Mister J. W. Blevins decides to flee.

But instead of fleeing, the road commissioner greets the sergeant and marshal comfortably seated at his desk. He addresses the uniformed officials with smug arrogance, echoing the mail clerk's words: "You can't arrest me, I've done nothing wrong."

Marshal Skyles says, "Please get up and put your jacket on and grab anything that you may need."

"I do not think so. You have no authority here."

"I have a warrant—a federal warrant—for your arrest. You've been identified as a member of the Ku Klux organization. We have ample evidence."

Blevins holds fast to his desk, refusing to rise.

"Mister Blevins, we can do this the easy way and you walk out of the front door with me. Or, I can call in the squad of soldiers that are outside of this building. The decision is yours to make."

In response, Blevins rekindles his rant. He asserts that no jury in Georgia would convict him of anything, ever. "They all know that Mister J. W. Blevins serves his neighbors, his people, and his state with honor and dignity. And that he will do so until his death."

The marshal turns to Sergeant Porter. "Sergeant, please call in your troops."

Sergeant Porter steps backwards to the door without taking his eyes from the quarry. He opens the door. "I'll need two of you."

Mueller and Belville step into the office with their long rifles and rucksacks. Mister Blevins, former rebel soldier, now stands. He puts on his jacket, then discreetly grabs a small purse from the desk. He walks through the door, held open by the two privates, Sergeant Porter and Marshal Skyles on his heels.

In the yard, the marshal asks, "How come your laborers are shackled?"

"They are not laborers, they are prisoners. Some are vagrants awaiting trials, the rest are thieves. The sheriff up in Trenton lends them to me. I need help with the roads. These boys know how to work." Puffed-up pride.

Sergeant Porter says, "Private Mueller, please shackle Mister Blevins before we walk back to the depot." Mueller leans his long rifle on the building's wall and drops his rucksack from his back. The rifle rests within two feet of the prisoner's right hand. Blevins pretends not to notice, giving his attention to Mueller opening his pack. Spying a potential problem, the sergeant executes a *pas de deaux*, working around the young private to fetch it.

Blevins, who had been carefully and deliberately ignoring the rifle, immediately responds verbally. "Don't you all see what is going on with our country? With your country? With your people? It is unnatural and against God's laws."

The soldiers remain quiet.

"I'll be home to my wife, our chickens, and my office as county road commissioner within the week. You have wasted your day. But what do I care what you do with your day? There's nothing you can do to me."

Mueller closes the cuffs on his wrists, twisting the lock with a key.

As he and Paul return from the rear of the building, Henry explores the accuracy of Blevins's words. The quartermaster issued each man a few rounds of ammunition and one day's food, just enough supplies to leave the garrison, but not enough to survive on. Blevins can either face a white jury or a black jury under the Freedmen's Bureau. Or, using the Enforcement Act passed in April, they can hold Blevins without *habeas corpus*. He would just rot away in a jail, suspended between the rights granted to a citizen and someone with no rights.

The McDonald clan suffered nearly a century of similar legal indignities from English kings. Henry had heard these stories since toddling free of swaddling cloth. Following the Jacobite Uprising of 1745, the English government outlawed Scottish highland culture, forbidding the use of the Gaelic language, highland dress, of highlanders engaging in sport or military training. Scottish highlanders opposed the union of Scotland and England. To some, religion stood at the core of the struggle. Many followers of Bonnie Prince Charlie practiced Catholicism, but England and the English king imposed a new state-run Protestant religion. Centuries prior English kings destroyed monasteries and churches. The Catholic pope in Rome excommunicated Henry VIII in the 1530s, and two centuries later, Catholics and Protestants continued to struggle for power on the British Isles.

After the 1745 uprising, the McDonalds fled—carrying their Catholicism with them as they scattered. The span of a century means little to a family, their stories, and their beliefs. Fleeing the highlands, the family hid with an assumed surname. Henry's father, Charles, finally claimed his own proud name of McDonald upon sailing from Dublin to New York in 1820. New York, and the U.S. Constitution, promised religious and personal freedoms now forbidden to the highlanders.

A quick survey of the men in Henry's squad provided hints of American founders' constitutional plans: Porter, Abrams, McDonald, Sturtevant, Belville, Donovan, and Mueller. Names from various European communities, now living as Americans. Each of these privates enlisted in the Army from recruiting stations in New York, Chicago, Boston, and Philadelphia. Each of the privates enlisted for five years. Each man swore the same oath. Each signed the same enlistment papers. Each man assumed that their duty would take them south to assist the government.

Fireside stories from Henry's father Charles and uncle Michael revolved around government treachery, lost lands, lost opportunity, and a lost home. In one famous massacre, the McDonalds had been invited to feast with the neighboring Campbells. In a now distant Scottish valley, members of the Campbell clan and the British army attacked the McDonalds during revelry that had been intended to celebrate a promised peace. Surviving members of the McDonald clan became outlaws. Henry grew up on stories of battle, of lands with cattle, and the duty of a chief and leader. Stories of warrior ancestors and warrior tactics whispered generation to generation, father to son. Skills practiced in isolation; skills invested in an unknown future. He absorbed them all.

Blevins's words, his sentiments, reflect both present and ancient conflicts. "A jury of my peers will look upon me with understanding and respect."

Blevin, now wearing a jacket, walks with his hands loosely shackled in front. Marshal Skyles orders the detail to return to the depot, whereupon Blevins starts complaining again. "I can't walk that far. I got shot in the war. My leg won't hold out."

"It is barely a mile."

"You need to let me be carried up in a wagon. It is only fair." The shackled white prisoner starts yelling at the shackled black prisoners, barking orders to fetch a team of mules and a wagon for him. Several of the yard men start moving to unhitch the team of mules until Marshal Skyles yells at both the laborers and Mister Blevins. The marshal informs all that a brief walk to the depot will do everyone good. He encourages Blevins's movement with push to the small of his back, knocking the balance from the mildly overweight man.

Blevins makes a show of dragging a lame foot through the dust with each step, giving up time and distance and splitting the squad into two. Marshal Skyles, now frustrated, yells at Blevins and hits him across the head with an open hand.

"Pick up the pace. Maybe I should string you up over that tree the way you did with that family in October? You lynched a man and his son. No, I get it, I ought to place you on a work crew without trial. Would you like that? You think you deserve a fair day in court? What about those men in shackles, do they get a day in court? Maybe I should have Private Mac shoot you while you try to run from us? We're going to make the noon train. So, move."

Blevins speeds up marginally, striding at a pace that is still slower than church ladies ambling home on a Sunday. The station comes into view before the distant whistle of the train echoes from the small hills, chugging slowly north from Alabama towards the depot.

Sergeant Porter commands the detail to push forward to the station, to make sure that the train waits for them. "You three, on me, at the quick."

The four soldiers quick march up the road, the long rifles banging on the legs of Belville, Sturtevant, and Mueller as they run to keep up with the long-legged sergeant.

Henry and Marshal Skyles walk at Blevins's pace, prodding and pushing their prisoner up the road. They watch Sergeant Porter greet the engineer, clearly providing instructions with animated hand gestures toward the three walking now a couple of hundred yards from the depot.

From the south, three men come riding hard and fast on horses toward them. Both Henry and Marshal Skyles hear them at the same time. Skyles slams Blevins to the ground. Henry spins, lifting his carbine to his shoulder and discharging two rounds into the ground in front of the running horses. One horse rears, spilling his passenger. One horse turns rapidly. The third horse does not respond to the sound of gunfire, indicating that this horse is a war veteran.

Henry aims his rifle dead center of charging man's chest, unwavering as horse and rider charge, but does not fire. The rider feigns an attack, gradually fading to the other side of the road. Spinning back south, Henry aims his rifle at the next nearest man, steady and calm.

The marshal calls out, "I hear this fellow is a crack shot. He won't miss you at that range."

Skyles lifts the prisoner back to his feet, then gives the man a push, and Henry follows, walking backwards with his rifle aimed south. Their attackers cannot shoot the marshal or the soldier without risking the prisoner.

They reach the carriage. Skyles guides Blevins up the first stair and onto the train.

The train leaves the depot, chugging north.

5 | Danes, Vikings, and Pilgrims

SAM'S JOURNAL, FEBRUARY 2006

B,

You know that stupid moment when the TV stations put their weather people out on the beach during a big storm? That's me. *New York Times* rules, right? Wanna know who knows the least about the stormy weather? That reporter in the yellow sou'wester holding a microphone while waves crash, and rain pours, and wind screams. I know what that experience is. I want to know what is going on and when it will end. Show me the mother-lovin' map and give me hope.

"Hey, LT, take four and run to X. Report back."

"You got it, boss."

The world reduces to about one square meter with wind, and rain, and waves.

You know more about this war than I do. You may even see the weather maps. Oh, right, there is no weather front, stationary front. No front at all.

Someone someday is going to ask me the important questions. What was this about? Can you help me understand this war? I've got the skills, the specialized training. I am here, on the ground. I find a TV to watch *Al Jazeera*, *BBC*, *CNN*, or anyone to help me see the battlespace from thirty thousand feet.

I guess this lieutenant is no different than any other lieutenant in any war.

This month, the commanding general said: "The fuse is lit."

I think that phrase got picked up by the media, too. "The fuse is lit."

The phrase harkens to a cartoon illustration of a wooden barrel, loaded with old-fashioned black powder. The fuse simmers slowly, two meters distant. In truth, Baghdad and Iraq resemble multiple powder kegs with multiple fuses.

I flew into a stalemate.

Saddam was captured by this same division in 2003. Some of those same soldiers are here with me today. Two plus years later, combatants swing at each other like two old drunk bastards with fading intensity. Things go boom in places where things tend to go boom. Home by Christmas, or winter solstice, was never our promise, but maybe I thought this could be our last solstice in Iraq.

Our neighbors throughout Iraq took to the streets to burn the Danish flag this month.

Seriously, the Arabs in the region hadn't thought about the Danes in a millennium. Why would you? There's Denmark up there in the chilly north, doing normal, modern Dane things. Here are the Arabs who, while not unified folks, do tend to broadly identify as Muslim, an umbrella term for a globally diverse body of religious practices.

This month, the world watched people in Iraq and throughout this region burn the Danish flag. I know you know the Danish flag, but most of the world doesn't. The last time the Danes really pissed off the Arab world was when they sailed and rowed down here in their long boats. They traded, and likely did the other Viking things, along the Tigris and Euphrates.

On the ninth of February, two million Shi'ah pilgrims walked to Karbala, Iraq. This is the third pilgrimage since the capture and arrest of Saddam Hussein. Suddenly, there is a bit of religious freedom here. Saddam forbade public observance of Shi'ah practices.

In the year 680 of our contemporary European calendar, Husayn ibn Ali and seventy-two of his confederates were killed in a battle. Husayn ibn Ali was the grandson of the prophet Muhammad. Ali had been killed during the Battle of Karbala. The Shi'ah regard his death as a martyrdom. A millennium and a half later, Saddam suppressed Shi'ah practices and strove to control the Shi'ah people. Following Saddam Hussein's capture by Americans in 2003, the Karbala pilgrimage returned. In 2006, we observed two million Shi'ah walking the roads in peace. The Shi'ah converged on Karbala, Iraq as a means of honoring Ali.

Three times feels like a pattern!

Dear censor: not strictly from a *NYT* article or *CNN*, but sure is public information that can be found on *Wikipedia*. Not history taught in American public schools, but if we are going to send a generation of soldiers, sailors, airmen, and marines over here, we might want to have a bit of understanding of the neighborhood.

A cartoonist in Denmark, not understanding Islam, nor these holy days, sparked a global brawl. The cartoonist drew the face of the prophet Muhammad, which is not done by Muslims. One does not make depictions of the prophet. To do so carries either the intent to offend or a blatant declaration of stupidity. Muslims regarded the cartoonist's drawing as an insult to the entire faith. A French magazine then published this Danish cartoon. While always a bad idea to insult the world's largest religion, the publication came during these days of mourning for Ali. People in the region, including Iraq, burned Danish and European Union flags.

To our west in Lebanon, Hezbollah organized protests to coincide with the forty-days of mourning spanning between Ashura and the pilgrimage. Hezbollah is an organization associated with the Shi'ah. To our northeast, in Pakistan, twenty-two people died in a bomb attack, attributed to sectarian violence between the Sunni and Shi'ah. In Afghanistan, people burned cars outside of mosques.

Rolling back nearly a quarter-century to 1979, the world watched an Islamic Revolution in Iran deposing the dynastic shah and his family. This revolution had been led by Shi'ah leaders, overthrowing a secular, wealthy, and west-leaning ruler. In the United States, we remember that fifty-two diplomats were held hostage for four hundred and forty-four days during the Carter administration. Iran released the hostages on the day of Ronald Reagan's inauguration on the 20th of January, 1981. The Iran-Contra Affair is part of our shared and messed-up history with these events.

In 1979, Saddam Hussein seized control of Iraq. Fearing an uprising of the majority Shi'ah in Iraq, and fearing the new government of Iran, he attacked Iran. Saddam thus started a decade-long war that killed millions of people. Iraq and Iran share a long border and a longer history.

In February 2006, this same month, Israel decided to unilaterally expand its authority in Jerusalem, also taken as an affront by Muslims in the region.

The time gap between 1979 and 2006 seems long. In America, we would draw lines breaking it into generations and decades. Here in Iraq, this pilgrimage commemorates a battle fought in 680, four hundred years before the Vikings sailed these rivers and traded on this land. Memories and stories stretch hundreds of years. Stories that are woven with rich color, character, tragedy, heroes, triumph, hope, and family. When the Fourth Infantry Division captured Saddam in Tikrit hiding in a hole, the Shi'ah expressed new freedoms in Iraq. Their stories, never forgotten, could be shared publicly.

Our military command and the western press identified the escalating tensions as sectarian. Articles and fingers pointed to strife between the Shi'ah and the Sunni. Someone needs to explore the role of external forces in Iraq. End of statement...*NYT* rules, sorry.

Are there Lebanese and Iranians in the crowds here in Iraq? I think I found that question in *Al Jazeera*. Hezbollah to the west and Iran to the east desire to support the Shi'ah majority in Iraq. Saddam had bolstered support for the Sunni minority for decades. In the north of Iraq, in an area informally called Kurdistan, is the land of the Kurds. The Kurds live in regions of northern Iraq, northern Iran, and southern Turkey. The land of the Kurds, "Kurdistan," is not recognized as an independent nation. Instead, Kurdistan is a region of people vaguely united culturally and linguistically. Saddam gassed the Kurds. The Turks, further north, also fear a Kurdish independence movement.

One cannot understand the cultural dynamics of Iraq from afar. Understanding the history requires an investment in study and knowledge. Being amongst these people, this history, humbles me. The global tensions and rekindling of Shi'ah practices caused both the civilian and military leaders to face their own limitations. Some in command have expressed a need to ensure the safety of the pilgrims walking to Karbala. Other leaders wish to avoid being perceived as allied with the Shi'ah or with the Sunni. The hybridized policy resulted in a confused set of instructions that involved patrolling without providing an escort. Standing ready to respond to a crisis, but not engaging in prevention.

As two million pilgrims walk to Kabala for the third time in as many decades, one of the soldiers in my Humvee said: "We can show the Danes what is to be hated in this world." When the United States shook Iraq by the ankles, removing a dictator and his idiot sons, we failed to recognize the adage taught to every child who walks into a store: "You break it, you buy it." While the United States expressed little desire to own Iraq, we're standing in these streets not knowing how to fix what we broke. The obvious corollary is: "You break it, you fix it."

Once upon a war, the enemy was the guy you saw through your rifle sight or aimed your arrows at. The enemy was the guy outside your castle; or the enemy was the guy inside the castle that you wanted. Once upon a war, the enemy came over the sea from Scandinavia in long ships. Friend and enemy have two components. There is the gang we call "us," facing the gang we call "them." We stood in Iraq, having removed Saddam Hussein from power, not knowing who or what our enemy was. We failed to install a government that served the people. We opened up cultural rifts spanning millennia. Not only do we not know who the enemy is, I understand now that the enemy keeps shifting.

The pilgrims, walking to Kabala, get food and water handed to them from volunteers present throughout the route. This recognition of Shi'ite history, forbidden by the Iraq government, now resumes. We know that funding, food, and support came from Hezbollah and Iran.

Our commanding general said: "Folks, the fuse has been lit." With the best intelligence resources on the globe, the general could offer little more to his soldiers than the observation that we stood upon powder kegs with a lit fuse. Laying down in the evening at our headquarters, I made a plea to an uncaring universe. First, I desire that Iran stays quiet with her soldiers on their side of the long border. Second, I wish that Israel says: "Just kidding," then offers an apologetic smile to the region. Third, we need a bit of reconciliation between the Shi'ah and the Sunni. Then we can resume the normal chaos of a war. Of course, until some Dane or French person discovers a new way to insult Islam with a pen stroke.

Instead of having any deity listen to my thoughts, I listen to inbound mortars and rockets. I told myself that not only would I follow the rules, but I would also delete any text that describes the stuff-that-goes-boom. That's not fair to you. On the flip side, you know I am in a combat zone. Stuff-goes-boom, end of.

My military intelligence unit got assigned to the divisional headquarters. I now have a small room in a trailer that I share with another female lieutenant. These trailers resemble construction offices and are the size of a standard shipping container. Our trailer has been divided into three rooms, each with a private entrance. Those with higher rank live in trailers that have been divided into two larger rooms. Colonels and generals live in an undivided trailer.

As a lieutenant leading a platoon, I get one roommate. My little room in my trailer is called "my hooch." We have one air conditioning unit, one overhead light, two beds, two desks, two chairs, two footlockers, and two standing lockers that serve as tiny closets. Most junior enlisted soldiers live four to a room—twelve to a trailer. We live in field of trailers, neatly lined up between a man-made hill and a man-made lake. The lake resembles the letter "Z." The hill, likely the spoil from digging the lake, serves the division as a platform for hundreds of communication masts and towers. Within the recent month, shortly after I moved here, someone turned on a red, flashing beacon on top of the hill.

The newly lit beacon echoes the general's statement: "The fuse has been lit." The beacon flashes with the brightness and regularity required by the Federal Aviation Administration, the U.S. agency responsible for flight rules in the United States. Back in the world, helicopters fly with flashing lights and use landing lights when approaching the ground. Here, in combat, the pilots rely on night- vision goggles, infrared sensor, and radar. The bright beacon provides the pilots with no value. If anything, the bright flash adversely impacts their night-vision goggles. Furthermore, it provides the enemy around us with a target reference point. They know that if they aim for red-flashing-beacon, they will hit something interesting. If the rocket goes short, or long, or left, or right, there is something American to hit. The mortars and rockets thump communications equipment, electrical services, offices, hooches, vehicles, or people. Surrounding this hill is our post exchange (PX), four dining halls, and Moral-Welfare-Recreation (MWR) tents for games, movies, socializing, and informal libraries. While we have trouble identifying the enemy, we presented a lit fuse to help them find our most important buildings. We announced to all: "Aim Here." It brings to mind the *MASH* episode, "Five O'Clock Charlie." The medical staff gather in lawn chairs at the edge of the mine field, looking towards the newly installed ammunition storage dump a kilometer away. At five o'clock each evening, an open cockpit airplane arrives to bomb the ammo dump. The aircraft's engine rattles with the waning energy of an out-of-balance washing machine suffering loose-bolt syndrome. Meanwhile, Radar collects bets and marks a grid. The one who owns the grid closest to the hand-tossed bomb wins the daily pot.

Here in Baghdad, we have posted a blinking light on a hill located in the middle of our Army's most valuable assets. With the regularity of "Five O'Clock Charlie," the rockets launch from beyond the dark. They aim for, then miss, the red beacon. Absent from my story are the fanciful cocktails sipped while sitting safely in lawn chairs. Instead, we became the targets under a rule-following fool's belief that a skilled combat aviator may crash into a small hill with one hundred antennae.

But the beacon complies with U.S. aviation rules, thousands of kilometers away.

In combat, one learns to keep score. A mortar hitting soft dirt sounds different than a mortar landing on a concrete pad or near a building. Our language fails to describe the subtly in these sounds: *whump, thud, crack*. One learns to judge distance from an explosion, too. Similarly, one learns the difference between the Kalashnikov AK-47, with its seven-point-six-two millimeter round, and our M-4 carbine, with the five-point-five-six millimeter NATO round. The

M-4 has a deeper, fuller sound, fires a bit slower, and with a more discernable rhythm. The AK-47 is higher pitched and carries a crack in the sound. The AK tends to fire at slightly irregular intervals when in full auto mode. Pistol fire sounds different from rifle fire.

The human mind processes, classifies, then stores these sounds with efficiency. They have become the sounds of my landscape; they have become the sounds that trigger the adrenal glands or permit the pressure of sleep to pull my lids down over my eyes. I must balance sleep with vigilance.

The brain learns: "That's an AK a goodly distance away and traveling away from me." The body responds: "Ho-hum." When the brain hears AK fire that gets closer or is sporadic, or AK fire intermixed with M-4 fire, then the adrenals squirt a bit of adrenalin into the bloodstream. One becomes more alert. Eyes dilate to see better. Heart rate increases. If entertaining thoughts of peeing, that sensation disappears. The body pulses with its own fight-or-flight-or-freeze-or-fawn response from the adrenalin, or epinephrine, we produce. Adrenalin stoppers small blood vessels, saving blood and stopping minor wounds from dripping. Adrenalin brings gentle moisture to the palms to help grip. When the tiger of the African plains leapt from the grass for a meal of human, adrenalin brought us the strength to run faster and further. Adrenalin staunched the blood flow from the cat's scratches on our backs. Adrenalin opened our eyes and warmed our muscles to make haste. Adrenalin bound the belly.

Not every crack of every gun, not every mortar round that lands on the hill behind my hooch, needs a one hundred percent response from my body. One must learn to calm the body, soothe the adrenal glands, and find a way to digest food smoothly and to sleep. We must train our bodies and our minds to untangle the mess of fear and risk, of inevitability and acceptance.

Even if we fail to recognize the enemy, our body can betray us. The body recognizes fear and risk with a tiny shot of a hormone that prepares us to survive. Watch the hands and eyes of someone while they face a sudden fright: a deer leaps into view from the margin of a car's headlights. The face flushes as blood accelerates. A keen observer can witness this flushing and warming of the face, the pupillary response, the small movement to wipe suddenly damp palms. That is our body telling us that it saw our own death, our enemy. This hit of adrenalin in our bloodstream often promotes chattering with repeated stories. The need for sleep and peeing disappears instantly. Many of these stories start: "No shit, there I was just minding my own business."

I am an American soldier. I am ensconced behind high walls. I am well armed, well fed, and sleep with a blinking night light above my tired head. I shoo the fears from my pillow. The blinking red light provides the enemy with an accurate means of finding me and all others at our headquarters. I force calmness. I tell myself these rockets are small and distant. I listen to the deep thump of a rocket landing in soft Iraqi dirt. I am safe.

In the midst of this global insanity, we watched Olympic curling matches on the Armed Forces Network. We sat in the dining facility as darkness settled. I knew people were watching Sweden and Canada because the room hushed during play. My fellow American soldiers sat unevenly distributed at the dining tables. When Canada knocked the Swede's stone from the inner rings, the room erupted in cheers. Armed soldiers in Iraq hooted and applauded great bowls, slides, goes, or curls, or whatever the action may be called. Leaning on Humvees and waiting for mission planning on sand tables, soldiers revisited the plays of the prior evening's curling match. Night after night this February, we watched curling at 1800 hours. Somewhere in Minnesota, six other people rose early to watch these same games. Little did Canadian, Swedish, or American curlers know that several hundred bored American soldiers studied and watched their matches with the same enthusiasm one might expect for football. Some of the guys bet on the games, spreads, and plays. Gambling may be prohibited by General Order Number One, but one-upmanship and the core values of competition cannot be regulated out of the soldier's existence.

In the middle of this month, February 2006, the last Mobile Army Surgical Hospital, or MASH, ceased operations. We gave it to the government of Pakistan. We left the facilities and equipment in the hands of medical staff and administrators. *Stars and Stripes*, the military's newspaper, informed me that the band played anthems and marches in accordance with military tradition. The band did not play the TV show's theme song, a tune called *Suicide is Painless*, which I believe was a missed opportunity. MASH units have been replaced with Combat Support Hospitals, which are pronounced "cash."

On the twenty-second of this month, someone blew up the "Golden Mosque" in Samarra. Samarra is 125 kilometers northwest of Baghdad. Locally, the mosque is called the Al-Askari Mosque or Shrine. Before the bombing, it had a brilliant golden dome. The mosque has been associated with the Shi'ah since the tenth century. The golden dome was added in 1905. The bombs were set by men wearing uniforms of the Iraqi Special Forces. The bombing destroyed the dome and most of the building. In response, or retaliation, at least 130 have been killed. Most of those killed were Sunni. A gun battle interrupted the funeral for an Iraqi journalist who investigated and reported on the bombing.

Shi'ah leaders such as Abdul-Asiz al-Hakim said that the attack on the shrine "does not represent Sunnis in Iraq." Shi'ah cleric Moqtada Sadr also urged restraint: "We are not enemies but brothers. Anyone who attacks a Muslim is not a Muslim." Protests and massive crowds attended prayers at the Abu Hanifa Mosque, Baghdad's most important Sunni site. Up and down Iraq—from Basra near the coast in the south to Kut and Mosul—people protested in unity, calling for calm and national reconciliation. Sunni and Shi'ah stood together pleading for peace while other factions forced wedges into thousand-year history.

External forces within Iraq attack Iraqis, which means that, while we are in the middle of our own Iraq war, someone else is incited a civil war on the same battlefield at the same time.

During my first tour, we patrolled the streets of Baghdad in unarmored vehicles, often painted the dark green and brown colors of northern European forests. In the early days of this war, the TV cameras rolled footage of American military muscle in an ancient city. The bad guys were brown-skinned Iraqis. We followed a script. The solution was democracy and the stained purple thumb worn by those who voted in American-led elections. We locked up Saddam Hussein. On

May 1st, 2003, the president of the United States stood on the deck of an aircraft carrier under a banner that read: "Mission Accomplished." Two years later, I was notified that my unit will attach to the Fourth Infantry Division for a one-year tour of duty in Iraq.

When I arrived for this tour, we were hastily slapping armor plates on vehicles. Soldiers asked families at home to ship high-quality body armor.

With armed soldiers on the ground, America discovered that Iraq's history involves centuries of strife between people who all look Iraqi to the American eye. These people all sound Iraqi to the American ear. American schools do not teach Iraqi history. Few American school systems teach students the history of Islam. We do not remember, or even know, that the British government drew these national borders following WWI at the end of the Ottoman rule. In attendance at a 1921 conference were Winston Churchill, T.E. Lawrence (remembered as Lawrence of Arabia), and Gertrude Bell. T. E. Lawrence noted that the conference and resulting boundaries "heralded a period of unrest in the Middle East which had been scarcely surpassed even under the Ottoman rule." In this region of Arabia, there had been a near-constant conflict between the Kurds and the Iraqi government, with active wars from 1961 to 1970, then again in 1974 and 1975. There was an internal Iraqi uprising during the 1991 invasion of Iraq by America and coalition forces. There was an Iraqi-Kurdish Civil War in 1994-1997. There are cultural and ethnic borders drawn by history we do not see.

Joe, the storybook American soldier, is white and Christian and carries stubble on his cheeks. Joe wears dusty fatigues while slinging his load with an easy readiness. Joe eats well. Joe marches with confidence and can identify the enemy without question.

I am an American soldier with smooth cheeks, a shorter stature, thick, dark, straight hair, and brown eyes. I grew up equally at home in the hills of Vermont as I was in the urban reaches of Boston, Massachusetts. On my body armor, I carry the same ammunition and medical kit as my fellow soldiers. I carry two thousand calories in dried fruit and snack bars. I carry three liters of warm water on my back. In my pockets, where some soldiers carry the American flag and a Bible, I carry a copy of the Declaration of Independence and the Constitution of the United States. Folded in this thin pamphlet are two poems: one by Longfellow and one by Frost, hometown writers whose words evoke images of my feet in the soft soil of a New England forest. Unlike the men, I carry a head scarf that I can rapidly deploy when my helmet comes off. I wear it to bridge cultural gaps and offer respect to those I meet on these streets. When I cover my head, I address people in poor Arabic. Yet, I am rewarded with smiles and trust.

Many of us strive to learn the language. We work to understand the people and the culture. We want to look back at our time with pride and a sense of accomplishment. My platoon, my company, this division, the United States military—we are here to do good. Sending armed soldiers may appear contrary to the goals of peace, yet we accept that. Soldiers become historians, students, storytellers, and linguists.

While I read the news of the day, I scour the internet for history. I fail to understand the community that I am standing in. I recognize that I am a foreigner here. I represent a long, long line of European soldiers who have stood on this soil before me, including my own Viking and crusader ancestors. When confused by the complexity of the strife here, I call to mind the history of the British Isles, where most of my ancestors came from. In the sixteenth century, Henry VIII broke from the Catholic Church of Roman. And in the 1970s, the world witnessed armed conflict on the streets of Belfast between Catholics and Protestants. The "Troubles," as they came to be known, flared up. The Troubles represented a history of conflict spanning two millennia. The parallels illustrate that history is non-linear, complicated, political, social, economic—as well as religious.

At once, I am a participant, a belligerent, and an observer here. I question if today's war may not be yesterday's war. At the opening of the month, two million Shi'ah walked a pilgrimage to Karbala. At the end of the month, a Shi'ah shrine exploded in an act of aggression, then hundreds of Iraqis lost their lives at the hands of other Iraqis—

or at the hands of Iraqis and others from the region. It is as if we came back from a television advertisement to discover ourselves in a new story. We woke from a brief nap to discover a new landscape.

Suddenly, our war is no longer our war.

6 | The Forgotten Armory

BRIGHID, FEBRUARY 2006

Sam's house falls a few miles north of the Massachusetts border. Few would observe the state line when crossing it. Massachusetts even put up their own brand of a town marker for the Vermont town. The sign, like all Massachusetts town signs, looks like an open book. Driving north along a Massachusetts state highway, you will see a Massachusetts-style town sign that reads: "Entering Trowbridge." The radio and few television stations in Trowbridge are Massachusetts stations. But Trowbridge is in Vermont.

At the western verge of the road stands a two-hundred- year-old granite pillar. Leaving Massachusetts, it says: "Mass." Leaving Vermont, it says: "VT." The pillar is backwards to modern eyes. When driving in a car, the pillar reads "Mass" when going north into Vermont. Today, travelers would expect the opposite: "VT" when entering Vermont, and "Mass" when entering Massachusetts.

I work in Massachusetts at the east coast campus of an employer I do not love. When possible, I live at Sam's home in Trowbridge. When the drive proves too long, or the work hours too long, I hunker down in my small apartment near campus. That apartment serves as my legal address for employment and my Massachusetts driver's license. When I say, "I am going to Vermont this weekend," people around campus assume I will be driving for hours to a cottage or condo at a well-known ski resort or in Burlington. Most in Massachusetts think that driving to Vermont requires effort, planning, camping gear, and a safari vehicle. Instead, I drive along the Massachusetts state highway, pop north over the line, and park. I never leave pavement.

So I've started saying, "I am going to the farm." This prevents the confusion caused by New England geography. I suspect that many New Englanders may secretly prefer the once-derogatory term, "Yankee." Except few here wish to confuse their loyalty to New England sports teams with the New York Yankees, a rivalry that has lasted a century. This is the Red Sox nation; home to the New England Patriots, the Boston Celtics, the Boston Bruins, and the New England Revolution soccer club.

Frankly, I like the term. It reminds me of the warm reception our troops got overseas in World War II movies: "Hello Yank" and "Here come the Yanks." Even during our poorly executed and poorly timed interference in Central America and the Caribbean, locals held signs protesting, "Yanqui go home." During the American Civil War, those fighting for the south against the U.S. government called members of the U.S. Army "Yankees." The author E. B. White, a long-time resident of Maine, once wrote:

"To foreigners, a Yankee is an American.
To Americans, a Yankee is a Northerner.
To Northerners, a Yankee is an Easterner.
To Easterners, a Yankee is a New Englander.
To New Englanders, a Yankee is a Vermonter.
And in Vermont, a Yankee is somebody
who eats pie for breakfast."

I occasionally refer to Sam's Trowbridge place as home. I say it aloud at the office. In my heart and mind, I can call myself a Yankee—as long as no one thinks I root for a New York sports team. And with a Massachusetts driver's license, maybe I qualify as a New Englander. If not now, then when? How many years of residency are required? Or is the term earned by lineage and ancestry?

I pull to the curb near the Worcester Armory, which now serves as the Massachusetts National Guard Museum and Archives. I put these thoughts of self-identity aside as I park in front of this castle-shaped building.

Last month, I paid for an official death certificate for Henry McDonald, my great-great-something ancestor. The green form, embossed and signed, states that Henry was a married white male who died at the age of forty-five years and five days. He died on the 25th of May,1900 while living at 46 Park Ave in Springfield, Massachusetts.

The modern death certificate issued by the City of Springfield left the veteran of foreign war box unchecked. I am here to verify the facts in my dossier of Captain Henry McDonald.

I enter the museum, holding a notebook and folder of loose papers. Starting first with the most obvious element of Captain's Henry career, I ask about the Spanish American War. The host greets me warmly. He introduces himself as lieutenant colonel, retired, of the Massachusetts National Guard. He appears to be the sole occupant of the facility. I sit with him at the desk and open my folders, introducing him to my Captain Henry and explaining that I would like information about his service with the Massachusetts National Guard and the Spanish American War.

That's where my host stops me. The Spanish American War brings two images to mind: a newspaper headline screaming that we are to "Remember the Maine," and the charge of Teddy Roosevelt and the Rough Riders up San Juan Hill. Following the Spanish American War, the United States government annexed the former Spanish colonies of Puerto Rico, the Philippines, and Guam. My host says: "You'll not find much about the war. Massachusetts sent nearly six thousand men to sit on the beaches in Florida where they all got sick with tropical and social diseases." He ought to have completed his statement with a dismissive hand wave.

"Well, my guy seems to have been injured in Cuba and linked to the Teddy Roosevelt, San Juan Hill action."

"Every family has that story."

"Seriously, I had no idea my guy existed. My family never had any family lore about this man. I discovered him during my research." I open my folder. I slide the obituary across the table to him. I point to the section that says he served with Company B of the Second Regiment.

I read aloud, "He went with his company into the war in Cuba. The great battle of El Caney was fought. Company B distinguished itself and the troop was waiting outside Santiago. Then, yes, it seems he slipped in the mud 'when danger was practically passed.' Further down, it reads that his company faced gunfire and that after the commander of Company K was shot, my guy managed both Company B and K."

"You are right. What was your name again?"

I offer my hand. "Brighid Doran."

"Lieutenant Colonel Whitney."

He studies the obituary again. "Either this obit is incorrect, or it is correct. Let's find out."

One point for me.

"Others have come in saying that their Massachusetts ancestor rode up the hill with Teddy Roosevelt. After a few minutes, I showed them that the battalion never left Florida. Two-hundred-thousand men had responded to the call to arms for a war that lasted ten weeks. This should be pretty easy. Your guy was an officer and company commander. Officers tend to have more written down about them. Maybe we have something?"

We move to a file room.

"By the early 1900s, the state militias, like your guys, formed into National Guard units and got federal funding."

"What were they before that date?"

"State-run military forces made up of volunteers who elected their officers and protected their communities. Before the early 1900s, the units were part of the Massachusetts Volunteer Militia, the MVM. They met for training, some monthly, some less frequently. Some units met weekly. Our history with militia goes back to the earliest days of the colony and even back to the English system of militias. If you were a young man and able bodied, you were required to serve. Do you know the name Myles Standish?"

"Sure, Plymouth and pilgrim and all that."

"Plymouth, yes. Pilgrim, no. Standish shipped over having served as a military officer in an English militia. The Pilgrims understood that the colony would require a militia, so they brought Standish along as their guy-with-a-gun. Many of the people on the Mayflower were not religious but traveled with specific roles as tradesmen, servants, and—like Standish—as military.

During the American Revolution, the militia here earned the

nickname 'minutemen' for their ability to muster quickly."

"A long and proud legacy?" I want to sound respectful, but I am not sure I get my tone right.

"I found his officer card."

He pulls it from the drawer and places it on the table. The card reads:

McDonald, Henry, Springfield
Birthplace: New York, N.Y.
Military Record:
2d Battle Inf. B, Sept 26, 1876; corpl., sgt, 1st sgt.,
1st lt., Apr 2. 1887; com. Vacated; Jan 11. 1882,
decision sup. jud. court; re-elected May 15, 1882;
capt. Feb 9, 1889.
2d Inf. U.S.A., C, Mar 11, 1870; dis.,
Oct 23,1874; corpl., sgt.

At the bottom of the page was a columnar form. It described his rank as major with Company B of the Second Infantry Regiment, Brigade 1. Retired July 26, 1899. Then typed in bolder and dark letters, as if with a fresh ribbon or different typewriter, it read:

Deceased.
Mail returned Nov 16, 1909 marked deceased.

I read it a few times, twice with my finger, following the lines of abbreviations. The colonel offers to translate it for me.

> "Henry McDonald enlisted in the second infantry battalion of the MVM in September 1876. When he joined, they gave him the rank of corporal, likely due to his prior service with the U.S. Army. Then, during the next decade, he was promoted to sergeant. He served for a while as the company first sergeant, the top non-commissioned sergeant in the unit. Then the men elected him to be a first lieutenant, at which point he was commissioned. Don't ask me what happened in 1882. It appears his commission was vacated, then the issue went to the top court in Massachusetts, the Supreme Judicial Court, where the decision

was likely reversed. He was promoted to captain in May 1889, then served as a captain until he retired."

"Why then do some records call him a major?"

"I'd say they promoted him to major on the day he retired. It is a way to honor a long serving officer. He served as a captain, but upon retirement, he gets the benefits and recognition of major. This card confirms that he was captain, and likely company commander, for B company of the Second Infantry Battalion of the Massachusetts Volunteer Militia."

"What is the difference between this second infantry and the other second infantry that he served with?"

"In 1870, your guy Henry enlisted in the United States Army, the *regular army*, as a private. He was assigned to the Second Infantry Battalion. Therefore, one unit was the Second Infantry Battalion of the Massachusetts Volunteer Militia or MVM, and the other was the Second Infantry Battalion of the United States Army. This would not happen today because the state militia became part of the federal structure in 1903. Units got re-designated. For example, when heading into World War I, the Massachusetts units formed into the Yankee Division, the 26th Infantry Division."

"Can I have a copy of that document?"

"Certainly, but let's see what else we can find." The colonel works through various drawers of neat files. "Here is a record of the mustering for the war. It seems that the unit traveled to Framingham." He pulls the card.

Name: McDonald Henry
Company: B
Regiment: 2 Massachusetts Infantry U.S. Volunteers
Rank: Captain
Age: 46
Height: 5 feet, 10 and ½ inches.
Complexion: Medium
Eyes: Blue
Hair: Dark
Where Born: New York City N.Y.

Occupation: Chief of Police
Enlisted: May 3, 1898
Where: South Framingham
Residence: Springfield Mass
Mustered In: May 10, 1898
Mustered Out: November 3, 1898
Remarks: Term two years

The LT adds, "This card shows that he reported to the state muster in early May of 1898. This card shows the transition from a state militia to a federal fighting force. At this point in our history, the regular army, the U.S. Army, only had twenty-five thousand soldiers. The government did not want to keep a standing army of an effective size."

"He and the company arrived in Framingham, what...via train, I suppose?"

"Sure, train from Springfield to Framingham. The rail line runs the same path as the Mass Pike."

"They arrived, then what?"

"Then they got processed, most likely. They probably got health inspections and fitness checks. There were likely political things going on in Washington. Then Henry and his company agreed to a two-year hitch as members of an infantry regiment that was funded by the federal government. These men started drawing pay as full-time soldiers."

I ask the colonel about the rest of the records in the Massachusetts National Guard Museum and Archives. He gives a professional shrug.

"The Mass Guard has a lineage and history going back to 1636, as part of the Massachusetts Bay Colony, then the Dominion of New England, then the Province of Massachusetts Bay before the Revolution. This war lasted two months at the end of the nineteenth century. In that century, we fought the War of 1812, a war with Mexico, and the Civil War. Historical records and letters often disappear when the wars end. Officers keep some for their memoirs. Others want something to prove that they were there. The records were only bits of paper. And then who gets them? The National Archive, the

U. S. Army, the state militia keeps them? It gets confusing. Nobody wants them initially, then eventually everyone wants them."

"I am super pleased with what you found. We've confirmed that he was in the militia and served for years. We've proved that he mustered for the war."

The colonel touches my arm. "And I might be able to go one step further."

He logs into a library system and then searches for various terms, including Cuba, Spanish War, and so on. He finds a book in the archive's library called *Correspondence relating to the War with Spain and the conditions growing out of the same.* The title continued, identifying the *Insurrection in the Philippine Islands, China Relief Effort.* The Government Printing Office published the document in 1902.

With the digital document open, he then searches "infantry;" "second infantry;" "Massachusetts;" and "El Caney." On page 543, he finds that the Second Massachusetts Volunteer Infantry had been placed within the Second Division. He looks at the screen.

"I think you've got what you came looking for."

"Really?"

I step around, leaning closely over his shoulder. With a quick scan, I can see the core elements of the story told in the obituary. The paragraph reads:

> Massachusetts Second Regiment organized and mustered into the service of the United States at South Framingham, Massachusetts between May 8th and May 10th of 1898. The regiment included 47 officers and 896 enlisted men. Ordered to Tampa, Florida on May 13th. Arrived at Lakeland Florida May 17th and temporarily assigned to the Second Cavalry Brigade, Fifth Army Corps. Changed trains from Lakeland to Tampa on May 30th. The regiment was then assigned to the First Brigade of the Second Division, Fifth Army Corps. Sailed from Tampa on June 14th; arrived at Daiquiri Cuba on June 22nd. Participated in the Santiago Campaign and in the battle of El Caney July 1. Transferred to the Third Brigade, Second Division, Fifth Army Corps. Left Santiago on the 21st

> of August. The Regiment arrived at Montauk Point, New York with 44 officers and 797 enlisted men. Casualties while in service: Officers—killed in action, 1; wounded, 3, died of disease, 2. Enlisted men—killed in action, 4, wounded, 41, died of wounds, 4, died of disease, 86.

After I read it completely, the lieutenant colonel says, "Given that the United States mustered about two-hundred-thousand soldiers, very few of them saw any action. In a war that last ten weeks, your guy was in the center of the action in Cuba. If you look at the numbers, this Massachusetts unit lost about fifteen percent of its force in a few days due to death, injury, and illness."

Navigating to *Wikipedia*, the colonel shows me that in the Battle of El Caney, Cuba, eighty-one men died during combat. With a finger, he points at the numbers. "There is no real accounting for these numbers; for example, we don't know if they included death-from-disease in the killed number or not, or do they show as wounded, or were the soldiers incapacitated with disease ignored in the reporting? Our little fighting team from Massachusetts gave what they could and left a bloody mark during that battle."

The colonel, now attracted to my mystery and my ancestor, gives another push on the document search. He comes up with a bound book called *Annual Report of the Adjutant General of the Commonwealth of Massachusetts for the year ending 1892*. On page 123, I read the names of every member of Company B, Second Regiment Infantry. The document lists them by rank and provides their scores at the rifle range. Henry was there! Another document for my dossier on Henry McDonald.

The colonel leafs through the small collection of documents in my folder. "This is cool," he says, holding up the death certificate. He feels the embossing, then looks at the signature. "Official, huh?"

"Why not? It took long enough to find."

He studies the death date and the cause of death, then asks, "Do you mind if I look at the obit again?"

I hand him the document.

The colonel says, "It looks like he dropped dead on the bedroom floor?"

"That's what it says."

"I am suspicious of this. He suddenly drops dead less than a year after returning from combat operations? If I had a medical education instead of artillery, I might wonder if he tossed a blood clot from the injury. The timing and his age are a bit odd. You will never know, but you might find a story buried in there."

"Okay. Great. What about the rest of his record? Thoughts about how I can verify or learn more?"

"Not really. I'll guess you should head to the national archives. As I said, the paper records get scattered from here to there, burned, tossed, or carried home as keepsakes."

We copy the two documents he found: the muster record showing that Captain Henry joined the Second Massachusetts Infantry, and the officer record that showed his various ranks as a member of the Massachusetts Voluntary Militia. We shake hands while I express my gratitude for his investment in my research project.

During our morning, not another soul entered the museum.

Having gathered my folder, I return to my car. If I head west on Interstate 90, the Massachusetts Turnpike, I will follow the path of the train that once transported soldiers from Springfield to Framingham. Following that path takes me to Captain Henry's home. I turn west. Driving the highway, I ask, "What can Springfield give me that I do not yet have?"

Two answers come at the same time. First, having just walked out of the old Worcester Armory, I would like to see the building where Captain Henry and his men met and trained. Second, I should discover his grave. The list builds itself as I drive. If he was the police chief, then a police station.

Pulling off the interstate at Springfield, I start searching my phone for "Springfield Armory." I drive to the location my phone points to.

Located in Armory Square, the building and related complex looks huge. Getting closer, I recognize the logo of the National Park Service. The brick building hosts a clock tower, and, upon the clock tower, a large American flag. The sign reads: "Springfield Armory National Historic Site."

It resembles the Worcester Armory in that both are brick buildings, and both have military—or castle—stylings. I wind my way towards the entrance, thinking this facility was managed by my ancestor. Questioning it, really. It appears rather larger than a militia company would need for meetings and training.

I start asking questions to the first uniformed member I meet.

"Is this the Springfield National Guard Armory?"

"Not sure what you are looking for. Do you want the National Guard facility in Springfield?"

"Maybe, I guess. I don't know. I am looking for the building where the old militia unit trained. Was that here?"

"No."

"What is this facility?"

"This is a national park."

I wait a beat, then two. "What was this facility?"

"This was the Springfield Armory where the government made weapons."

"I just came from the Worcester Armory. How is that different?"

"I don't think that they made guns in Worcester. What do they do at the Worcester Armory?"

"It is a museum, but it used to be home to a militia unit. Let me try asking again...if I wanted to find where the old state militia met and trained, where would I look? Or what would it be called?"

"I think you are looking for that national guard base."

"Okay, I'll go there."

"It is just up the road. Go up State and take a left on Roosevelt."

I find a single-story building on the right side of the road. The flags and tank help me identify it. The building is thoroughly modern. I pull in, expecting instant attention from a gate guard, but none exists. I park at the front of the building and ask the first soldier I see. Of course, the first response suggests that I return to the National Park Building. I say no, been there.

Then I see the soldier come up with a new idea.

"There is an old community center that looks like it was once an armory, back in the day."

"Tall, brick, looks like a castle?"

"Yes."

"Do you know where it is?"

"It is right downtown, but the neighborhood is a bit sketchy. The building is in rough shape. It is south of the rail and Memorial Bridge, but it is kind of near the river. Look around the area of State Street and Main Street."

"Do you know what it is called?"

"When I was a kid, it was a community center, probably named for someone we've all forgotten about. Or maybe it was 'South End Community Center?'"

I offer my hand, then return to my car.

I follow the directions, coming to a neighborhood that earns top marks for neglected. Plywood boards cover the windows of the old armory building. The brick façade looks age-worn and tired. When I spy it, I know it is the correct building. In relief above the main door, it reads: "Armory M-V-M," a phrase I now recognize as "Massachusetts Volunteer Militia."

I park and walk around the building. I find a cornerstone covered in debris and dirt. It informs me that the building was built in 1895. Scanning my notes, I see that Henry McDonald was promoted to captain on February 9, 1889 and retired in 1899. Henry had been company commander for six years prior to the laying of this cornerstone and for three years following.

This is my Captain Henry's building. He would have been the first company commander of the first company that served in this facility. The men of this company volunteered for a two-year hitch to wage a war against Spain. The war lasted only ten weeks. During that ten weeks, men of this company faced bloody combat against Spanish soldiers on the island of Cuba. Henry and the men of Company B returned to Springfield as heroes of a foreign war, a war which influenced the 1900 election of President Teddy Roosevelt and resulted in the United States taking Guam, Puerto Rico, and the Philippines as territories.

Damn. He is my guy.

That this entire history should be captured in this shabby, neglected building just off Main Street in Springfield, Massachusetts surprises and disappoints. Another few years of neglect and this building will drop to the ground under its own weight.

In a state—and region—that takes such pride in history, I recognize the difficult decisions people must make each day with buildings, urban landscapes, and history. One hundred years ago, soldiers from Massachusetts fetched home stories of tragedy and victory. This castle- like militia building passed from a state function to a federal function when that militia morphed into the modern National Guard. Global wars eclipsed our memories. This building, once a celebration of a region's place on the global stage, became a financial burden to an industrial city in western Massachusetts. As the city's status and economic prospects declined, so went the condition of this building and the memories of the men, and families, it once served.

We choose what wars to remember. We choose our heroes. We build statues and preserve the history that affirms our present. Massachusetts has its Old North Church and Boston Common. Massachusetts has the U. S. S. Constitution, "Old Ironsides," the oldest commissioned ship in the U.S. Navy. Massachusetts has Plymouth, Lexington, and Concord—even Salem.

As I read Sam's journal entries, I see parallels between the Iraq War and this war with Spain. Once upon a time, a U.S. Navy ship exploded while at harbor in Havana, Cuba. William Randolph Hearst and Joseph Pulitzer excited the national body. Hearst published: "Remember the Maine, To Hell with Spain!" The newspapers called the Spanish "murderers" while identifying the explosion as an "atrocity."

Sam is in Iraq, for the second time, because we did not like Saddam Hussein. We created a cloud of lies related to weapons of mass destruction as a means of legitimizing an invasion. The yellow journalism of a century ago resembles the lies told by our government then retold by the news media today. For this reason, Sam leads a small military intelligence unit out on the streets of Iraq.

I decide—while looking at this forgotten building, a memorial to forgotten men—that I may have found a home here in New England. This is Captain Henry's building. The years before it was built, he served here with Company B, the Springfield City Guard. The day the foundation stone was laid, he served as the company commander. He left for war from here, and thus returned. He was the boss of the building for the first years of its life.

When I touch this building, I am touching part of my own Captain Henry. My touch spans a century.

7 | Trenton

HENRY, DECEMBER 1871

The train chugs north, leaving the Rising Fawn depot behind. Marshal James Skyles holds two prisoners with the help of Sergeant Porter and his squad of six soldiers: McDonald, Donovan, Sturtevant, Belville, Mueller, and Abrams.

McDonald, with his short carbine rifle, remains standing by the carriage door. Marshal Skyles paces the center aisle. Their spy, Asa Boydston, rides north on a horse.

They travel the ten miles to Trenton, the seat of Dade County, Georgia. The train whistles and slows as it enters the yard at Trenton. The squad rises. The prisoners, unaware of the next evolution, complain loudly about their treatment and refuse to get up from their seats. Marshal Skyles provides physical and verbal encouragement to them.

Belville and Donovan step to the wooden platform first. Followed by Abrams. They position their rifles at the ready. The mail clerk, Hale, steps down. Then road commissioner Blevins gains his footing on the depot's deck. Henry lets himself out of the rear door of the carriage, stepping to the ground while making a wide assessment of the depot, the town, and the terrain.

Asa Boydston watches the proceedings from horseback one hundred yards to the south. The marshal, having seen Boydston, walks towards him. With a flick of the hand and a quick, furtive glance towards the county road, Boydston warns him off. He has alerted the marshal to new dangers. The marshal nods in acknowledgment.

"Mac, keep it tight. Stay vigilant," the marshal says to Henry, then motions Sergeant Porter to the signalman's shack. "Sergeant, I think we have a reception committee waiting for us on the other side of the depot. I'll hazard a guess that several men from Rising Fawn rode ahead of us."

"Thoughts?"

"I've got one more warrant to serve today, for a gentleman named Haney. Asa says he knows him. And I'll need Asa to point the finger before I arrest him."

"Maybe we should have stayed on the train and come back another day?"

"We didn't though, did we?" Both the sergeant and the marshal watch the slow-moving train depart the switching yard, continuing north towards the safety of Tennessee. The steam and smoke will be visible for several miles. The train travels faster than a small infantry squad with two shackled prisoners could run. Escaping Trenton by train is no longer an option.

Sergeant Porter offers a plan. "I can take over the depot and telegraph Lieutenant Dempsey. We're only twenty miles from the post. A mounted squad could get to us in a couple of hours."

"And we can take the next train."

"I think the next train goes back south again. I am not too keen to head into Alabama with the Ku Kluxers chasing us. The next northbound train is not until 7:00 p.m. or later."

"Too bad we don't have Army trains like we did under Sherman. The general could whistle one from the ether. During the war, we had our own engineers and our own locomotives."

"You served down here, Sergeant?"

"I did. I tended to follow Sherman around. Or maybe he followed me around. I first served under him in Mississippi. We worked on the gunboats up and down the river. Then I got posted here before the big push to Atlanta."

"You were part of that March to Atlanta?"

"Me and several hundred thousand men. I used to ride these rails up and back from Chattanooga often. We would deploy to Acworth, Marietta, Atlanta, and back north to Chattanooga. The furthest I made it was to Macon. We had to garrison every depot in Georgia back then. We shuffled men, horses, supplies, and artillery."

"We can garrison this depot then, just like the old days, huh?" These old days were only six and seven years ago.

"I supposed we will have to."

The sergeant and the marshal return to the depot building. The depot hosted passengers on the northern half and a freight warehouse in the southern half. The platform reaches wraps around the building.

The marshal opens the sliding freight depot doors. The freight warehouse has one small window to the south and no windows facing the road to the west. The soldiers bring the prisoners to the door and the sergeant speaks to them quietly.

"We have company on the other side of this building. Donovan, take up a firing position by that south window but do not show yourself. Belville, guard Blevins. Mueller, you have the other prisoner, Haney. Don't talk to your prisoners. Sit them on the ground in the dark near this back door but in the corner. In fact, put them in opposite corners. Keep them apart. Understood?"

Each private acknowledges the instructions, then stands waiting. "Go, move. Quietly and quickly." Donovan, Mueller, and Belville round up the prisoners and sneak into the darkened warehouse. "Sturtevant and Abrams, you are with me. Abrams, you'll watch the back door and railyard from behind the door. Sturtevant, you keep your eyes on the passenger side. Mac, you are going with the marshal. He wants to get one more prisoner here."

"Understood, Sergeant." The squad deploys into the freight warehouse. Abrams pulls the sliding door closed, or mostly closed, leaving a small gap through which he can aim a rifle and watch his sector.

Marshal Skyles walks up to Henry, and—looking over his shoulders—watches the quiet railyard.

Henry asks, "Got a plan?"

"Not much of one."

"Do you know where your guy is?"

"No. For all I know, he could be part of the crew in front of this building. You are pretty good with that carbine of yours?"

"Fair enough. I hit what I aim at."

"Go conceal yourself on the north side of the depot. Keep out of sight and keep that rifle of yours ready to fire. I'll go through the depot and walk into the street from the center of the building. We'll see what happens from there."

Henry thinks, *true, not much of a plan.*

With forty rounds each for each soldier, limited food rations, and trapped in a small wooden train depot, the soldiers will not last long if the fighting gets intense.

Wordlessly, Henry walks to the north edge of the building. He scans the road for riders or men hiding in concealed firing positions. Before coming to the corner, he silently places his rucksack on the ground. He positions his ammo box at his left hip. He also liberates a small shaving mirror and tucks this into his shirt pocket. In the bottom of the rucksack, he reaches for his spare ammo box, adding another forty-two rounds to the forty-two issued for this mission.

He positions himself against the wall and stills his breathing. With each exhale, he slows his heart rate and opens his ears with the intensity of a hunter hiding in the woods.

He hears Marshal Skyles open, then close, the front door. He imagines the marshal standing with his right hand near his holstered pistol, back to the depot door.

"My name is United States Deputy Marshal James Skyles. I am ordering you three to disband immediately." The marshal speaks loudly enough to communicate to both Henry and Sergeant Porter inside the building that three mounted men await the soldiers in the road. Henry uses his small pocket mirror to survey the situation.

"If you do not disband and depart immediately, I will arrest you for interfering with governmental operations. You've got several rifles trained on you right now." In a clear voice, the marshal continues, "Remember the young private who did not shoot you in Rising Fawn. He's got you in his sights right now. He could take the three of you down before you finish your next breath. Please go home to your families."

The men on the street yell back at the marshal. They instruct the marshal to unshackle their friends and release them, in colorful language rich with terms used during the recent war. Henry knows that these men had not yet accepted—may never accept—that the war ended. That the Confederacy lost.

In response to the vitriolic language, the marshal addresses the armed riders with stiff, short words that could be safely written in a training manual. The yelling continues until the marshal shouts to Henry, "Hey, Mac, do you mind giving these guys a demonstration?"

Henry steps into plain view. He adjusts his rifle aim from the three men on Montague Street to the church spire two blocks distant. The first shot spins the wind vane. The second shot rings the bell. The third shot hits a fire pail that immediately drains itself of water. Henry makes the three shots within the time it takes to count to two. Three accurate shots made within one breath from a Spencer repeating carbine. He brings the rifle to bear on the face of the middle-most man.

The street falls silent. The sound of the three rapid shots echoes in the ears of everyone in the town. Henry sights over his barrel, regarding his target with both eyes open. He breathes regularly and evenly.

"Gentlemen, he is only one of our soldiers. Please ride home to your families safely. I've never known this man to miss anything, ever."

The man with the rifle pointed to his face backs his horse. Horse and rider take three steps back, breaking ranks with the other two men. Then all three turned south towards Rising Fawn.

Henry relaxes his posture but keeps the rifle at his shoulder.

The marshal moves away from the door. "Sergeant, I am going to take the private with me. We will return directly. Seems okay out here." Asa, still mounted, appears into sight from his hidden position and rides towards the courthouse square, stopping in front of a restaurant on the north side. He points towards it with an open and flat hand. Henry and Skyles approach.

At the door, the marshal says, "Mac, wait here."

Skyles enters the restaurant and addresses a middle-aged man seated at a table. "My name is Deputy U.S. Marshal James Skyles. I am arresting you for violation of several federal statutes. Please rise and walk with me." The gentleman complies immediately. He stands, puts on his overcoat, then strides to the door. Before opening it, he says, "Della honey, I'll square up the bill when I get back. I won't be too long."

Outside of the building, Skyles asks, "Are you Mister Robert Haney of Trenton, Georgia?" The man answers confidently, "I am." Asa Boydston nods from horseback in agreement.

"We are going to take you into federal custody pending trial for violations of civil rights acts and violations of the Ku-Klux Acts. This private is going to place handcuff on your wrists." Unlike the other arrests, Mister Haney adds nothing. He does not complain. He does not puff out his chest with bravado. He demonstrates pride in being arrested by a federal officer and a U.S. Army soldier. His silence, his calm, and his willingness to comply introduces a touch of fear to Henry.

This man is a real risk, Henry thinks.

Townspeople gather silently around the square watching the arrest. As Henry and Skyles walk their prisoner to the depot, they follow, the crowd swelling as they head down Court Street. The street pushes the people together. Some young kids and younger men run down the parallel Church Street, keeping level with Henry and the marshal.

After Mister Robert Haney reaches the depot platform, he pivots to the gathering crowd. They had spread out along Montague Street and the depot yard. They keep out of reach but within the range of an easy pistol shot.

"Neighbors, dear friends, worry not for me. These northern gentlemen will take perfect care of me. I am certain my old friends Foster Blodgett and Colonel James Smith will help us all untangle this unholy mess. I won't be but a day or two. We will clear the matter up in Chattanooga where I have a lot of good friends—and so do you all. Pray for me and pray for these poorly educated soldiers of the north. These young men, they never knew the war like we did. Most of these soldiers only started shaving last year." The prisoner looks at Henry. "They'll take good care of me, I promise you all that. While I am gone, let's make sure that Missus Haney does not worry for me. You all know how she loves her garden and her tea. Be generous with her. Give her the support she needs. I am alright now. You all go back to the shops and your homes."

Haney, skilled at speaking in front of a crowd, makes eye contact with his audience from his makeshift pulpit. He walks to the passenger side of the depot then stands like a trained dog with his cuffed hands hanging loosely over his belly. He waits for Henry to open the door for him, then enters, taking a seat on a bench opposite the station master's window.

Mister Haney asks Deputy Skyles, "Deputy, why don't you bring the other two men in here and let them sit in these benches? It must be dusty and cold in that old warehouse." Henry recognizes that Mister Robert Haney had prior knowledge of his own arrest and of the soldiers' arrival.

Every action undertaken by the Army during this December day had been noted, communicated, and shared within Dade County. Dade County is shaped like a small triangle in the extreme upper left corner of the state, resembling a dog-eared page in weekly periodical: just a little fold in the northwest. Dade County ceded from both the State of Georgia and the United States of America a full year before the outbreak of the Civil War, or so the rumor goes at the post in Chattanooga. This tiny Nation of Dade held firmly to their antebellum economics, beliefs, and treatment of all those who did not share their white, Christian, European heritage. European immigrants took this land from the Cherokee through Georgia Land Lotteries. Sixteen thousand Cherokee were forcibly relocated from this region to the Oklahoma Indian Territories. The Trail of Tears started right here.

Mister Haney speaks loudly and clearly. "I assure you, deputy, that nothing will happen to us. We're all perfectly safe. Especially if our Dade County neighbors can see their beloved road commissioner and postman through these windows here." Therein hides the threat. Mister Haney threatens violence if the other prisoners are not soon visible through the glass windows. Marshal Skyles comprehends the unspoken threat.

"Sergeant, let's bring the prisoners in here. Abrams, Donovan, stay where you are."

Feeling a shift in power, prisoner Robert Haney then speaks to the station master. "Martin, how about a bit more heat in here. Let's take the chill off this day. Maybe you can send some of your boys to fetch us some firewood and maybe something to drink for our two guests from Rising Fawn. We want to make them feel welcome in Trenton, don't we?" Mister Haney, shackled prisoner, appoints himself the host.

The station master responds, "Good idea, Mister Haney." The station master enters the parlor, puts some wood into the stove, then steps out the back of the station. The room feels warmer immediately. The last phrase Henry hears from the station master is, "Where did those boys get to?"

Then the sergeant issues his own set of instructions, superseding those of the prisoner. "No one is entering or leaving this building. Understood, Mister Station Master?"

"I have telegrams to deliver."

"Not today, you don't."

"And my boys don't count. They move the freight. You can't mean them."

"I mean everyone. No one comes. No one goes."

The power in the room shifts back to the armed military. The soldiers settle into a newer, more relaxed configuration. Henry watches through the front of the station while occasionally looking to the rear windows and the railyard. The sergeant seats the prisoners on separate benches.

"Mac, follow me, will you?"

Together, the two men step out the front door and into the dark corner where Henry had been concealing himself. The sergeant asks: "Can you tap out a message?"

"No, Sergeant, I was never trained."

"Can any of the boys?"

"No, sorry, Sergeant."

"Well, the next time we do a simple one-day chore like this, I am taking a signals private with me. I am entirely confident that anything we give to that *good-ole-boy* will get shared with the entire Nation of Dade within five minutes."

Henry probes, "We should still try to send a telegram, don't you think, Sergeant?"

"On the one hand, it informs every rebel soldier, Ku-Kluxer, and moonshiner in the region that there is a squad of trapped soldiers. On the other hand, we could get reinforcements. I have my code book, but I am certain half of these station masters have the same code book."

"We can try the book to create a message. Maybe the station master does not have this version."

"Fine, but it only takes one person listening on the wire from here to Meridian, Alabama. If he has the current code book, we're up the creek. Within a minute of our request for help, someone else flashes 'six bluegill perch caught in Trenton.'" Six blue-bellied soldiers caught in a depot like fish out of water.

The sergeant thinks for a moment, then says, "Mac, put together a message and code it out for me, then get it sent."

"Will do, Sergeant. Would you like to know who is really good at these sorts of efforts? Paul Abrams, he's clever this way."

"Fine, ask for a special or an express to come down and hopefully before dark. Mister Haney is too full of *bon ami* for my taste. He thinks he is in charge. If you are going to get Private Abrams, go around back, like you are making a patrol circuit."

The sergeant presents Henry a small pad of paper and a stubby pencil. "Bring that back to me when you are done."

"Ok, Sergeant."

With his rifle loosely gripped in his right hand, Henry loops around the building. He calls quietly to Paul. Handing the code book, the pad, and the pencil to him, Henry commands, "Encode a message asking for a special train to Trenton. I'll be right back." Henry then completes a full circuit of the building, walking on the platform deck with an easy stance and his rifle at the ready in his right hand. This posture, and attitude, deliberately falls below Army standards for a soldier posting guard duty. He ought to have his rifle slung. His stride ought to be precise and measured. His cadence ought to be regular, with crisp, formal turns. To those watching, Henry's relaxed approach reflects arrogance, a measure of confidence in the control of the situation. But he is more alert than ever.

On the next loop, Paul hands him the pad, pencil, and code book.

"Keep the code book, pencil, and pad," Henry says. "Just give me the message."

Henry looks at the message. Fifteen letters arranged in three blocks of five letters each.

"What does it say?"

"Send special."

"That's all? Send special?"

"Do you want it to say more?"

"No, I guess not." Henry snorts. "Send special."

He makes another circuit of the building then enters the front, handing the note to the sergeant. The sergeant looked at the three simple blocks of letters.

"Is that it?"

"That's it."

"Well send it. Watch him while you do it, then wait for a reply."

Henry approaches the seated station master. "I need to send a telegram to the post."

"Certainly, sir. Do you have the message?"

"I do." Henry hands the note over.

"That's a short message."

"Just telling them we are safe and warm here."

"Very good. Now, who is this to?"

"The signals officer at the post."

"Well, I need a proper name for the records and to fill in the heading, you see."

Henry explores the options. He could send it to Captain Hood, the commander of E and F Companies. He could send it to his own lieutenant, Lieutenant Dempsey, the one who signed the orders for this adventure. Then, thinking of the number of Irish in this army, he decides to address it to Lieutenant Triobloit, which translates to "trouble" from the Irish language.

"Sir, hand me the note back. Let me write it down for you." The note came through. "Do you have a pen or a pencil for me to use?"

The station master offers Henry a pencil, with, "Now, you hand that back to me when you are done."

Henry writes: "Lieutenant Triobloit."

He hands the paper and the pencil back.

The station master sounds the name out. "Oh, that is a new name to me."

"He is new. He seems to be French or something." Henry pronounces it with an affected French accent: Trio-bloy, rolling the "r" with a Gallic trill. One of the dozens of Mics, Macs, O'Brians, O'Learys, or O'Shaunnassys will figure it out. Some young private will decode the message then say, "Do we have a Lieutenant Triobloit?" The private will run to a corporal and a sergeant repeating the name. Then the sergeant will run to the signals lieutenant. At some point, one of the ever-present—and nosey—Irishmen on the post will say: "Who's lookin' for Trouble?"

An acknowledgment returns quickly from the post in Chattanooga. "Well, sir, they got the message."

"What did they say?"

"Nothing, just an acknowledgement."

"Thank you."

Henry returns to the sergeant. "Message sent."

"Okay, let's have you take up a post outside."

Ten minutes later, the sergeant opens the door. "Message is back."

The header of the message reads: "To: Sergeant Porter and Squad Number 4." The message is comprised of a single block of five letters.

"I'll take it around back."

"Good, and this time, bring back my pencil."

"Right, Sergeant."

Henry makes a patrolling circuit around the building to Paul's post at the sliding door.

"We have a message from the post."

Paul looks through the book. "All it says is 'acknowledged.' And it is signed 'LT.' 'T.' Who is Lieutenant 'T'?"

"I made him up. It comes from the Irish for 'trouble.'"

"Oh."

"So do you think they are sending a train for us?"

"I do. And I think it will arrive at four o'clock."

"Oh! I see it."

"We're not squad number four, never have been. Someone on that end is just as clever as we are."

"We hold on until then, eh?"

"That's it, Paul. We hold on until four."

"We can do that, don't you think."

"I do, Paul, I do. Keep your eyes open. If they do try something, it will be after dark, before the evening train."

Henry patrols around the southern part of the building. He raps on the window, giving Donovan a jaunty wave. Back at the front of the building, he re-enters the waiting room.

Mister Haney speaks. "Hey, every time you open that door, the temperature in here drops."

Henry ignores the prisoner. He returns the codebook, the notepad, the pencil, and the message to Sergeant Porter. Written neatly, in Henry's hand, the note read: "Special due at 4p."

"I'll go back outside, now."

Henry opens the door wide. "Back into the cold for me, guys. Wish us luck." He gives the team a silly wave, then closes the door slowly.

At his normal post, Henry leans against a corner column, looking across the town of Trenton, the courthouse, the numerous small churches, the grid of village streets. He wonders how many eyes are watching him through windows. The garrisoned depot and the town look quiet and peaceful on the 12th of December 1871. The little lie of Dade County: a county at peace with itself, with its neighbors, and with the United States of America.

For most of the century, the county had been at war with the first inhabitants, the Cherokee. Cherokee landowners farmed and owned slaves like their white neighbors. They allied with the Americans against the British during the War of 1812. In the 1820s, the Cherokee developed a dictionary, improved the written form of their language, and translated and printed the Bible. And in 1829, the Cherokee drafted a constitution, modeling it after the United States Constitution. But the rich agricultural lands already growing cotton were just too appealing to white landowners, and the hill country of the region proved rich in gold and coal. In 1838, in violation of numerous treaties, Present Martin van Buren ordered the militias of the region to force the Cherokee off their lands. The U.S. Army supported the militias with pushing these humans west of the Mississippi River.

In 1860, months before the Battle of Fort Sumpter in South Carolina, this county had already ceded from the nation. In 1865, President Andrew Jackson declared the Civil War over. Interested in reuniting the states, he pardoned every rebel—given they had an estate valued less than $20,000. In effect, the president granted a pardon to every individual who had engaged in treason and insurrection against the United States. Six years later, these same individuals continue to engage in illegal and violent actions contrary to federal law.

With the new civil rights laws and two new amendments to the Constitution, men of the south could vote for representation in local, state, and national governments. This freedom to vote was granted to formerly enslaved people as well. In many counties, these men held a majority of the population and thus a majority of the vote. Politics in Alabama, Georgia, and parts of Tennessee become a messy fight over control of the government, schools, and representation.

Andrew Jackson owned slaves and hailed from Tennessee. The laws being passed by Congress created conflicts with the president's executive plans. This conflict resulted in contradictory policies flowing from the nation's capital. When General Ulysses Grant came to office in March 1869, he generally supported reconstruction and strove to help African Americans. People like these prisoners hindered progress through violence, intimidation, and voter suppression.

Marshal Skyles drags two chairs from the waiting room through the front door to the porch. He offers one to Henry, then sits in the other tipping it back to lean his shoulder against the building. Henry sits tentatively, laying his rifle across his lap.

"You're pretty good with that thing, Henry. What did you do before enlisting?"

"I was a waiter in New York City."

"That surprises me. I thought you were some farm kid from New England."

"No, sir. New York City, born and raised."

"Where did you learn to shoot like that?"

"My father taught me."

"What did your father do?"

"He sold tin and scrap metal from a cart on the streets."

"But he could afford a gun to teach you?"

"It was the second thing he bought when he could afford it."

"What was the first?"

"A Scottish-style broadsword."

Silence dominates the conversation. Henry maintains a heightened alertness. Sitting while on guard duty could get a soldier court martialed. He feels Sergeant Porter's eyeballs on the back of his head. From the waiting room, it must appear that the marshal and the private are relaxing on a porch as one might following a rich and filling Sunday dinner.

"Marshal, I can't sit when on guard duty."

"Sit."

"I can't."

"Sit. You are under my orders. I order you to sit. I'll inform your sergeant. Listen, private, I know that you are just as lethal and just as alert sitting in that chair as you are standing. I can't believe you rang their church bell on them. That sent a message. Did your father have you on a wooden sword when you were young?"

"Nearly as soon as I could walk, he put a play-sword in my hand, yes, sir."

"And he sells scrap metal on the streets of New York."

"He sells nice copper pots and tin wares such as lanterns and such now. It used to be just scraps."

"He came from Scotland, off the boat, then?"

"No, he was born in Dublin, but to Scottish highlanders. He's damn proud of that."

"I'd say so, to have you swinging a sword while in still in swaddling clothes."

"About right, sir."

The silence returns as both scan the buildings, the roads, the tree lines.

"What do you think? They will attack at dark?"

"I do, yes. That is my guess, but if they learn about our special, they may hit earlier. If we have to wait for the evening train, none of us will see moonrise." After a pause, he adds, "You might, Private McDonald, you might."

"Only if I ran, and I would not run."

"No, you would not run. You'd keep firing until you ran out of ammo. Then you'd swing a chair or whatever you could grab."

"That's likely. Let's hope they are sitting in someone's barn, drinking liquid courage and telling big stories of their war years."

"How old are you?"

"Twenty-one, sir." Henry reinforces the lie he told the recruiters.

"When did you enlist?"

"This year, sir."

"Listen, Henry, if you save my life one more time, you'll have to stop calling me 'sir.' I never made it past corporal during my war years. I kept getting shifted between units and commanders." Skyles tips forward, discreetly pulls his revolver from his holster and lays it on his lap. He employs his hat to cover the drawn and cocked pistol, then rocks back again into a leisurely posture.

"Maybe you should take another patrol?" he says. "Check on the others..."

"Certainly, sir."

Walking his patrol, Henry chats with Abrams then Donovan. He gets a report of "all clear" from each of them, then returns to the chair, feigning ease.

"You seem better trained than others, especially for having just enlisted."

"Thank you, sir. My father put me in a seaman's apprentice program with the Navy when I was fifteen. I did two years at sea."

"Like a midshipman."

"Sort of. We learned navigation and Navy discipline. We were ship's boys, cabin boys for senior officers."

"You left."

"I did. When my hitch was up, I returned to New York. I would rather be on land."

The sounds around them change. The two men alert, standing from their chairs and moving them away from the door. Skyles returns his pistol to his holster but does not fasten the cover down. Henry opens the top of his own holster.

Both men look north, scanning, tipping their ears and searching for the sound.

"Horses?" Henry asks.

"I think so. Being ridden hard."

"Maybe a train, too?"

"Maybe."

"I'll alert the others." Going south along the building, Henry moves quickly. He raps Donovan's window with some urgency. Then, to Paul Abrams, he whispers, "We got some activity to the north."

"Like what?"

"We don't know yet. Sounds like horses."

"Thank you, Henry."

Henry enters the passenger's waiting room through the track-side door. "Sergeant?"

"Yes, got it."

Henry observes the increased level of alertness in the room as he scans the prisoners. He peeks at the station clock which reads ten minutes to three. When Henry's eyes meet Mister Robert Haney, Haney smirks. His unspoken message communicates: "We've got you now."

Henry leaves through the side door and walks around the north side of the building as a means of completing his patrol circuit. He returns his rucksack to his back, slings the ammo box correctly and smartly. He half-opens the action of his rifle to examine the load. He confirms that he has in fact reloaded after the day's shooting. Two shots in Rising Fawn and three in Trenton.

"I do hear a train, don't you, Henry?" Skyles says.

"I was thinking so. But I also heard those horses."

"Maybe the horses are trying to outrun the train? To warn the others? Do you hear horses now?"

"No, nothing but the faintest sounds of the train. I don't see any smoke or steam either. I'll go around back." Henry walks around to the tracks and looks up them with a degree of hopefulness.

He returns to Skyles's side. The marshal asks, "Anything?"

"Nothing."

"Did you listen to the track?"

"No, sir."

"Try it."

"Try what?"

"Try putting your hand or your ear on the tracks. You can sometimes hear through the steel."

"Really? That always seemed like a fairy tale."

Back on the north side of the building, Henry uses the stairs to descend to ground level, staying out of sight of the road. Then, placing his rifle on the ground, he bends and places his head on the rail, his ear to the very cold steel. It feels as if his ear may freeze in place but he eases his head further down. Then, he hears a ping as if cold steel had been hit with a hammer some great distance off. He also feels, or hears, a deeper sound, something he did not hear when he was an inch above the rail.

And that is his report to Deputy Skyles: a distant rumble and a further, distant ping. In response, the marshal says, "Now we have a race, don't we, young Henry?"

Southern guerillas, or KKK members, have lathered their horses in an effort to outpace an unscheduled train traveling south from Chattanooga.

8 | Civil War

SAM'S JOURNAL, MARCH 2006

B:

Your Captain Henry relates to Killeen, Texas. How's that for an odd link across time? Your young Henry served as a private soldier near Chattanooga, Tennessee just after the American Civil War. There is a creek near Chattanooga called the Chickamauga. Confederate General Hood originally trained and served in the U.S. Army before rebelling against the nation. He lost his leg near Chickamauga in a battle against the United States Army. Earlier at Gettysburg, he lost the function of an arm. Adding insult to injury, Hood lost most of his battles. He violated his oath, fought against the United States, and proved to be a poor leader. In an effort to appease southern politicians, we named the Army post near Killeen after this guy. Fort Hood. You've been there with me. One of our nation's largest Army posts is named for a general of a rebellious army, and a treasonous criminal.

As you research this period of our history, you might keep your eyes open for names that seem heroic and honored, but are actually a hint of old political battles within our country. While fighting here in Iraq, my thoughts explore the closure and healing process that follows civil war.

At the end of our one-year tour here, these soldiers of the Fourth Infantry Division garrisoned at Fort Hood will move to Fort Carson in Colorado. These soldiers, who have been on the go since the wars began, have already been presented with a choice. If a soldier remains with the Fourth Infantry Division, they will return from combat to Texas and immediately move to Colorado. If a soldier decides that Texas and Fort Hood is their forever home, then the soldier must transfer to a different unit. But most of the units at Fort Hood who did not deploy this year will deploy to Iraq next year.

We've given our soldiers a Hobson's Choice. They must decide to move to Colorado or return to combat nearly immediately. Many of the soldiers have already decided and used their mid-tour break to pack up their lives and their families.

If a soldier decides to remain with the Fourth Infantry Division, then they move to Colorado, then they will return to these battlefields within eighteen months. The only relief is retirement, injury, schooling, or end of service. And yet, there are hundreds of serving soldiers here who have already retired or have found themselves in active units during their supposed "terminal leave." The Army holds on to skilled and experienced soldiers. I am here with a lot of overweight soldiers and soldiers who filed for retirement more than a year ago. Some do not expect to be released for yet another year.

Since 2003, our government has mobilized this division from Texas to Iraq then back to Texas then back to Iraq. From Baghdad, they will return to Texas, move to Colorado, unpack, then deployed again to Iraq or Afghanistan. I am counting the evolutions on my fingers: one, two, three, four, five, six, seven. That will be seven complete moves of a heavy infantry division in under a decade. A division is approximately fifteen thousand soldiers. Add family, support staff, vehicles, office equipment, households, and sundry...the number of humans involved ranges between sixty and one hundred thousand. In addition to the people, their households, and offices, the moves include artillery, hundreds of M1A1 Abrams tanks weighing between sixty and eighty tons, thousands of Humvees, and thousands of shipping containers.

Young soldiers in our ranks, people my age, have experienced combat action in two countries and have been in a theater of combat for most of their very short careers. When command offers a young soldier a coin or a written statement of praise, they do not appear to care much. Young soldiers, young privates already awarded a Silver or Bronze Star, roll their eyes at being made soldier of the month from their own company. They have already seen multiple combat tours. Tired soldiers seeing years of combat operations in front of them. Letters of recognition fail to instill motivation like they once did.

With Iran in the news with such frequency, and the increasing violence in Iraq, I hope that our government does not expect this Army to walk into Iran and solve the problems with Iraq. Iran and Iraq battled for a decade. Back then, Iraq was our friend and Iran held American hostages. Imagine the day when our elected officials announce that we are adding another battlefield. Such a decision will crush the souls and families of this generation of soldiery.

My boss's boss is Major Bowman. He was one of the first American soldiers into Afghanistan in the autumn of 2001 after the 9/11 attacks. This major—who specialized in logistics and was very fit and slender—was on a brief mission to Pakistan. As the Army prepared to send special operations teams into Afghanistan, the teams traveled through U.S. bases in Pakistan, pulling people they needed. My major stood near palletes of material in Pakistan one day and on a dark runway in Northern Afghanistan with Special Operations soldiers the next day. He spent months walking and riding donkeys. On his collar, he wears the wagon wheel, identifying him as an officer in the logistics branch. On his right shoulder, he wears the shoulder patch of the U. S. Army's special forces command. In the traditional Army, you would not see this combination of patches. A logistics officer would not normally earn a combat patch while serving with Special Operations.

Major Bowman, when suddenly assigned to the Fourth Infantry Division in 2005, decided to live in his van. He did not bother moving his family to Texas. They would only have to move again to Colorado. He skipped that process. Given the workload required prior to deployment, the major camped in a parking lot near a gym. He slept in a bag on the floor of his van most nights. When he told this story to a small group of us, a sergeant sitting with us said that she used her mid-tour break to move her mother and daughter to new quarters in Colorado. The major said: "I absolutely understand why the Army can't keep people. It isn't only the deployments; it is the time at home."

Four of us got posted to tiny Camp Falcon. It is a short distance from my normal base. All my stuff remains behind at divisional HQ. I live from my ruck, rotating between two uniforms and a handful of underwear and socks that I either launder in a sink or simply wear in the shower. I wash them with shampoo. I wring them out, then hang them the night. The following morning, they are dry. Regrettably, my undies hold the shape of whatever I hung them on; they are just that stiff.

I barely sleep at night. I had been excited to have this small building to myself, with its walls and door; I did not feel welcome with the enlisted females as I am the only female officer on this base, and the rules state that I cannot rack out with my own squad because they are all dudes. I failed to understand that dozens of Chinook helicopters come in most nights. Chinooks date back to the Vietnam war. They have two sets of rotors and a loading ramp like a cargo plane. We fly them at night now because they are vulnerable to ground attacks during the day. They are heavy, slow, loud, and explain why this small building remained uninhabited by the soldiers serving here. Nobody wants to sleep in the landing path of Chinooks.

Most soldiers rack out in two-story buildings. These two-story buildings are dressed in the khaki-colored stucco that matches our equipment and the soil. The ground story of the building has a layer of tall concrete barriers—called either Texas barriers or Alaska barriers—which resemble the Jersey barriers of highways back home, except they stand three meters tall. Each window on the ground floor has three layers of sandbags. Ringing the buildings between the ground floor and the top floor is an exterior concrete trough that carries basic utilities. Our troops use this trough to carry communications wires and stack sandbags. The second story windows also have three layers of sandbags unless there is an air conditioning unit.

The roof deck of the building is flat and made of concrete tiles on a concrete base. Antenna masts and antenna dishes are weighted down with sandbags. Additionally, one can observe the ghosts of former sandbags. Regrettably, a lot of the bags we have used for making sandbags had been manufactured out of nylon or plastics. The sun destroys these plastics within a few months. The sandbags get bleached, then corrode in the sun. The result is leaking and spilling sand. The dense sand remains in its neat, round pile while the plastic fabric fades to dust. Thereby creating ghosts of former sandbags.

Upon arriving here, I started learning new lessons, lessons that bootcamp should probably teach but did not. One layer of sandbags slows a bullet, reducing its lethality, but the dust and dirt from the sandbag enters a soldier's wound which can introduce evil infections. Three layers of sandbags stack with greater stability and stop normal bullets and most shrapnel from IEDs, mortars, rockets, and grenades. As many urban kids know before joining the Army, sleeping on the floor provides greater protection from bullets.

During my first tour into Iraq, a female master sergeant provided an informal class to female soldiers. One of the lessons was called feet-first. Before dressing, take care of your feet and treat for fungus. Then put on clean, dry socks. Do this before putting on underwear. The little bugs can't jump through your socks. The little beasties from the feet have a more difficult time traveling to the nether regions covered by the underwear. Listen to the infantry. Another lesson involved urinating into a plastic bottle. She showed us how to make an oblique cut on a plastic water bottle, which, when completed, makes an anatomical match. Stand or squad, she said. Pee, then pour the contents into a bottle with a screw on top. Toss. With the lesson, we joined the world of those who can pee standing up. It makes peeing on a C-130 Hercules, peeing when doing surveillance, and peeing with a small squad of male soldiers just that much easier. It also makes peeing at night easier, too.

Camp Falcon occupies a few city blocks. It has a three-story wall, made from Iraqi brick. It already had guard towers, so I assume that this facility was once an Iraqi military post. This is an urban base. The sounds of Baghdad remain constant and close.

The nightly body count in Baghdad approximates fifty citizens. That's fifty Baghdadi folks, not U.S. troops; Iraqis killing Iraqis. We seem further from an end that we did when I got here. We appear to be traveling backwards, away from peace, the longer we are here. In the summer of 2003, when I deployed here for a few months as a sergeant, I believed we approached the end of the war. Instead, peace keeps retreating from Iraq.

I acknowledge that my foul attitude is due, in part, to living in quarters that would be condemned in any U.S. city. In Iraq, I call it home-for-now. I have made a nest in the corner. I fight with mice, ants, bugs, and spiders to defend my crappy piece of this room.

I noticed a dramatic down-tick in my emotional state when I read about a man in Afghanistan who converted to Christianity. I read that the government of Afghanistan now wants to execute him because of his conversion. In a country where we committed U.S. soldiers, we are faced with a government that wants to execute someone because of a religious preference. I am incensed by this. My stack is blown—as in, remains blown. Aren't we here to defend freedom? Freedoms of religion and of the press, freedom from unwarranted searches, freedom to vote?

The fact that I carry the Constitution and Bill of Rights with me, even in this miserable place, expresses my desire to stand for these values. I do not wish to have American soldiers fighting to restore power to a government that completely eschews our soldier's oath.

I know I am in Iraq, but the fluidity between Iraq and Afghanistan amazes me. Between Iraq and Afghanistan is the nation of Iran. Presently, Iraq and Afghanistan are two different battlefields against two different enemies being fought for two different reasons. Yet it is the same few Americans that deploy into, then out of, these two wars. Most Americans do not know the difference. Most Americans cannot point to either of these nations on a map.

I read what I can about Afghanistan. If I am not going there next, I'll return here. I am certain I will see Afghanistan at least once.

At this moment, NATO is taking over forces in Afghanistan. Our troops are about to fight under a British general for the first time since World War II. At the same time, we are in a diplomatic fracas with the Mayor of Kabul (oh, I mean the "President of Afghanistan," forgive me). Under Karzai, opium production is better than it has been in decades. Their constitution does not provide for a distinction between state and church, nor does it provide itself the ability to supersede traditional Islamic law. Under the new rulers, Afghans can return to lopping off the hands of thieves and stoning women.

The Taliban's strict enforcement of Islamic law inspired the destruction of the ancient Buddhist sculptures carved into the mountain side. The Buddhas of Bamiyan were considered idolatry and sacrilegious by these religious zealots. Therefore, the Taliban—then standing as the Afghanistan government—blew them up. They filmed it. They filmed the process of destroying artifacts created in the sixth century. One stood thirty-eight meters tall, the other fifty-five. "One should not let idols stand," said the nation's boss, so they blew them up.

Let's admit that part of the Islamic code remains as rigid and archaic as Leviticus. Imagine a nation run by the rules of Leviticus? If someone decided that America must be a truly Christian nation and follow the teachings of the Christian Bible, where would we be? Yet the U.S. government seems to be stumbling around with our proverbial knickers at our ankles. We must stand for real religious freedom; instead, we support a government that has outlawed converting to Christianity. We plea for a life sentence or an insane asylum in lieu of death. We are negotiating with the government we installed, the government presumed to be more liberal than the Taliban.

Let's observe that we negotiate the sentence whilst ignoring the underlying law. We have put American soldiers into the line of fire so that this new government can codify laws that limit religious preference. None of this follows the tenants of my oath—our oaths—nor the words written in that slim document in my breast pocket. What is the difference between the Taliban or this new Afghanistan government if they both use the same laws and tactics?

Soldiers express shock, anger, and dismay over this issue. Things heated up on the anniversary of the Invasion of Iraq. Many here thought that Afghanistan was a model for success, a model that demonstrated to all of us how this war in Iraq could come to a good end. Victory by U.S. forces can never, ever tolerate religious persecution. That is the first of our amendments. 1791, the same year Vermont joined the union, the following words were written and accepted as law:

> "Congress shall make no law respecting an establishment of religion, or prohibiting the free exercise thereof; of abridging the freedom of speech, or of the press; or the right of the people to peaceably assemble, and to petition the government for a redress of grievances."

The authors found that freedom of speech and religion were exactly that important. We do not drain our blood, our credibility, our nation's bank account, and destroy American families so that some damn government can just lock up—or kill—a guy with a Bible, a Koran, a Torah, a Bhagavad Ghita, or any other document. That is not in the bargain. We serve to support our values and our Constitution. We shall not yield the life of a single American soldier to support a government that would execute or imprison a citizen for his religious beliefs.

Reporters in Afghanistan tend to focus on the military as the story. The bodies, the tactics, the weapons. The news has not yet made an issue out of the limitations of the laws in Afghanistan. The reporters, and politicians, need to see past the Humvees and the patrols.

But you have to be here to see beyond. Footage of the most recent bombing is the same here as any other place: flashing lights, a reporter yelling into a mic while wearing a blue flak vest, a bloom of smoke over his shoulder and bits of car and debris all over the place. We've seen it. You've seen it. It is not news.

We should be reporting on stories that matter. Let me offer several. I mean, no one is listening, are they? But if I could research and write stories, I may start with one of the following.

> **Story option one for the world press:**
>
> When I was flying last week, I traveled repeatedly over the major roads that go from Baghdad to Karbala. I wish I knew the original Iraqi names for these roads; we've renamed them all for our own purposes. I think of this highway as I-95 running north to south through the major cities. Hundreds of thousands marched from their homes to Karbala. They marched in

a way we could never know. Old ladies marched alone in their black clothing. Kids marched. Everyone marched. For days, they marched towards Karbala. No packs, no bags, no cars. Every few kilometers, there was a way-station with food and water. These way-stations had been built from ancient trucks or mule-carts or upturned crates. Anything that could host food and water. I traveled almost one hundred kilometers in two days by Blackhawk. We flew up and down I-95 from mission to mission. I was amazed. I was in awe.

How did all of this get organized? Who did this? How did the people know? How did the people know to trust their neighbors and that there would be food, water, and bedding along the way? How does this happen?

That's a story. It highlights a change since Saddam. It documents a means of communication unique to this area. It illustrates how people can simply walk a highway with trust. The pilgrims were rewarded with kindness, food, water, and shelter. I saw no violence. I would know more if someone in the media researched it then reported on it. It illustrates new religious freedoms.

Another story option for the world press:

Why are the counter-Iraqi forces winning at the PsyOps game? PsyOps is Army-speak for Psychological Operations. The U.S. is prohibited by law from doing propaganda. So, we call it PsyOps instead. We do it. They do it.

Only, they do it more effectively.

The enemy is a bad guy. His tactics work. These bad guys stand for a type of totalitarianism and religious regime governed by Islamic law. They may not win hearts and minds, but they do control the community with fear.

The Bad Guys capture people and torture them. They film this, then burn the images to DVDs. They then duplicate the DVDs and distribute them throughout neighborhoods. The Bad Guys will kidnap the family of another fellow and repeat the process with the filming and the DVDs and the midnight distribution process.

If a Good Guy lives in the community and wants the nation to progress towards democracy, then this Good Guy finds his family held captive by a Bad Guy. The Good Guy becomes compliant. So do his neighbors. The DVDs show images of people who had once served tea as friends and countrymen, now acting with unbelievable violence towards these same friends and countrymen.

This technique is highly effective. It sends a strong message. And given the electronic nature of the message, it is untraceable. They scrub the location and equipment metadata from the video feeds, then reproduce with inexpensive DVD cloning machines. There is no internet address to chase. It is a brilliant application of technology.

A third story for the press to explore:

Let's write an article, or create a short documentary, about our enemy. I'd like to know who he is. Who is the enemy? Are we fighting bin-Ladenism? Are we fighting an Islamic reactionary force? Are we fighting against a backdrop of traditional tribal war? Are we fighting foreign insurgents from Iran, Jordan, Syria, and Turkey, all of whom have interests in controlling this region? Turkey is afraid of the Kurds gaining autonomy. The Iranians seem to be supporting an Iranian-esque Shi'ah Islamic government. And the states to the west are likely to support the Sunni with an Islamic government. There is a soldier in Iraq who would like to know the answer to these questions.

Many Iraqi I meet state some folks just want "The Chair." They simply want power. They want to be rulers of their part of the land. "The Chair" seems to be a local term for throne or seat of power. They simply say, "The Chair." Here, "The Chair" means power, and that means wealth, corruption, and respect. All of the above.

I offer a fourth story that the media could tell me:

I am a soldier on the ground, eating Iraqi dust, wearing underwear that I can wag in the air like a stick. Please define success for me. What does the end of this war look like to me and to the Iraqi people? What would they consider a natural state? What are their priorities? In my conversations, all I hear is security. With security comes all: utilities, benzene (gasoline), economy, family, growth, politics, and everything else. Without security, there is nothing.

I recognized my definition of the end when I thought through the question today. This conflict is over when I can walk out of Forward Operating Base Falcon and walk back to the division headquarters. I can see the hill next to the Z-shaped lake when I stand on a roof here. Imagine that I could step out of these gates, dressed in either my uniform or civilian clothing, then walk back to headquarters. If I could stop at an Iraqi bodega for water and a snack, greet people on the street, and make it the other side of my journey safely, that would be an accomplishment. I would accept that as an improvement in security.

Instead, I listen to frequent gunfire around me. In the morning briefings, we are informed of fifty dead Iraqis, or some other dreadful number. The evidence of kidnapping, torture, and street-based executions can be found in the DVDs we gather.

Blue fingers and elections don't matter. Especially when the election can still result in the death of a man because he changed religions.

There are other stories like these that aren't being investigated, that aren't being told. And someone must. We've been at war since March 2003 in Iraq. It is March 2006. Therefore, we have entered the fourth year of this war. Where are the checks-and-balances in our culture to examine the situation? Like why fifty percent of our "fighting" force is contractors? How do we explain to U.S. citizens that a reduction in military presence here will be countered by an increase in U.S. contractors, filling roles traditionally held by uniformed military personnel?

If you do bump into any answers, please provide them to a dusty and tired soldier. Someday, I can sleep in a comfortable bed, then, in the morning, dress in soft underwear that doesn't feel like cardboard.

Recently, when the daily death count of Iraqis killed by Iraqis escalated, we started describing our battlefield as a civil war. Our coalition forces stand on this same battlefield. All sides attempt to leverage us. They come to us with a whisper, an accusation, and sometimes proof. "Hey, old Freddy here, he was the one that mortared your base three days ago. He bought some weapons from the Iranians that came from China. I can show you." We investigate. Do we arrest Freddy? In the early weeks, we did. We'd bang down doors, zip-tie or kill folks in Freddy's building. We have wised up a bit. Maybe Freddy was set up. Maybe Freddy and Barney had a falling out. Maybe Barney is the real Bad Guy. We lost track.

Right now, we don't know. Anyone who says otherwise is lying.

We did not necessarily understand we stood in a civil war. We took intelligence from people we knew and trusted and had served good intelligence before. This environment can be like drug wars in U.S. cities, where one rival gang provides information to the cops about another gang. The result is that the gang making the reports gains territory and trust with the police. The police earn recognition for seizing drugs and making high-profile arrests. If the police side with one gang or the other, they escalate the violence and corruption. But if the police do not act on intelligence, they fail to curb the violence and movement of drugs. We find ourselves in that situation here today. The bosses have not yet said: "This is a civil war." The politicians have not said it either. The dead bodies on the streets tell their own story. The gunfire at night tells its own story.

I came to Camp Falcon because a counterintelligence team found a metric ton of anhydrous nitrogen. While this liquid product is used by farmers as a fertilizer, we believe that this stash was to be used for improvised explosives. Certainly, we have thousands of local farms growing dates and other fruits. They would love to get their hands on this fertilizer for their fields. Yet, the manner of storage and the location of the find indicates that someone planned on making hundreds of bombs from this material. To make a bomb from this anhydrous nitrogen, we need a trigger and a detonation source.

One of the dining facilities I have visited during my travels displays the makings of various improved explosive devices (IEDs). Someone mounted the wiring and detonation system for IEDs on a sheet of powder-blue plywood. A black marker described the components and how they work. I remember one that used an egg timer; one that used a Nokia mobile phone; one that used the timer from an electric clothes dryer. We stood in line for our meals studying these diagrams. I learned and memorized more from these boards than I had in classrooms. Reinforcing these lessons was the knowledge that these bits of wires, timers, and diagrams had been picked from IEDs that exploded near the base. The soldiers who made these displays used crime scene evidence to make functional diagrams of explosive devices. Soldiers waited in line for breakfast learning how to either make one, or, more importantly, how to recognize one.

A ton of explosive fertilizer, a small battery, a timer or trigger, then an ignition source...that's all a bomb maker needs. When investigating a ton of explosive material, I tend to ask myself: "What did we miss?" I am working with Jim and Kyle, members of a human intelligence support team, or HST. Jim pays the guy who pays the guy who pays the guy who gets the information on shipments of bad-stuff and the location of these explosives. Kyle tends to write reports, analyze the data, and talk with bosses. Jim and Kyle created a team of two that has proven effective, even in this bizarre battlespace. They seem to be savvy enough to avoid the obvious attempts at passing on sectarian-based—or revenge-based—data. At the edge of this world, where spies do not call themselves spies, Jim and Kyle spy.

I look forward to yielding my corner back to the rats and bugs from whom I stole the space. I hate this hooch and do not feel very safe at Forward Operating Base Falcon. I never thought I would look fondly on a room that occupies one-third of an aluminum trailer. But back at that base, contractors do my laundry. I drop it one day, skip a day, then fetch my laundry. That's the counter in my head: drop, skip, get. The clothing returns clean and with a hint of fluffiness. Life is better when dressing in soft underwear and a properly cleaned uniform. When I walk into the D-fac for my breakfast, the fellows at the griddle know my order and treat me well. I know I have it good, nestled in with the division headquarters staff. It is not Vermont, and I see them pour eggs from a carton. My morning egg comes from a shelf-stable egg-like product that pours from a box. In Vermont, eggs come from a chicken that scratched the dirt near someone's home. In the ranking of good-better-best, Vermont remains at the top of the list, and it is best because it is my home. The divisional headquarters ranks as good. I acknowledge it as the best of all possible options when in Iraq. Camp Falcon is still better than sleeping rough and better than the conditions in which a lot of our soldiers live.

FOB Falcon greeted me with two familiar insignias. First, the four green ivy leaves of the Fourth Infantry Division. Second, an artist painted the shoulder patch of the 506th Infantry Regiment, part of the 101st Airborne Division. During World War II, it was known as the 506th Parachute Infantry Regiment, abbreviated "PIR." The shoulder patch displays six white parachutes in a blue sky near a green hill. Below the image is the word "Currahee." The HBO series Band of Brothers followed the men of "E," or Easy Company, of the 506th PIR through World War II. This unit is now here in Baghdad with us. Many soldiers serve anonymously and quietly. We do take pride in our efforts, and the heritage of our units. The men and women of the 506th landed during D-Day, parachuted into the Netherlands during Operation Market Garden, slept in the snow during the Battle of the Bulge. In the spring of 2006, they fly their colors at this urban outpost in Baghdad.

I shan't complain about stiff underwear I wash in the shower, because I have access to a shower. So many do not. I shan't complain about a morning egg that pours from a carton, given we often have to rely on ready-to-eat meals. I shan't complain about displacing rats and bugs to create my own nest on a floor, because it is better than sleeping outdoors or in a tent. But maybe I should wonder about invading a nation without much of a plan for either building the nation's government or the possibility of creating a civil war in our own battlefield. This month, I know of one ton of explosives that will not be used to kill hundreds of Iraqis. Regrettably, if there was another ton of explosives a kilometer away, I would not know.

9 | Private "T"

HENRY, DECEMBER 1871

Henry slowly patrols circuits around the Trenton, Georgia train depot. On the trackside of the building, he checks on the two soldiers hiding in the freight warehouse. Private Paul Abrams monitors the railyard through a small opening in the sliding door. Private Donovan monitors the southern reaches and the tree line through a window.

The squad stands alert. They prepare for a fight based on scant evidence: a noise heard by both Henry and Marshal Skyles. Both thought that they heard the sound of a locomotive at a goodly distance. Both thought that they had heard the sounds of horses galloping from the north. While a train indicates salvation and rescue in the form of a relief force of soldiers from Chattanooga, galloping riders means trouble.

One of the three prisoners seemed overly confident during his arrest and detention. He put forth airs that he would not be leaving the county in the company of soldiers—not this day, nor any day. His confidence and calm has infected the other two prisoners: the county road commissioner, and the postal clerk from Rising Fawn.

Henry had witnessed earlier in the day how the road commissioner, in cooperation with the Dade County Sheriff, used shackled men as free labor to maintain the roads. Blevins claimed that the black men were all awaiting trials for various charges of vagrancy and theft. If convicted of vagrancy, these men, and their families, could be forced into unilateral labor contracts with landowners, as a result of new laws passed in the region. The new law required formerly enslaved peoples to work, if vagrant, then forced back to plantations as if still enslaved. The wages in contracts with supposed vagrants typically equaled the cost of clothing, food, and shelter, thereby keeping families trapped in a cycle of debt and poverty.

Skyles tells Henry that these men—their prisoners—and others of this county, had burnt a neighboring settlement to the ground, a village of families recently released from bondage who had established a small farming community west of the railroad tracks. The white leaders hung two men who had recently voted. The KKK beat a teenage boy who rose to defend his father. After beating the boy, one of the Ku Kluxers raped the boy with a stick. The boy died within a week due to infections in his bowel. All fit adult men in the village had been taken into custody. With houses burned and crops destroyed, these families became vagrants. And with the new laws, vagrants became slaves again.

A village dog barks, for the first time all day. This means that during the day, everyone remained at home and the dogs saw no strangers. Henry turns towards it.

"Stay here," the marshal says. He kicks one of the two chairs from the depot's platform, demonstrating a hint of anger. He opens the door. "Sergeant, let's get the prisoners and the station master into the warehouse. We've got visitors coming to town."

Mister Haney stands. With a voice that is a touch too sweet, he says, "Let me talk to them. I can help."

Sergeant Porter retorts, "Not this time, Mister Haney. You've done enough. 'Take care of my wife' and that nonsense about gardens and tea. I don't know what you told them, but I am certain that you are not intending to help us one iota. Now move. Move into the warehouse. You too, station master."

Belville assumes a post inside the waiting room.

"Naught to do but wait with your carbine." The marshal gives Henry a gentle tap in the ribs with his elbow. This time the waiting did not include conversation. Just quick looks of confirmation.

It went, "Did you hear that?"

And, "Yes, I did."

A small group of men furtively sprint across Court Street from the north to the south, hiding behind the courthouse. When the quarter-chime rings from the church spire, Henry and Skyles hear a rhythmic beating of sticks, a slow, regular drumming sound moving closer. The approaching men attempt to remain concealed but occasionally appear briefly while moving from building to building. Henry notes that the sound and the movement feels like being swarmed, like a Viking attack with men pounding on shields. An effort to amplify the magnitude of the opposing force.

None of the soldiers doubt that they are under attack. Each man has forty-two rounds of ammunition. Each rifle can fire twenty rounds in a minute. If every shot hits a target, they could kill hundreds of townsmen. If the soldier's shots go wild, or they shoot too rapidly, their makeshift garrison will become their own prison, surrounded by armed and angry villagers, vestiges from the recent war.

Henry makes a quick circuit around the building. To each of the men he visits, he says, "Don't shoot unless you can kill. Aim low, fire slow."

Around the building.

"Donovan, aim low, fire slow."

"Paul, aim low, fire slow and, for God's sake, kill what you hit."

Opening the track-side door of the waiting room, he says, "Belville, aim low," and Belville answers, "Fire slow."

The moment for trick shots and demonstrations of force is over. A wild, whooping call comes from the courthouse lawn, answered by barks and wolf calls from around the town. Whooping cries come from the tree line surrounding the railyard. Noise comes from all points of the compass.

The firing starts. Chaotic firing of rifles and pistols, at first making only noise, but as they get closer and closer to the depot, the shots occasionally ricochet off various objects and bounce up off of the dirt. One bullet hits a luggage trolley. Most bullets seem to have been fired into the air. Henry looks around. There was no safe side of the building to fire from. The wolf calls and gunfire came from all quarters. He considers laying down. This reduces the risk of being hit and improves his aim and range, but it limits his ability to maneuver and bring his rifle to bear in a full circle. He opts for a squatting position with his rifle on his knees. He can command most of what he sees from this position, and hit anything that moves.

Ten men walk down Court Street towards the depot. They are heavily armed. Most carry long rifles and side arms. Some wear their

Confederate grey uniforms in a show of defiance. They halt fifty paces from the depot.

The center man shouts, "Deputy?"

"I hear you."

"Deputy, if you let your three prisoners go, we will give you until nightfall to get out of town. If you do not turn over your prisoners, you will not live to hear the clock chime again."

Everyone can infer the remainder of the message. The United States Army faces an adversary who has them outgunned and outnumbered. The former insurrectionists will be fighting on their home soil. The village men have known years of war. These are men who fought as regulars in the Confederate Army or as guerrillas in support of the Confederacy. These men have already proven their willingness for violence by attacking freemen, burning a village, and lynching American citizens. And three of these men had attacked the squad during their morning maneuvers in Rising Fawn.

"Deputy, I will give you a count of ten to make up your mind. If you open the door and show us our friends, you will live."

Inside the building, Henry hears his squad mates chanting: "Aim low, fire slow." The guys in the warehouse start, "Aim low." The guys in the waiting room answer, "Fire slow."

"Aim low."

"Fire slow."

"One." The self-appointed commander of the rebels starts his count.

The men on Court Street back away from the depot.

"Two."

The men spread out, taking cover behind buildings.

"Three."

The counting man retreats further from Henry's rifle.

The shooting starts somewhere around the number eight or nine. The counting man is too far away for Henry to hear, but still close enough to shoot. The glass window in the door shatters. Henry looks over his barrel, following the sound of the closest shot, and sees movement from a man hiding behind a wood pile. Henry aims at an oak log, thinking he could launch it towards the fellow's head. Then he sees that the logs are stacked on flat rocks. Henry points the rifle to the leading edge of the rock and eases off a shot. Flakes of rock fly upwards. The hiding man screams in pain.

Henry calls to the team: "One."

None of the other soldiers have yet pulled their triggers. Henry is pleased. Most of the gunfire comes from a distance greater than two hundred yards. The yahooing and wolf calls return.

One of the soldiers behind Henry squeezes off a shot. Henry hears a horse cry and fall. Belville says, "Two."

When a man runs across Court Street, Henry places a bullet in his thigh. He drops in the middle of the street.

"Three."

Henry draws a bead on a dog, following the dog and letting the dog go. He scans with his eyes, then moves the rifle barrel through an arc that describes half of a circle. The marshal takes up a laying position with his revolver.

"I am sticking close to you, kid," the marshal offers up to Henry as Henry alerts to movement again. This time, the movement is on the church spire. A good place for a sniper to set up. The sniper snuggles down into a firing position after leaning his rifle on the black iron railing. Henry puts a bullet into the firing mechanism of the rifle, then places a second shot on the wood below the shooter's face. The wood slivers tear into the man's face and shoulders.

Donovan takes a shot through the south window. He yells: "A clean miss. Damn." Within a minute, he yells again. "Nope. He's going to limp for a long while. Five!"

The men inside the building give another and more enthusiastic round of their "aim low, fire slow" chant.

Henry hears the sound of a locomotive. "Marshal, do you hear that, too?"

"I do."

So do the others in town. They increase their pressure and their rates of fire. The sound of gunfire and the wolf calls gets closer. The insurrectionists feel emboldened by the approaching train. It became a now-or-never moment for the men of Dade County.

The train starts whistling. The smoke becomes visible. The train itself is alive with the sounds of rifle fire.

Abrams yells from his position behind the freight door, "She's backing down the track!"

Henry says, "Marshal, I'll cover you while you get inside. We need to get off of this platform." Skyles rises from his supine position. Two shots crack. One from the second story of a house to the right and another from the left. Henry returns fire, then spins to the left, looking for another shooter. Skyles leaves the door open. Now in a standing position, Henry inches toward it.

The gunfire from the train is continuous. Rounds thud against buildings all over town. The soldiers on the train possess zero discipline. They fire at anything because they do not have to worry about running out of ammunition. Henry retreats further into the waiting room, crosses it, and steps onto the train platform backwards. He puts the wooden wall between him and the town before turning to assess the rest of his squad.

Paul Abrams has the warehouse door fully open. The train, slowing now, had traveled backwards from Chattanooga. The rear carriage is a freight car. The relief soldiers are firing from both open doors. The soldiers in the passenger carriage stand between the benches, shooting through the windows. The train had been peppered with shots. One can see raw yellow wood everywhere. Slivers of wood litter the floor.

Sergeant Porter pushes the prisoners into the passenger carriage. Meanwhile, Henry takes the extra time to reload his rifle while surveilling the depot and the town one more time. As soon as the train comes to a stop, it starts going forward again.

Henry steps up to the moving carriage, observing that the carriage is filled with spent gunpowder fumes and brass casings from hundreds, even thousands of rounds. The carriage has absorbed hundreds of bullets. There are holes in the wood, either from bullets that traveled through the windows or through the walls. One private, newly arrived with the relief force, sits in the front with his arm heavily bandaged.

The men on the train talk excitedly. The relief force was under fire for ten minutes, maybe fifteen. Insurrections fired from the woods and horseback as the train puffed backward. The little squad, who had survived a day under siege, says nothing.. They do not have the energy to compete with the loud, anxious, banter of the fresh soldiers.

This band that traveled to Rising Fawn have become veterans. They tasted the fear, and joy, of combat. They had survived the day against overwhelming odds. They had been outnumbered, outgunned, and trapped in a small wooden building in enemy territory with no means of escape. Sitting on the floor of the train, they listen to the rescuers tell and re-tell their own story of a brief train ride into danger.

With haste, the rescuers turned a freight car and a passenger carriage into a combat platform. They steamed into danger. When the bullets flew, they turned into a lethal porcupine. Instead of sharp quills with tiny barbs, the soldiers shot back with lead. Like a porcupine, the bullets came from every possible angle, every surface.

When needing rescuing, one should never begrudge the story of the rescuer's adventure. McDonald, Abrams, Belville, Donovan, Mueller, and Sturtevant listen to the rescuers and thank them. Donovan and Abrams—who spent their day staring into the woods for an unseen enemy—fall asleep.

Shapes in a woodlot and a railyard shift and change during the day. As the sun wends its way through the winter sky, shadows change shape. Colors change. One studies a shape, convinced it is a head, a shoulder, a rifle. Then the sun shifts. A hat becomes visible. Light dances from a steel barrel. The chittering of squirrels warns of movement. The raven's caw causes the soldier to bring his rifle to his shoulder. The soldier spends hours convinced that there exists a man hiding in the wood, working closer and closer to the garrison. The sun shifts again, and suddenly your man and his rifle reveal themselves as a stump, a stick, and a bundle of leaves.

A shot-up carriage with noisy rescuers brings an end to this exhausting watch.

It is the enemy they fail to recognize who threatens them all. The one-hundred percent intensity drains soldiers of their reserves.

Henry quietly restocks ammo in the bottom of his rucksack. He puts several extra boxes into the packs of his squad. Sergeant Porter admires the stealth movements of the young private. The next time the men are issued forty rounds for a simple mission, each of Porter's soldiers will have an additional one hundred to two hundred rounds hidden in their packs. Never again will these men complain about the added weight.

Uncertain if the quartermaster will require an accounting of every bullet, Henry also provides each soldier with a box of forty-two. This spare (stolen) box will be handed to the quartermaster, thereby keeping the books balanced.

During the siege, the soldiers experienced the near horror of running out of food, water, and ammunition, while not being able to communicate.

In the irony of military accounting, the rescuers will not undergo the same tallying and reviews of Sergeant Porter's squad. Sergeant Porter's squad had been issued one day's food rations and forty-two bullets. Upon return, they will be expected to turn in forty-two rounds or explain where the bullets went. On the other hand, knowing that the American soldiers were in trouble, the rescuers pulled everything they could carry from the warehouse. They tossed crate after crate of ammo and rifles onto the rescue train. After the mission, the quartermaster will examine the empty crates and the condition of the railcars, then will adjust his inventory with a brief entry: "rescue mission for besieged squad." But when Sergeant Porter takes his men through the front door of the quartermaster's facility, the quartermaster will require a detailed accounting for each item issued.

Two standards. Two sets of rules.

The train slows and whistles as it enters the Chattanooga railyard. Bullets had shattered the locomotive's lamps. Pock marks from bullets are visible from the front of the engine, down both sides, along the coal tender. Bullets redecorated the passenger and freight carriages that follow. The shunted train passes the depot, then switches to a military siding. The sergeant leans over to Henry.

"Mac, get the squad up and ready to go. I want them sharp. All eyes will be on us."

Henry passes between the railcars, finding the rest of the squad. Most have found a corner or a smooth part of the floor. Their men, their squad, gather at the front of the passenger car.

"Clean it up," the sergeant barks. His bark, while as barky as any other bark, conveys a sense of pride in the team. Working in twos, the men dust off their blue uniforms. They adjust their tunics and get their rucksacks to lay neatly.

"We're off first. Step off the train, then form two files ten yards from the edge of the last track. The prisoners will follow with Marshal Skyles. The other squad will help the prisoners down. Six of their men will provide escort to the prisoners as we march."

The squad waits for the prisoners to alight from the carriage. Skyles has to, again, provide motivation. Six of the rescue squad, including a corporal, form up around the prisoners. Porter observes the preparations. The other squad's sergeant remains to help clear the cars, get his wounded soldier to care, and account for the ammo crates. With a set of nods between the two sergeants and the U.S. marshal, Sergeant Porter speak softly to his men: "Alright boys, tighten it up. Look your best, heads high."

Then loudly for the assembly, "Forward...march." On "march," feet lift and drop in unison. The squad leads the prisoners and rescuers on a march down the middle of the street, creating an impromptu parade for themselves in the early twilight of a December afternoon. The sound of their marching echoes from the façades of the buildings. Men and women of Chattanooga encounter a cadre of professional and well-trained soldiers. These soldiers demonstrate discipline. They were well-uniformed, well-kitted, and well-armed.

Entering the Chattanooga Garrison, Captain H. C. Cook, Lieutenants C. A. Dempsey, and William Wolf meet them at the parade ground. Sergeant Porter's men respond perfectly to the close-order commands which bring them to attention directly in front of the post command, post adjutant, and company commander. The squad listens to a few words from Captain Cook about accounting well for themselves and the United States Army. With a quick call to attention, Sergeant Porter dismisses the men.

Once in the barracks, Henry aids his comrades in stashing the extra supplies of ammunition. Donovan reveals a bottle of moonshine bourbon purloined during a prior raid. The attitude of the men remains quiet, somber, and reflective as they share illicit sips of an illicit liquor. Unlike the rescue party, the squad does not engage in the high-energy retelling of a shared adventure. Instead, they nibble the hard biscuits that had been issued as part of their day's rations and each enjoy their own quiet. They rapidly hide the bottle when someone knocks on the door of the barracks. Had it been a soldier assigned to their barracks, he would have just walked in.

Henry stands as James Skyles enters. He waves his hands for the men to sit and closes the door quietly, then approaches the cluster of beds serving as a gathering place.

"What are we drinking?" The marshal asks the question gently, indicating he would prefer to be included.

"A bit of bourbon, Marshal."

The marshal accepts the bottle, studying it from all angles. "Donovan, lad, this bottle seems familiar."

"Whether it does or whether it does not, I could not say, Marshal. It is a fair bourbon, even if a bit raw yet."

The marshal takes a nip, then passes it.

"You did well, boys. You kept your heads and stayed focused. I was lucky to have drawn this squad today. That's something I'll swear to."

The soldiers offer a smattering of thanks and grunts. "Maybe a just a bit less hot next time, though?" says Donovon.

Paul Abrams adds, "I'll second that, Marshal. That was no walk in a city park."

When the bottle comes around again, the marshal raises it. "To Mac and his famous Lieutenant T."

Donovan then says: "Henry, I didn't know you had the Irish."

"Not much, I've got a few words though. I do know trouble, as my father said. So, he gave it to me in the Gaelic—troub-let—and sometimes spelled with his belt."

The marshal chimes in. "Oh, is that how it is said? It is spelled how?"

"T-R-I-O-B-L-O-I-D, with a bit of an accent of that second 'O.'

Sure, it comes out troub-let, or even tru-bloid, depending."

"It sounds like the American for trouble, doesn't it?"

During the evening of drinking, the men try out new monikers on Private Henry S. McDonald. They call him Lieutenant T, Henry T. McDonald, T-Mac, then just settle on T.

Henry gets his own adjutant in Paul Abrams. Every soldier knows the story of the telegram coming in from a train depot addressed to Lieutenant Trouble and how Signals Private O'Brian recognized the Irish word then alerted command. Within two days, the whole garrison calls the young man T. The sergeants yell for "T," "Go fetch T," "Tell T he's going out again on a mission."

Henry stands for trouble, and Command does not hesitate to put him in trouble's path. Skyles continues to request him—and Sergeant Porter—for his ongoing missions in Georgia and Alabama chasing the Ku Kluxer.

But between missions, Trouble can be found with the blacksmith, pumping bellows and reading the news.

"Mos, the only paper I could find today is the *Daily Union* and *American* out of Nashville."

"That's alright, Henry."

Henry has sent telegrams to newspapers throughout the south advertising for Moses's family. He buys any newspapers he can when he travels, and as papers come through the rails in Chattanooga. With Moses, he looks through the pages endeavoring to find people, including Moses's wife and two sons. When the searches fail, Henry reads the paper aloud.

"Alrighty, Moses, under the heading Washington, let's see what is going on....We have a new commissioner of Internal Revenue. And a Mister Waters became the Assessor of Internal Revenue for the third district of Tennessee. No doubt he'll make my life interesting, just like these marshals."

"No doubt, Henry."

"A Mister George Bancroft has been appointed Envoy Extraordinary and Minister Plenipotentiary to the German Empire. That's a mouthful and a title. From Texas, it looks like they sent a fellow named Clark and Herndon to represent them in Washington. The election committee said that these two are entitled to be sworn in as members pending any contest for their seat.

"*Utah*, Delegate Hooper returns to Utah next week. He favors the formation of a state constitution acceptable to Congress, and preliminary action by that body for the admission of Utah.

"*Fishy*, the House Committee on Foreign Relations, paid Secretary of State Hamilton Fish an official visit today. The secretary returned thanks to the gentlemen of the committee for their visit and friendly wishes but gave no intimation of an intention to resign his office. His decision upon that subject he said must be reserved. The story continues. The situation has changed within a day or two, and the question is no longer as to how soon Mister Fish will retire but rather as to how long he will remain.

"The *Carolinas*, military arrests to be tested before the Federal Supreme Court. A dispatch from Raleigh states both branches of the legislature held excited debates on the recent arrests for alleged Ku-Kluxism. The general assembly authorized the attorney of state to apply to the Supreme Court of the United States for a writ of *habeas corpus* to test the legality of the military arrests. In Columbia, South Carolina, the United States Circuit Court, R. Hayes Mitch of York was arraigned under the Ku-Klux law, on a charge of conspiracy. The jury consisted of two whites and ten blacks.

"Ohio, Cincinnati, December 12th, George Anderson and John D. Patterson were charged with the murdering of Edward Cremming last week at Evon, Ohio and arrested at Ashborn yesterday while passing Evon. The citizens of that place attempted to lynch them but were prevented by the officers in charge. The affair created excitement in the area.

"A young lady was heard to remark lately that she was glad the cold weather had come because now the mosquitoes must quit us.

"Buy a lottery ticket by all means. A Memphis man who invested $1,000 has just drawn two prizes of five dollars each.

"A Vermonter has discovered a method of tanning with leaves. Small schoolboys are often tanned without their leaves."

Moses speaks up, interrupting the lad's recitation. "Henry, sir, slow yourself down. Listen to the room. Listen to your own heartbeat. Listen to the rhythm of Teo's hammer and my hammer. This room has its own beat and its own rhythm. Find it, hear it. When you do, you can speak on the beat. Hit the beat with your words. Let 'em ring like my hammer. For effect, you can come off the beat, but you gotta find it first. Remember, breathe from here"—Moses taps his own stomach— "then make your voice in here"—now tapping his chest.

Henry continues, sitting up a bit taller. With greater focus on breathing and cadence, Henry speaks:

"Havana, Cuba. December 12th, today and hence-forward, regular troops will garrison the Moro, Cabanas, and Principe forts in view of reinforcements from Spain to relieve the volunteers from their arduous service. Spain will send to Cuba this month four battalions of troops of the regular army of Spain, and 10,000 reinforcements are to follow in one year. Senior Moreno, the new Governor of Havana, has begun suppressing the gambling houses."

In a section titled *Tennessee Legislature*, Henry grabs onto the tail end of a story. He reads the editor's words aloud. "Your committee said it before, and they say it again, peace reigneth undisturbed and profound throughout the land. The war is over, and the quiet of a summer evening in gentleness rests upon all our hills and in all our valleys. Walk lightly, my friend, and stay that ruthless hand that would disturb our slumbers. *Let us have peace.*"

Henry picks the articles based on his own interests, for humor, and for insight into the people living in the south. He projects his voice to bear over the sounds of the smithy. While reading, he keeps foot-pumping the bellows.

Henry's self-appointed adjutant comes in. "Henry?"

"Yes, Paul?"

"We're going out again tomorrow. The sergeant wants you."

10 | The Long War

SAM'S JOURNAL, APRIL 2006

My war has a new name. What we called the *Global War on Terrorism* became *The Long War* this month. Remember that old lie soldiers were always told when marching to war: "Home by Christmas." We'll knock the teeth out of the rebs, the Huns, Krauts, the Reds... by Christmas. We kiss our loved ones with that promise. Even then, all but the stupidest people recognized the lie. Home by Christmas stood for: "Home soon," and "I'll be home safely," and all of the other sentiments that a soldier possesses when leaving home. The calendar flipped over. Year three closed without being "home for Christmas," at least not as a fighting force. If one soldier remains on the battlefield, then we all discover that part of ourselves remains standing on that battlefield, even when home. "Home for Christmas" means "peace by Christmas." It means peace. It means hope.

At year three, plus a month, I now fight in a war called *The Long War*. There is no "home for Christmas" implied or hidden in the confines of that simple name. Long means long. *The Longest Day* is a day during which thousands of American soldiers died on the beaches of Normandy on June 6th, 1944. *The Longest Day* remains, in our memory, as their last day on earth. *The Long March* and *The Long Walk* each tell of heroic efforts upon which the outcome remained uncertain. That is what "long" means. *The Long Trail* starts in Massachusetts then travels the length of Vermont. *The Long Gray Line* celebrates generations of student-soldiers at the United States Military Academy at West Point, New York. *The Long Gray Line* is not intended to end. *The Long War* stands now for my heritage, my present, and the future of my career. The first truthful thing said about this war since before it began. This war shall be a long war.

Back at division headquarters, I realigned with the officers from the Judge Advocate General's team. Oddly, JAG seem to be dominated by female officers. Their admin soldier is a male. JAG decided to host an Easter party. These ladies and their invited guests, which included me, grabbed hard-boiled eggs from the breakfast buffet. One of the JAG officers had ordered coloring kits, Easter candy, baskets, and silly decorations with bright colors, bunnies, and images of an unrealistic spring from home—better than the perpetual khaki. Someone shipped in a smoked salmon. A good European cheese appeared, too. The rules, which we all followed, prohibited even near-beer from being served in the headquarters' building. And we had no music. We created a party of food, coloring eggs, looking at colors, and enjoying each other's company.

JAG officers tend to be lawyers. Their branch insignia involves a quill pen crossing a sword, overlaying a laurel wreath. These officers are often portrayed in movies and television shows investigating crimes and participating in courtroom dramas. Here in Iraq, their duties involve the challenges of fighting a complicated war.

Daily, these lawyers get phone calls from battlefield commanders asking for rulings on whether their troops can return fire. Without the aid of video and while listening to the environment via a terrible mobile phone connection, they interview the commander: "Are you taking fire now?" or "Are you or your soldiers in imminent danger?" Thus on down through the checklist of requirements. Meanwhile, soldiers shout, "Can we fire?" The commander yells back, "Hold on, I am on the phone with JAG."

One officer, a graduate of U-Mass ROTC who then earned her juris doctorate at Purdue, oversees the legal issues related to prisoner detention. The Fourth Infantry Division's area of operations includes the infamous Abu Ghraib prison. Prior to our invasion of Iraq, Saddam Hussein used the facility to hold fifty thousand prisoners, many of whom were tortured and executed within the facility. After our invasion, we used the prison to house a mix of people, including common criminals and enemy combatants. A year ago this month, the world learned that American soldiers abused prisoners behind these walls. As the Army prepares to move detainees to the facilities at Camp Cropper, we still house prisoners at Abu Ghraib. This lawyer has the responsibility for overseeing the treatment of the prisoners, making rulings about prisoner punishment, and inspecting the guards. She is on duty or on call twenty-four hours a day.

Few of these lawyer-soldiers are older than thirty.

I'll step backwards to explain that we are not allowed "near-beer" in the headquarters building because the generals on the upper floor do not want visiting dignitaries to think a soldier is holding a beer while on duty. We can sip fake beer when away from this building (we are never allowed real beer or real booze). The generals fear that if we are seen holding a "near-beer" and a senator, congressman, reporter, or state department official walked by, they would not know the difference. Therefore, no beer cans are allowed in the building, even if fake. We are not permitted music, even playing softly, because music and partying during combat operations is seen as disrespectful.

During our party, not drinking fake beer, and not listening to music, we ate salmon and good cheese. Then someone dropped a purple marshmallow Peep on the concrete floor.

The first game involved testing how far down one could squish a Peep while still having it inflate to its normal form. This lonely purple Peep got joined by others: yellow and orange. Someone stacked them for a photograph. That photograph likely foreshadowed the next activities. It ought to have served us all as a warning.

Fashioning a cigarette from a toothpick, one lawyer posed two Peeps to recreate a now-famous photo of Private Lynndie England. The lawyers put Peeps on dog leashes and made a pyramid of colored Peeps. Each tableau resembling famous photos published globally in the media.

If photos of these lawyers torturing Peeps got released, then every soldier at our party would be disciplined. I rapidly wished that the digital camera would disappear. The fine line of playing with Peeps and mocking prisoner torture rests only with the observer. If no camera existed, I would have laughed more freely, *New York Times* rules be damned. Instead, I remember the line from *MASH*. "Every once in a while, you just have to pull down your pants and slide on the ice." An observer from afar, or a reporter, or a two-star general, would fail to recognize the human need to process the insanity of our lives.

This is a war during which bullets are inventoried monthly. If a soldier fires a weapon, an investigation follows. This much I know from firsthand experience. I carry weapons, face dangers, then I interview soldiers after they pulled a trigger. I have interviewed soldiers that should never have been placed into positions of responsibility or been deployed into a combat theater of operations. My little team of three flew to a unit to interview a soldier and his commander. This private had begged to be left home. He knew he was unfit for duty. His bosses begged for him to be left off their rosters and be transferred to a unit that could care for him and his needs. Senior officials determined that this private would deploy to Iraq.

Now in Baghdad, armed with a loaded rifle, he started self-medicating. His previously unstable mental health issues blossomed into a crisis. In one scenario, command could have—should have—shunted this man towards medical units for treatment. Instead, this soldier had been hit with multiple charges under the UCMJ. The military police locked this unfortunate soldier in a detention barracks. While several soldiers in the detention barracks had significant mental health issues often compounded by learning or developmental disabilities, other soldiers in the detention barracks were cold-blooded killers and rapists.

Why would a combat commander call a lawyer prior to having a soldier pull a trigger? Instead of being the setup for a bad joke, it is reality. The combat commander had been told by his unit commander, who had been told by their commanders, to precisely follow the Rules of Engagement. If you fail to follow the Rules of Engagement, you get investigated for possible violations of the UCMJ. If you called a lawyer before pulling a trigger, then the commander followed the rules and protected their career.

The United States fights two wars in two countries using two techniques. In the Afghan War, the one we celebrate as going well, opium production exceeds all past levels. That's our benchmark for current success. In my war, here in Iraq, we pour money into the most corrupt organizations I have ever heard of. We ought to recognize corruption as our enemy here. Weekly, the Iraqi army and the Iraqi police fight against each other in the streets. A brigade commander captured a group of Iraqi Police officers and a similar number of Iraqi army soldiers. He tossed them all into his detention facility. Before locking them up, his soldiers stripped them of their uniforms, forcing them into the orange jumpsuits worn by prisoners. I heard this brigade commander give a brief after the action. He said: "I'll sort this all out later. I am too damned mad at them all to deal with it tonight. They will sleep in our cells wearing their new orange outfits until I cool off." Yeah, okay, so a story not in the *Times*.

None of this will improve with an invasion into Iran, nor if Iran invades Iraq.

In the face of these pressures, I could see the Army and the press making a big deal out of a picture of a soldier—a lawyer—torturing a Peep. The unseen irony is that the lawyer posing the Peep happens to be prosecuting military police officers for torturing Iraqis. It is both tasteless and hilarious. It is inappropriate and outrageously funny.

At the party, everyone's favorite egg had been colored light purple. Written with a neat, careful hand, a lawyer wrote "TNT" on the egg. It had a small fuse coming out of the top. Another lawyer made an I-Egg-D. Obviously, I took the task too seriously, trying to make colorful zig-zags with dots and striving for the intricacy of Fabergé. I was channeling my inner you, Brie.

The building guards put a yellow Easter egg near a nest of sandbags at the guard shack. This yellow Easter egg divided the headquarters staff into three groups. The first group saw nothing out of the ordinary. The second group recognized a potential IED at the guard shack. The third group recognized an Easter egg. Please know that the most dangerous group was those who saw nothing.

The yellow egg had been colored by the drummer in the divisional band. The Fourth Infantry Division brought the divisional band into Baghdad. With their instruments locked in an armory, these soldiers held rifles at the perimeter of the division headquarters. The young woman who checks my ID most mornings plays the piccolo. Imagine that young woman's mother. Army musicians get extra money, travel extensively, and get treated very well, unless the division gets deployed into *The Long War*. In that case, the piccolo player says to the military intelligence officer, "Good morning, Lieutenant Musgrave, can I see your ID?"

Several years ago, this young woman said, "Don't worry, Mom, I am just going to play the piccolo."

The rain came. Roads flooded. This part of Iraq turned to mud. The Bad Guys stopped tossing stuff-that-goes-boom. In other words, we got a reprieve from mortar and rocket attacks. During the worst of the weather, the daily murder rate dropped, too. Mud limits movement and the mosquitoes take up the fight from the Bad Guys. Iraqi mosquitos are as bad as anyone else's mosquitoes except these guys wait a year to hatch. During the dry and hot times, one worries about nasty bugs in the sand and scorpions. When it rains, Iraq gets swarmed by a year's worth of mosquitos with an unrestrained life-lust. I got sent back to Forward Operating Base Falcon for more investigations.

I must remind myself that I find the following story funny because of the inherent racism and ongoing idiosyncrasy of my employer, the United States Army. The U.S. government hired a division of Halliburton called Kellogg, Brown, and Root—KBR. Halliburton gained notoriety for its long connections with Vice President Chaney and because their contract is a cost-plus contract, meaning the government put no checks-and-balances on the contract. Halliburton/KBR pays what they pay, they jack up the price, and bill Uncle Sam for it. KBR provides a massive amount of logistical support to the Army. They build the bases, feed us, and have created the infrastructure that we require to live.

KBR hires firms to provide services. For example, they hired Toifor from Germany to haul and handle trash. They hired several catering companies to prepare and serve our hot meals. And they contracted with PPI for unskilled labor. KBR positions itself as a project management firm and the source of skilled and unskilled labor while in this combat environment. The trades—such as carpenters, plumbers, earth movers, and electricians—now include a posse of PPI unskilled laborers that follow along.

PPI travels to the poorest parts of India, Sri Lanka, and Bangladesh recruiting men. Universally, they are tiny: short and skinny. Most appear two weeks from malnourished. PPI hires them. KBR flies them into Iraq. They wear ridiculous orange safety vests everywhere, typically over dark blue coveralls. While soldiers wear camouflage, these men wear highly visible, highly contrasting clothing. You can see them a kilometer away. They pick up trash in parking lots, clean things, and even sweep the dust outside the division headquarters. We call them TCNs. TCN means "third-country nationals." We can admit that TCN is a shabby word that obscures the fact that we employ the poorest men of southern Asia to take on hazardous and miserable jobs. In the phrase "third-country nationals," we recognize that North American and Europeans together stand as the "first" party, our friends and allies. North African and Arabic peoples then are the "second" party—our enemies, as it were. Thus, poor, south Asian men provide a foray into the "third country." India, Sri Lanka, and Bangladesh are not combatants in this fight.

Our language segments the world. We interact with HCN or LNs. HCN is a host-country national whereas an LN is a local national. That's the language we use: Host Country National and Third-Country Nationals and "us." And who stands in the "us" circle? Americans, Brits, Aussies, Poles, and on through the list. When you meet a Serbian here, is he an HCN or a TCN? Is he a Host-Country National? No. Is he a Third-Country National? No. He is one of us. He is in the "our nation" group in our three-nation image of the combat theater. If you are member of a coalition nation or working for the military or you work for KBR, you are a member of "us." If you got hauled in as cheap labor from Malaysia, Thailand, India, Sri Lanka, or Bangladesh, then you are a TCN.

TCNs have their own locked compounds within our compounds. They have their own dining hall within their compounds. The handy bit of this process is that when darkness comes, we sort people based on skin color. HCNs (Arab men) get removed from the bases. TCNs (South Asian men) get locked into their sub-compounds, surrounded by chain link fencing. They often sleep in shipping containers that had once been used to haul freight. When walking by, you can see dozens of pairs of shoes outside one shipping container door.

Life gets tricky for some members of the "us" crowd. Some of the "us" crowd are Arabic or south Asian. When evening comes, soldiers try to round these men up and point them towards various gates. Arabs out. South Asian behind the fences of the PPI compound. The nightly ritual of showing IDs and proving that you are a member of the "us" team happens. The neat effort of color-coding human beings does not work well and has not for centuries. Soldiers and contractors who fail to look "American" get treated badly.

Frankly, I have fallen in love with the TCNs I see on my missions and on my daily duties. I hear, "Hello, Ma'am," and get a salute. The salute involves raising the right hand skyward with the palm showing forward. It is like a static wave, a very stiff movement. I have adopted the wave, offering it back to the men. They always smile. Sometimes I shout out "namaste" as well.

I have been watching ten men prepare a new paved sidewalk during recent days. They haul dry cement and gravel in a crappy wheelbarrow that most Americans would have long ago tossed to the curb. Then, on the ground, they mix the concrete with sticks. At the edge of their worksite, they have removed their shoes, in near pairs creating a straight line. They work barefoot. I have seen these guys down on their haunches, holding shovels by the neck and digging a hole. I had been taught by my Aunts to stand at a shovel and use my foot to cut the soil. I then use the length of the shovel handle as a lever. The soil in Vermont remains moist and soft when not covered by winter snow. In Iraq, one digs by scraping the earth. Maybe these fellows are illustrating an ancient way to dig hard-packed soils.

I hear rumors that PPI holds the personal paperwork of their employees in secure vaults. While this sounds like a service, it also approaches forced labor. The PPI men do not have access to their passports. For this reason, many soldiers, including me, call PPI "Prime Prisons Incorporated." I suppose the name fits, given we lock them into a fenced enclosure each night, all night. Very prison-like.

I started working with another human intelligence guy this week.

This HUMINT specialist spent most of his career in Germany before the end of the Cold War and the years that followed. He is fluent in German and Russian. We got to talking about languages spoken and heard here. He said, "It doesn't matter. If a Russian gent wants to talk with a Japanese gent, both will speak English. This is not your grandfather's imperialism. Everyone has adopted the language of the internet and business." I think I can still catch a pretty good whiff of old-fashioned imperialism. I am in a war in Iraq. The rest of the fighting army is in Afghanistan. European powers have fought over this terrain for more than a century—or is that a millennium?

We just forgot to use the word "imperialism."

The United States designed a new flag for Iraq. Let's observe that the colors of flags throughout Arab lands share similar properties and colors. Many have red, black, and white as dominant colors. Black, white, green, and red have been recognized as Pan-Arab colors for over a century. Each color represents a dynastic legacy and/or caliphate in Arabic history. Many have strong horizontal bands. Look at the flags of Egypt, Kuwait, and Syria. Even Iran's flag is similar.

The United States presented Iraq with a new flag in 2004, filled with important symbolism and inclusive colors. White for purity. Two blue lines representing the Tigris and Euphrates rivers. A golden yellow borrowed from the yellow sun of the Kurd flag. In the middle was a pale blue crescent moon, the size and shape of the present Turkish flag. Created by idiotic foreign officers or civilian intelligence with no understanding of the symbols, rivalries, feuds, and cultural impact of this color or that shape.

The present Turkish flag with a crescent moon once flew over Iraq when Iraq was under the fist of the Ottoman Empire. They don't want a reminder of the Ottoman Empire. But we give it to them with a pale blue crescent moon ("Hey, it isn't white."). Please let us present you with your new national flag carrying the heritage of your former Turkish overlords. To take the insult further, the new flag had the colors of Israel. Can you imagine a day when an Arabic nation adopts the white and blue colors of Israel? I suspect that day doesn't land in 2006 or even 2007.

Not sure how smart people thought that designing a flag for Iraq using Israel's blue-and-white colors and the Ottoman's crescent moon would be successful. Just another thumb imposing their vision on an ancient peoples. Just another form of a boot-heel pressing down on the neck of Arab Muslims.

Surprise! Our Israeli/Ottoman-inspired flag failed to gain support from Iraqis.

On their present flag, the top third of the flag is red. The bottom third is black with three stars in the middle white band. Written in Arabic was the takbir. It reads "God is great" or "Allahu Akbar." Shall we observe that we have similar statements on our currency, from the lowly penny on up: "In God we trust."

Having failed at installing our own blue and white flag, we ordered millions of lapel pins printed with flag version 2.0. American politicians love pinning the Flag of the United States on their lapels. Therefore, Iraqis will too, right? We suggested that Iraqis attach this small pin to their clothing as a source of pride in the new nation of Iraq. The United States government, by printing these pins, communicated acceptance of the Iraqi government's decision to remain with their own flag.

Except...the United States government refused to print the takbir on the flag.

Our government paid a Chinese company to manufacture these pins for us. The Chinese manufacturer had a quality control issue. Several thousand of the pins were printed only in solid green. Solid green ignores the Pan-Arabic sentiment found in the use of multiple colors. Solid color flags often get carried and waved by separatist and rebels. The solid green banner is recognized as Shi'ah. The remaining thousands of pins got printed with the right colors and the three stars, but ignored God, thus insulting all we had not yet insulted with the green-only version.

The manufacturer put each pin in a small plastic zipper-topped baggy. Each baggy had a gold sticker that read, "Made in China," written in English, which we then gave to Arabic-speaking Muslims in Iraq.

Well done, team.

The fucked-up solid green pins with the outline of Iraq communicates to all Arabs that this is now the land of the Shi'a. Oopsy-daisy.

In our efforts to foster unity and create a sense of national pride, we have blundered repeatedly.

Officially, some in leadership stated that we did not use the *takbir* as seen on the flag because it was written in Saddam Hussein's handwriting. Others said printing the *takbir* would be too small to read, therefore we left it out. Let's admit that some other cultural or religious based bias might be present in this decision.

Imagine that the next overlords who invade America decide to print our currency without "In God We Trust." I might not miss it, but someone will. Could cause a stink, you think?

11 | December 1871

HENRY, DECEMBER 1871

On the morning of December 15th, 1871, Private Henry "T" McDonald meets Deputy U.S. Marshal James Skyles at the detention barracks. The Army's collection of Ku Kluxers exceeds the capacity of the garrison's stockade. As Army units had arrested members of the Dade County Ku Klux organization, the detainees got moved into a barracks building. Sixteen men lived in the detention barracks, with four remaining behind bars in the stockade.

Sergeant O'Rourke's squad is in the railyard, preparing a train to transport prisoners and guards to Atlanta. They affix three carriages to the end of the trainset that makes the daily run to Atlanta. In the freight car, they load a few crates of dry rations and coal for the stove, extra ammunition, and two empty, wooden crates. In the two passenger cars, they start coal fires to heat the area.

Marshal Skyles teases Henry upon seeing him at sun-up: "Hey T, I debated asking for you. On one hand, if I bring you, I've invited trouble. But if I leave you behind, trouble may find me anyway."

Henry, not enamored by the moniker, lets the greeting slide. He speaks with a formal tone. "Good morning, Marshal Skyles. How are you, sir?"

"I am well." The marshal feels like Henry ignored his jocularity and warmth. "Have you seen the orders?"

"Yes, sir, I read them. Sergeant Porter handed them to me. We're transporting the prisoners to Atlanta, handing them over, and returning with our shackles."

"That's it. Like a Sunday walk in the park." Skyles's hand taps Henry on the back. Henry does not flinch, neither does he slap the marshal's back in return.

"Are we on a special or an express?"

"No, the Army decided it could not afford a special or an express.

We're running down the road on the schedule. Sergeant O'Rourke is preparing a few extra cars for us. His squad will help us load." Three soldiers push a handcart loaded with steal shackles. As the soldiers park the cart, the marshal says, "Let's get the prisoners shackled."

Henry reaches for a set of irons, intending to help the other privates. The marshal says, "T, you are with me. Let them do the shackling. Help me manage the prisoners." Like the marshal, Henry had been present for the arrest of most of the men in the room. The prisoners had either seen Henry and his rifle at work, or they had heard the stories of the young private who the other soldiers called "T," "T" for trouble.

"When you shackle them, check them for weapons and bourbon. We don't need knives or drunks on the road with us. Hey, private!"

All of the young soldiers within five feet of the marshal stop and look at him. "You, run to command and ask where our omnibus is."

"The prisoners are not marching?" Henry asks.

"No, they'll drag their feet and cause a ruckus on the street. We'll haul them to the yard and load them." Shackled prisoners come out of the barracks in pairs, each of them grumbling and complaining loudly to the marshal. Without fail, they each state in plain colloquial English that they will not walk to the station.

Henry says nothing to the prisoners. He wraps himself in his warrior's posture, projecting a no-nonsense attitude. He stands alert. He listens to everything but the prisoners' words. He sees everything the prisoners do. Prisoners Hale, Blevins, and Haney step into the cool sunlight. Henry's team arrive. Privates Belville and Donovan join with the other privates shackling the prisoners.

With a whisper, Henry says, "Mueller?"

"Yes, T?"

"Prisoner Haney has something in his boot, left boot."

Mueller and Sturtevant remove Prisoner Haney from the line. Mueller leans over. He lifts the trouser leg and pulls a five-inch sheath knife from inside. Mueller hands the knife to Sturtevant, then checks the other leg.

Marshal Skyles, watching the movement, says, "Mueller, check them all, please." Sturtevant hands the knife to Henry. The pair then work down the line of prisoners. Both Skyles and Henry observe a small glass flask of bourbon slide into Mueller's pocket after being removed from a prisoner's boot.

Sixteen prisoners load into the mule-drawn omnibus. The soldiers load four prisoners into the garrison's open coach. With twenty prisoners accounted for, shackled, and loaded into transports, Sergeant Porter organizes all members of E Company into an escort. Fifteen men of E Company are required to remain at garrison duties and two are at the infirmary, one still healing from a wound to the shoulder from the foray into Trenton, Georgia the prior week. A detail of ten soldiers form the lead escort. Another ten form the rear escort. Henry, Donovan, Sturtevant, Belville, Mueller, and Abrams form a loose cordon around the two vehicles. Like Henry, Sturtevant, Belville, Mueller, and Abrams each now carry the shorter carbine-style rifle — an honor presented to the privates after their heroics. Sergeant Porter positions himself at the forward left flank.

In a loud, clear, parade-ground voice, Porter commands, "Company, forward...march." Men, mules, and horses step forward. Unlike close-order marching drills, the escort has a staggered start. Mules and horses do not step smartly with their right foot on command. Unlike soldiers, the progress of mules cannot be measured in neat, thirty-inch strides. Mules move at a mule's pace.

By the time they reach the garrison gate, they have found a cadence that works for both man and beast. Most of the soldiers in the escort party march with rifles slung on their shoulders. The men in the rear group wear rucksacks with blankets rolled on top. The men at the fore travel lightly. Henry and his team keep their shorter rifles in their hands, flanking the parade. They do not march with formal discipline. Their eyes scan the buildings and streets. They walk with the careful strides of hunters at the ready.

Reaching the railyard, Sergeant O'Rourke's men of F Company form two ranks, creating a broad alley down which the prisoners will be walked. Henry's squad created a loose, roving outer ring. All other soldiers unload prisoners from the omnibus. These sixteen get loaded into the train car, two-by-two, each set of men occupying a bench. Two soldiers stand at the front of the carriage, armed only with pistols secured in leather holsters. The omnibus wheels clear the work zone. The four prisoners on the open carriage alight, then get marched to the train. The forward escort and Sergeant O'Rourke's men of F Company form ranks, then return to the garrison. The rear escort detail, those burdened with rucksacks, blankets, and provisions, enter the second military carriage. These soldiers will provide a rotating cadre of guards, and a fighting force if the train were to be attacked between Chattanooga and Atlanta.

Henry's squad operates independently. Sergeant Porter has detailed Henry and "his" five to follow the orders and guidance of the marshal. While stationary on the military siding adjacent to the warehouse, Sergeant Porter organizes the guards, setting patrols and rotations. Henry's squad sit separately and operates under casual discipline.

All soldiers on the train understand that in case of action, these six veterans of the Ku-Klux battles will take the lead.

Henry sits on the right side of the rear-most carriage against the window. His men feel special due to the special treatment. Instead of exercising their freedoms and independence, they follow Henry's lead. They sit silently, one man per bench. The train lurches, jerking forwards, settling backwards, then rolling down the track, never exceeding the pace of a slow walk. It approaches the depot and the whistle shrieks.

Henry's men stand. Each opens the door they have been assigned. Three walk to the back side of the train, three to the front, patrolling the exterior of the train. Donovan, now known as "Backdoor," stands between the tracks at the rear of the train. "The Adjutant" Abrams follows Henry out to the depot side. Mueller pushes forward through the depot toward the locomotive. Unseen, away from the depot, Belville takes a position next to the locomotive. Each man has his carbine rifle in hand, modelling Henry.

Civilian passengers settle into their carriages. Depot staff load freight and the post into the freight car. The doors of the military's freight car open with a narrow gap to provide sightlines to the outside world.

The whistle announces their departure. The train pushes east out of the yard.

Henry's men, as if they had worked the rails since boyhood, swing up to the moving cars, each in their turn. Backdoor Donovan loads first, then Abrams. The final two, Belville and Mueller, who had taken posts near the locomotive, swing up onto the carriage's iron stair. The train gains speed, heading to Boyce Station about one-half mile from Chickamauga Creek and Harrison Pike. Boyce Station also serves as a signal and switchyard. It switches to the Western and Atlantic track that will carry all to Atlanta. Henry's men again drop to the ground, taking positions around the train until it chugs from the station. Curving around the northern edge of Missionary Ridge, Henry takes a seat on the left side of the carriage so he can catch glimpses of the Chickamauga.

The train enters the battlefields left by months of war fought between the U.S. Army under William S. Rosecrans and rebel forces led by Braxton Bragg. This battle, fought in September 1863, marked the end of the Army's advance into Georgia. The Army lost sixteen thousand men, with nearly two thousand killed and ten thousand wounded. About five thousand were captured by the rebel forces. The loss of life in this battle was exceeded only by the Battle of Gettysburg, fought in July of the same year. The Chickamauga serves as a reminder of a significant loss, while also marking the opening of General William Tecumseh Sherman's advance to Atlanta.

Starting in May of 1864, six months after the Army's defeat near Chickamauga, Major General William Tecumseh Sherman invaded Georgia. Sherman used the rail for everything: to advance fresh troops, to carry weapons, ammunition, food, horses, and wagons.

The enemy tried to cut off this supply line. They heated and bent the rail. They burned the wooden sleepers. They blew up the road.

The soldiers rebuilt it.

During Sherman's advance through Georgia, soldiers garrisoned each station moving south. Injured soldiers and rebel prisoners were transported north along the rail. In 1871, Private Henry S. McDonald rides over these same tracks, looking at relatively fresh battlefields.

Henry wears the same blue woolen uniform as those who came before him on this road. Twists in the creek and turns made by the train permits Henry to study the terrain from his window. He can see scars made by running skirmishes, hastily dug redouts, and trenches. These remain etched into the land.

Only seven years separate the days that Sherman's men fought to gain control of this region during the summer of 1864 and the winter of 1871 when Henry escorts still-rebellious prisoners to an Army garrison in Atlanta. Seven years prior, Sergeant Porter fought here and guarded supplies and depots along this same road. It took Sherman's Army five months, from May until September, to advance to Atlanta, a route traveled several times daily with the Western and Atlantic Rail. The distance between Chattanooga and Atlanta approximates 120 miles. Sherman's campaign took 150 days to travel those 120 miles. They advanced approximately one mile per day into hostile territory.

Sherman's legacy remains on this scorched land and in the bitterness of some people. Even those liberated by General Sherman have expressed new frustrations as their freedoms blossomed then rapidly eroded.

Henry imagined sitting on this train during the war years. He pictured enslaved peoples running towards this rail line, running towards the United States Army, running towards Sherman's men. Once making it to the lines, enslaved people became free. They fled with nothing. They carried little or no food. The elderly and the very young arrived carried by those that could keep going. Upon encountering a uniformed soldier, they crossed the threshold from enslaved to free.

These events manifested acutely for Henry because of Moses, the blacksmith, who ran from Trickum, Georgia, south of Catoosa Station. Moses had been sold in 1862. During that sale from one slave owner to another, he was forced away from his wife and two sons, one son still suckling at the breast. Although the distance Moses traveled was short, his wife was sold and removed to Dalton. Without letters, telegraph, or visits, Moses lost his wife and his family. Once making the line of U.S. soldiers, Moses picked up a hammer. Since that day, he remains as close as possible to the last spot where he saw his wife and two children.

First, he laid rail. When rebel forces destroyed a section, Moses and a team rebuilt it. He forged nails and shoed horses. Officers observed him building tools and repairing nearly anything at hand. His skills earned him attention. Moses still refers to himself as "The General's Blacksmith." Those around him call him, "Uncle Billy's Blacksmith." Instead of following Sherman further, Moses remained in Chattanooga, opting to continue his work for the Army.

A dozen men in a dozen ranks separate Henry from General William Tecumseh Sherman. In 1871, General Sherman is the se-nior- most officer in the Army. Henry, as a private, holds the junior-most rank in the Army. At the first tier stands Sergeant Preston, who knows the general and served under him twice. Then there is their own lieutenant, then Captain Cook, the commander of Companies E and F of the Second Infantry Regiment. Then the regimental commander, then the battalion commander, then the commander of the Department of the South, then, finally, General Sherman. General Sherman serves as the commanding general for the United States Army, thus boss to all soldiers.

Henry asks himself how many times General Sherman traveled up and down these rails during 1864. With the Army proceeding at one mile per day, he likely walked and rode horses back and forth, then sat in a carriage like this one. Henry cannot envision the general enjoying a plush and ornate carriage. Maybe an austere office with a field cot. He imagines the soldiers greeting their commander with friendly yells for their "Uncle Billy," a soldier's soldier.

When the whistle announces the coming of a station, Henry's squad members each rise from their seats. They drop to the ground from the moving training. They establish themselves at their outside posts, alert for insurrectionists desiring the freedom of their fellows. As the train departs each station, they leap, or swing, back onto the various cars.

The train passes through Tunnel Hill, Tilton, Resaca, and Calhoun. Some of the older soldiers tell quiet stories of their battles along this road. The prisoners also tell stories of their days fighting at Nackajack Gap, Armuchee Creek, and Pine Log Creek, referring to each other by their prior ranks in the army of the confederacy. Men in civilian clothing bound by steal shackles use the honorifics "colonel" and "captain" in the train car.

Approaching New Hope Church, Picket Mills, and Dallas, the memories of war become more intense. Rebel soldiers rekindle stories of their efforts to keep Georgia free from northern aggression. They share stories of the wealth, opportunities, freedoms, and beauty of their Georgia. In their telling, everyone knew their place in society and in the economy. Georgia stood for culture and grace.

"You boys are working altogether too hard," the prisoners say to their guards, who rotate throughout the carriage. "You should relax. We're just going to Atlanta. We've got nothing to worry about."

The prisoners tell Henry and the others that neither the Army, nor the United States Marshal's Office, has sufficient jurisdiction in the State of Georgia.

"Private McDonald," Prisoner Haney says, holding up his shackled wrist in a display of bravado, "I've got nothing to fear from the men of Georgia. These men, these prisoners, followed state laws, local customs, and more importantly, God's laws. This trial won't be like those other trials in the Carolinas. We will face a real jury."

Henry walks away from the rest of the sentence, leaving the words unheard. Haney's sentiments seem to be shared with all of the prisoners. None of the twenty fear the courts or the jury, nor do they contemplate being convicted of any crime in Georgia. The prisoners plan for a dinner served to them at a hotel, attended by state and local officials. The prisoners say as much as this train transports Georgians to an impromptu regimental reunion.

Henry gauges the waning enthusiasm from his squad as they pass Allatoona. They are slightly more morose and less speedy clearing the Ackworth Depot. A small team of U.S. Army soldiers meet the train at Marietta, traveling via horseback from the Atlanta Garrison. In Marietta, they provide a security perimeter while passing intelligence to the marshal and Sergeant Porter. Porter informs Henry to expect no resistance along the road, nor in Atlanta. At Vining's Station, Henry's men rise from their seats, taking posts within the cars. Their time for swinging acrobatics quietly ends.

"Sergeant Porter?"

"That's me."

"We're instructed to tell you that you and the prisoners are to remain on board at the civilian depot. The train will be shunted to our military siding. You all will alight there. Okay?"

"Sure."

The prisoners, with freedom in sight, move rapidly and willingly. They ignore the paraded soldiers. Within an hour, the prisoners had been secured into a barracks block. As soon as shackles are removed and doors locked, dignitaries arrive from the community. Black servants follow the dignitaries, carrying warm food and picnic hampers for the prisoners. The prisoners eat the best of what could be carried to them from the wealthiest kitchens in Atlanta and drink from bottles hidden in hampers and coat pockets. Meanwhile, the Chattanooga soldiers eat cold mess and pass the small bottle Mueller lifted from a prisoner's boot earlier in the day.

The following day, the soldiers return to Chattanooga in their own military carriage. They chug back up the rail with shackles, weapons, and ammunition.

On Thursday, Private Henry McDonald sits next to Moses's forge. He reads the article in the *Daily Union and American* privately to himself. It starts with, "Outrages upon personal liberties in Georgia." The article, published the day prior in Nashville, traveled via the post, on the 7:00 p.m. Central Short Line from Nashville, arriving at 3:13 a.m. in Chattanooga.

Moses prompts Henry, "Stand up straight."

Henry stands with greater formality. He tries to keep the bellows pumping as he read the story a second time:

Outrages upon Personal Liberties in Georgia
The following dispatch was sent from Atlanta GA
on the 11th Instant to Foster Blodget in Washington.

Moses asks, "Who is Foster Blodget?"

"He was the mayor of some town in Georgia, then sent to the U.S. Senate by Georgia. The government refused to seat him in the Senate."

"So, he is their Senator?"

"I don't think so. I think Georgia thinks he's their Senator, but the United States Senate won't accept him."

"Alright, continue."

> Twenty Ku-Klux arrests have been made in Dade and Walker counties. An investigation is now proceeding. The evidence implicates a number of the members of the Georgia Legislature and others as high in the order. The organization is being developed as powerful in Northern Georgia. Signed G.B. Chamberlain, Chief United States Deputy Marshal.
>
> It appears that these men were arrested by Federal troops stationed at Chattanooga. Mr. R. H. Tatum, one of the parties arrested, published a card in the Atlanta Constitution, on the 13th instant, in which he stated that he did not know what offense he was charged with until he arrived in Atlanta. There he had been confined for ten days, and bail was refused. The total number arrested at different times was about thirty-five, some comprising of the most respectable citizens of Dade county. It appears that these men were arrested by Federal troops sent from Chattanooga. These troops invaded a peaceable State, arrested citizens without warrant and without informing them of the charges upon which they were arrested, and then brought them into this State, where they are held as prisoners pervious to being sent to Atlanta. It is not pretended that they could not have been arrested by the United States Marshal alone, on the contrary, there is every reason to believe that the simple service of process would have been ample to have secured their attendance at Atlanta to answer for any charge preferred against them. Now for the sequel to this raid upon these citizens of

Dade county by Federal troops from Tennessee. The Atlanta Sun of the 17th instant says:

"We had opportunities of conversing with the prisoners, witnesses, and other citizens of Dade, who were not arraigned in this examination, and from them we have obtained the following reliable and impartial explanation of the unfounded prosecution of the honest and innocent citizens of the county of Dade.

"It seems that one Asa Boydston, living on the line of Alabama and Georgia, but within Alabama during the war, too cowardly to volunteer as a soldier, frequented the mountains, and at every opportunity committed thefts, robbed defenseless women and helpless children, and ravaged the homes of families of soldiers in the army, and was guilty of innumerable depredations not tolerated by any civilized government. After the war, being several times detected in thieving and other misdemeanors, he soon forfeited the respect of every honest man in the vicinity. During this winter he very suddenly left the county, but returned about two weeks ago in company with one James Skyles, who seemed to be employed by the government for arresting parties under the Ku-Klux acts of Congress, under the proclamations of Bullock, to get the rewards offered.

"Arriving at Trenton, Dade County, Boydston pointed out Mr. R. Haney, who was immediately arrested and placed under guard of a squad of United States soldiers. They then proceeded to Rising Fawn and arrested the postmaster, J. G. Hale, in the act of distributing the mail; J. W. Blevins, Road Commissioner, in the act of writing out his report; and fifteen or twenty more, who were closely and busily engaged in their respective duties, who were not allowed time for preparation in the bitterly cold weather that was then prevailing. Many of the prisoners were compelled to pass the frigid night without shelter and without blankets around a smoul, which was but a poor protection in the tempestuous winds that howled among these mountain regions.

"The party next proceeded to Chattanooga, where all were committed to prison except T. W. Sharrock and W. P. Sharrock, who were last seen with the United States Commissioner. It is supposed that, by cajoling, threats and promises, these two persons were persuaded to turn Government evidence. They were treated with clemency, and even with special kindness, while all other prisoners were allowed a bare pittance of filthy food and were confined in cells which barely admitted the body of lying on their sides. One of the prisoners testified that, while lying down, it was impossible for one man to move without the simultaneous movement of every inmate of the room. While there, the officer and commissioners used every device and all of their eloquence to persuade one of the younger sons of Colonel R. H. Tatum—a man of extended influence—to turn Government evidence, doubtless hoping that a confession or treacherous and malicious testimony from such an esteemed and reliable source would convict a host of innocent citizens. They urged that he ought not 'in the bloom of his youth,' to accept certain imprisonment, when the opportunity was presented to escape. Young Tatum, with indignation, replied that he would suffer the horrors of a life-time imprisonment before he would testify against his own neighbors and involve them in a crime, which, if ever perpetrated at all, was not only without their countenance, but without their knowledge. His malicious tempters said they would make no more efforts. "If the younger Tatum would not yield, it was useless to appeal to the older." So their efforts in that direction were baffled; but they were more successful with the two Sharrocks who both turned Government evidence.

"The prisoners were then brought to this place, and all, with the exception of a few, were committed to prison. They all assert that they were arrested without being notified of the reason or the cause of the arrest. The officers intimated that they were subpoenaed as witnesses. Their treatment afterwards was such as to make them feel they were regarded as galley slaves."

> The United States Commissioners held W. P. H. Tatum and G. W. M. Tatum in bonds of $2,500 each for their appearance at the United States Court, because, he said, according to the Atlanta Sun, "the liberty of Sevier Powell had been violated, but he did not state that his rights, under the enforcement act, had been infringed upon under which act along the warrant was issued." The prosecution of all the other prisoners was abandoned, the counsel for the government stating that there was no proof against them. Two citizens of Dade county, H. T. Wilson and M. Nichols, appeared before the Commissioners and stated that they had been arrested, but knew not why. There were no charges against them, and they were told they could return home. Here we have a specimen of the outrages committed upon unoffending citizens of Georgia. They are arrested by Federal soldiers, and taken under guard, first to Chattanooga, and then to Atlanta, there to be told that there is no proof or no charges against them. And yet these citizens, who were treated as felons while in charge of the troops, and imprisoned without the privilege of bail when taken to Atlanta, have no redress for these indignities and outrages. If these things continue to be winked at by the men who hold power in Congress, the time will come when the North will be made to feel this despotism as severely as the South now does.

Henry carries Moses's paper back to the barrack to share with the men who had risked their lives during the campaign to clear the Ku-Klux members from northwestern Georgia. They escorted white prisoners who traveled on heated trains and were met by warm company and warm food. These prisoners now claimed that the soldiers had treated them with the violence and low regard of a "galley slave," while asserting that their own efforts to clear lands of formerly enslaved people was an appropriate and supported act. Hanging a black man, raping his son, and burning his home are not crimes in Georgia, not any longer. Georgia, once again a member of the United States of America, will not be subject to occupation by federal troops nor will the white citizens of the state be subject to federal laws— federal laws recently passed to grant the rights of people who had recently been bought and sold as property by these same honored families of the south.

Sitting on Army beds reading by candlelight, the men debate the facts of the article. Henry, half listening, debates the future role of the U.S. Army in Tennessee and Georgia. It makes no sense to spend money and time enforcing unpopular laws, especially if the prison doors open following their arrests.

Henry feels the routine of a garrison life closing in. Each morning starts with reveille, then stable call. At six in the morning, the bugler makes the breakfast call. The buglers break the day into segments, like the chimes from a clock tower or church steeple. Drill call at ten and dinner call at noon, on through the cycle until retreat, tattoo, and taps at nine in the evening.

During company inspection, which is attended by Marshal Skyles, Captain Cook asks Porter to call Private Henry S. McDonald to the front of the assembly.

Sergeant O'Rourke bellows with his parade voice, "Attention to Orders."

Lieutenant Dempsey then reads:

> Be it known to all present, that the Commanding General of the United States Army William T. Sherman has reposed special trust and confidence in the valor, fidelity, and excellence demonstrated by Private Henry McDonald. In view of these qualities and demonstrated leadership potential, Private McDonald is advanced to the rank of corporal effective 24 December 1871. Signed Captain H. C. Cook Second Infantry Regiment, E and F company, commanding.

12 | Monday

SAM'S JOURNAL, MAY 2006

During these months, I repeat the line: "Every day is Monday." Not true though, is it? Some days are birthdays. Some are anniversaries, or graduation days. Some days are Sundays.

I sat with my captain, Brian Ufner, and two lieutenants. When one of the women got up for a bowl of ice cream, her battle-buddy and friend leaned over, saying, "Today is her birthday. If we start singing, everyone will join us." I looked around the D-Fac, observing that soldiers were watching a spelling bee on the ceiling-mounted television monitors. In my hundreds of meals now eaten in Iraq, in a dozen forward operating bases, I had never heard soldiers sing, even the cadences.

Lieutenant Simmons starts us. One hundred soldiers join in. This young lieutenant has spent three of her four most recent birthdays in Iraq.

Brian's birthday is the 20th of May, but oddly, he would prefer if his birthday were on the 5th of May. Brian loves the number five. It shows up continuously in his life. He always gives assignments and writes emails with five bullets, even when three would suit. Brian's first, last, and middle names each have five letters. If he could move his birthday to the fifth day of the fifth month, it would bring symmetry to his life. When you spend between five and twenty-five hours per day with another person, the conversations tend to cover everything in life—almost everything.

In recognition that every day is Monday, the PX does not sell birthday cards. The dining facilities do not make special cakes. The only stores are the same stores we see every day. We can buy bootleg DVDs for three dollars. We can buy fake French perfume, fake Rolex watches, or computer parts that will either break in a week or infect every system with wretched viruses. At the PX, you can buy fake beer, brown towels, real DVDs, and bad paperback books. I think about doing something for Brian for his real, or imagined, birthday. The T-shirts are not funny enough: "Who's your Baghdaddy?" written in both English and Arabic. The "Camp Liberty Country Club" requires explaining when back in the world. In the months that we have been here, we know every product sold by every vendor at every military installation in the greater Baghdad area. We are supposed to run background checks on these vendors and track their movement. Some vendors provide us with good intelligence.

Shopping for a friend proves difficult when the effort is nothing special. Brian and I have made our fair share of pity purchases. Additionally, we make purchases that obscure payments for information. If I buy a movie, Brian watches it after me. If he buys a movie, I watch it after him. If Brian wants a Snapple Apple, he gets two. One for me.

We traveled south to Forward Operating Base Kalsu. Brian and I think part of our summer will be spent working in that region, attached to the Second Brigade Combat Team of the Fourth Infantry Division. The camp was named in honor of a professional football player who was killed in action while serving in Vietnam as lieutenant in the 101st Airborne Division. Bob Kalsu played for the Buffalo Bills and was the rookie of the year in 1968. He was one of two professional football players killed by combat in Vietnam. As Brian pointed out, Pat Tillman was the first football player to be killed in these new wars.

Camp Kalsu, unlike most of the FOBs I have worked from, felt like the real desert. Most of my missions involved working in and around metropolitan Baghdad, a city of eight million people. FOB Kalsu stands adjacent to the highway that connects Baghdad with Kuwait and the south. We call it "Material Supply Route" Tampa, or MSR Tampa. This is the road I privately call I-95.

Kalsu sits on a canal that carries water from the Euphrates west of the camp. The canal originates on the Euphrates between Karbala and Iskandariya, or Alexandria.

While FOB Kalsu was named by fans of the Buffalo Bills football team in honor of a hometown hero, Iskandariya was founded and named after Alexander the Great, *Al-Iskandar* in Arabic. Alexander traveled this region 2,300 years ago and left his mark. Iskandariya and FOB Kalsu both reside the Babylon region of Iraq.

Kalsu is almost equidistant between the Tigris and the smaller Euphrates. In southern Iraq, the Euphrates and Tigris meet to form the Shatt al-Arab, the River of Arabs, also called the Arvand-Rood. South of Basra, this river serves as part of the boundary line between Iraq and Iran.

The temperature in the Blackhawk flying to FOB Kalsu was over 110 degrees F/43oC. The doors were closed, and I had a half-liter bottle of frozen water in my thigh pocket. I feel it melting aggressively. The bottle was wedged between my leg and my neighbor's leg. We didn't speak. First, it is simply too loud to hear anything. Second, the thawing bottle was getting both of us slightly damp. That makes the opening comment a bit hard to formulate. "Lieutenant, ma'am, I believe you have a leak somewhere. It is getting my leg wet."

We are two hours into a forty-minute flight. We should not be this far west. The pilots have demonstrated very odd behavior. We've flown in circles, made a quick landing, then remained on the ground doing nothing.

We both ignored the issue.

Most of the guys on the flight were from Criminal Investigations Division, or CID. No doubt they recognized our branch insignia as Military Intelligence. We all experienced a tense truce between these two alpha-dog units.

We landed at Kalsu, then Brian and I walked for six hours in the early summer heat under a blistering sun. When in Baghdad and traveling the regions between the two rivers, the sense of living and working within the Fertile Crescent feels real. When traveling west of the Euphrates, one experiences the desert in the most classic sense. We're sixty miles south and west of our division headquarters. Together, Brian and I recognize that our little team has been pledged to missions in the summer heat at the edge of the Iraqi desert.

Summer, and the new pressures of a growing Iraqi civil war, has expanded our mission. We are a small military intelligence unit attached to the Fourth Infantry Division, but not a permanent member of the team. As such, we also do not have a permanent assignment. We go to where the action is, or to where the action is not. Back in Baghdad, most of my friends in the JAG unit have rotated to new positions. All of the new lawyers are male, and their admin-assistant is female, a complete reversal from the prior months. The brightly colored parties disappeared.

Parties do not belong here anyway. When planning a party, one must continuously remember that an American soldier just died or is about to die. The tension here is so thick and the violence on such an ugly climb that one cannot wish it away. The best hope rests with spontaneous fun.

With an overeager sense of play, Private Pettigrew ran through our office in the division headquarters with a squirt gun. Private Pettigrew showers a lieutenant, me. I got hit with cold water. The water dripped down inside my uniform, down the back of my neck I laugh. Some grumble about her maturity. I got hit with cold water. The water dripped down inside my uniform, down the back of my neck. I saw her stalking Brian, a captain. It seemed unwise on several fronts. Least of which involves assaulting your company commander, but the real risk was Pettigrew's crush on her captain. I gave her a "psst" and suggested she take a walk with me.

With the bluntness born of being a Yankee, I called her out, warned her of having thoughts about her commanding officer, and acknowledged how entirely unfair the Army was to friendships, love, and sex. No, Pettigrew, you are not permitted to have a crush on our boss. And no, Pettigrew, you are not allowed to shoot him with your squirt gun. And no, I gave her no opportunity to speak, explain, or discuss any of the above matters. I spoke, she listened. Then I instructed her to get me a cold Coke from the PX. I gave her too much money and several of the plastic coins we called pogs. We both knew that I said, "fuck off," at least for a while.

When I was outside with her, I witnessed a new unit on the march. I stood staring at the chaos that I saw. The unit was comprised of sixteen members in two files. An NCO marched them. The unit contained a mix of Navy uniforms, Air Force uniforms, and a few Army uniforms. The NCO wore an Air Force uniform. The detail came to a ragged halt at the guard shack. The divisional drummer—gate guard—greeted the Air Force senior master sergeant.

"Sar'n't, can I help?"

The divisional drummer did not resemble the classic tin soldier one expects at a divisional headquarters building, and while the drummer grew accustomed to seeing four-star generals, politicians, and the occasional famous performer visiting Iraq, the motley crew of U.S. enlisted military personnel fell outside of the norms.

"We are a new platoon within a civil affairs company. I am the company first sergeant. We have been told to report here for badging and orientation."

I listened to the conversation. The sergeants rank insignia included the white diamonds that designed him as the "first shirt," or top NCO, of an Air Force unit. In the Army, he would be addressed as "top" and would have been recognized as the company first sergeant. A unit's top sergeant rank patch includes a black diamond.

I approached the sentry. "Sergeant Jefferson, can I be of assistance?"

"Yes, Ma'am."

The introductions started as if I had never heard a word. When completed, I eyeballed the crew, then in a command voice, said, "Welcome to the United States Army."

Some came to attention, some did not. Rather a few said: "Yes, Ma'am."

To the Air Force *first shirt*, I said, "Come on, Top, I'll escort you inside. I'll introduce you to the G-9 staff. They will get you sorted."

No doubt that the Army's G-2, military intelligence section, will expand by incorporating both enlisted and commissioned members of the U.S. Navy and Air Force. After years of transformation and reorganizing for the modern battlefield, the United States Army finds itself improvising. Oops.

On the third Monday of the week, which was probably Wednesday, I took a quick mission with the Jalopy Humvee we use when we are inside the wire, operating within the massive Baghdad airport complex. I took Private Pettigrew with me, as my battle-buddy, and again providing distance between her and trouble. Trouble being my friend Brian. We were following a contact who works at a telecommunications facility within the Baghdad International Airport grounds.

I drive this Humvee because nobody else will. First, this Humvee is not safe beyond the protection of our walls. Second, it is not cool, which to me, makes it cool. This Humvee resembles the best of all farm trucks in Vermont, complete with bumps and bruises. The cab hosts two and the back is flat and open like a pickup. The roof is a bit of thin fabric, the hood fiberglass, and the body and back are made of steel. The doors, front windshield, and side window have been up-armored. These windows are made from layers of bullet proof plastics. Bullet proof doors and window, but a fabric top. And the floor is thin steel.

Once upon a time, this noble little vehicle served as a communications truck or something else. It carried a big box in the back, like you might see with a civilian camper mounted on a pickup truck. That communications box is likely standing on the ground in Iraq, surrounded with plywood and a little flight of stairs. What was once a portable communications vehicle, a squad pulled apart. The communications box became a shed for some outpost that needed a place to house radios. The vehicle now looks like a snail without its shell.

We have learned about improved explosive devices that get hidden on the roads. They tear vehicles apart from the bottom. The newest trucks to the field have v-shaped bottoms with heavy plates. This style of Humvee served as the darlings of the 1991 invasion of Iraq and was to be the replacement of the World War II Jeep. New wars bring new threats. The thousands of light-skinned or un-armored Humvees provide no better protection than the standard American sports utility vehicle, except Humvees are more expensive, use more fuel, and are less safe.

A proper combat vehicle has radios and Blue-Force Tracker. Blue Force Tracker identifies a vehicle or team's position on a moving map. The operators know where they are. Friendly forces are blue dots on maps. Bad guys are in red. Sadly, Blue Force Tracker does not provide instantaneous updates of the bad guys. If we had such a tool, we may call it Red Force Tracker. That is the job of military intelligence and others. We strive to find the bad guys, discover what they are doing, and such. With Blue Force Tracker, a team can update command with status information and make requests.

My Jalopy does not have any of these. It provides no radio tracking. It provides no real protection from IED threats. But it does provide gentle protection against a random bullet shot towards me. Granted, bullets can fall through the fabric roof or be aimed through the fabric roof from a building or any other tall object. But my Jalopy gives me freedom.

Until I felt a strong pull to my right, as if one wheel were in a ditch. I stopped. Pettigrew and I got out and discovered a slice through the tire from rim to tread.

Our unit of military intelligence officers and soldiers are attached to the Fourth Infantry Division. To be attached means we fall within their command structure during deployment. When this deployment is over, we return to our normal command structure. We are borrowed forces, just like the Air Force and Navy personnel who have been added to the Army's ranks. While at Fort Hood, we took courses in preparation for our year in Iraq. I took a course called "Advancing against Direct Fire," another called "Advancing against Indirect Fire," and one called "Driving Laws of Kuwait." I sat through twenty slides showing me the most common street signs and courtesies for intersections. Each time the instructor, a sergeant first class, came to an important slide, he would stomp his foot and say, "You may want to remember *this* statement."

I aced that test. Most of the soldiers in the room aced the test. But I, Lieutenant Sarah Ann Musgrave, did not attend the Humvee maintenance courses. Neither did Private First Class Emily Pettigrew. Together, we looked at the sliced tire with rapid recognition of several problems. First, my Jalopy does not carry a spare tire. Like everything else theft-able, the spare was repurposed for a real, operational Humvee. Second, the Jalopy, identified on inventory records as "Three-Zero X-Ray," does not have a radio, Blue Force Tracker, nor anything needed to phone home. The name: "Three-Zero X-Ray," written "30X," designates the vehicle as being owned by the headquarters of the Third Infantry Division. The division that departed five months ago. This little buggy failed to qualify for the expensive ride home to the United States.

Had I taken the Humvee Maintenance and Operations course, I would have learned that I could have operated the Humvee safely with the sliced tire. The tires provide run-safe technology that protects the rim. It makes sense. It is unwise to have a crew of four or five soldiers standing at the verge of a road, changing a tire. The basic rule of driving a Humvee through trouble is: Just Drive. Keep Going. Having skipped, or missed, or not been invited to that course, I did not know to "keep going."

I wanted to take care of my little buggy. I had grown attached to this orphaned vehicle. We returned back down the road, finding our way to the Army Corps of Engineers headquarters. The Army Corps hired Gorkha to protect the compound. One might expect that the U.S. Army Corps of Engineers would have soldiers from the U.S. Army as part of their defense force. But it appears that we ran out of soldiers. Therefore, they use an international firm named Aegis for the protection of their job sites. Construction sites in Iraq are guarded by Columbian gunmen and former Irish Republican Army soldiers.

Gurkhas guard the Corps's headquarters facilities. Gurkhas are the most respected commando fighters on the planet. They have served in military units in Nepali, British, and Indian armies since the early 1800s. The British army of today includes several Gurkha battalions, as does the Indian army. There is a contingent of Gurkha in Singapore and Brunei. The United Nations, out of respect for the skills of Gurkha soldiers, exempted them from the definition of mercenaries. Under UN protocols, Gurkha must be given all of the courtesies provided within Article 45. In short, Gurkha must be treated as legitimate prisoners of war and entitled to all related rights. The Columbia and Irish soldiers may not get this same treatment.

The back of my military ID informs others that if I am captured, I fall into the Geneva Convention Category III as a company grade officer. In the event of capture, I am entitled to fifty Swiss francs per month. Frankly, we all know that anyone captured in Iraq by the enemy forces will be subject to the same treatment. It is more likely that my head will be removed from my body while being videotaped.

I telephoned Brian at headquarters, asking for assistance. Pettigrew and I spent the waiting hours listening to stories from the Gurkhas around us. They recounted stories of travel and training with units around the world. One of the guys remarked that he did not like Mexico because they did not speak English. Yet, when asked what languages he spoke, I got a list of Asian and European languages as long as my arm, including Mandarin and Hindi. The list did not include Spanish.

Brian and Sergeant Rodriquez arrived at sundown in a non-tactical vehicle. NTV represents a suite of cars, trucks, and SUVs that, like my Humvee, are not safe beyond the walls. A real Humvee followed them, having been dispatched from our motor pool.

Turns out the motor pool sent Private Goober and Private Dumbass out to rescue us. These "experts" bolted the two Humvees together with a towbar, then towed my favorite little Jalopy with the front wheels turned strongly to the right, because the steering wheel was still turned to the right from my right turn into the Army Corps of Engineer's facilities.

Within a few hundred meters, the mechanics had shredded the sliced tire. Then the sidewall of the other front wheel started to give up as it got dragged sideways across the hard Iraqi ground.

The decision, when I called asking for help, was that I do not drive the vehicle on the run-flats as I may do more damage to the wheels and vehicle. Instead, I watched two professionals destroy two tires and likely two wheels while dragging my buggy towards their shop.

The following morning, I walked to the motor pool, where I meet Staff Sergeant Rizzo, a name I am borrowing from the TV show *MASH*.

"Sergeant, how long will it take to build a wheel for my Humvee?"

"Don't know." *Spit.*

He had already decided not to salute me nor come to attention when addressing me. When answering a direct question from me, he left off the required "Ma'am." Army regulations require that Sergeant Rizzo address me as "Ma'am." The salute can be tricky. The rules state that he does not have to salute me indoors nor in a combat environment. Those two exceptions provide Rizzo with enough wiggle room to avoid giving me that courtesy. If I insisted on the courtesy, he will retaliate. I knew that my lovely Three-Zero X-Ray would languish forever in his motor pool awaiting an elusive part, the famed Flux-Capacitor, or some other imaginary bit of unobtainium.

"Sergeant, can you provide me a time estimate? I have missions I must return to, and this is the vehicle I've got."

"It takes"—*spit*—"an operator as long as it takes." *Spit.*

"Sorry, Sergeant, I do not understand you. Can you speak up? I have a hearing problem." Saying this causes idiots like Staff Sergeant Rizzo to shout.

"It'll take an operator"—*spit*—"just as long as it takes an operator to build a wheel." *Spit*—"can't tell you how long it will take"—*spit*, "an operator to build a wheel"—*spit*.

"Sergeant, what is an operator?"

Spit. "An operator is an operator. Someone who drives a vehicle is an operator. That's what an operator is." *Spit.*

Therefore, an operator—according to the motor pool—is a non-mechanic. An operator, in this localized definition, operates the vehicle when the vehicle had the problem. Staff Sergeant Rizzo strove to tell me, in a roundabout way, that I was an operator. He had been trying to tell me that the wheel will be repaired when I fix the wheel.

"Staff Sergeant Rizzo, when I return, will someone teach me how to use these tools to build a wheel?" He looks at me blankly. I continued, "Sergeant, will someone show me where to get the parts?" Rizzo's look morphed to disbelief and impatience. "Sergeant, will I be provided a safety orientation to your shop? And will you provide a detailed safety check prior to my operating of the vehicle again?" I paused. "I believe, Sergeant, you are telling a platoon leader and a lieutenant that I must drop what I am doing to repair my own vehicle without the guidance, support, or expertise of motor pool soldiers?"

"Someone will be here." *Spit.*

I returned at 1330h with Captain Brian Ufner. Not one soldier used the words "Sir," "Ma'am," "please," or "Thank you." No manual was provided. I enjoyed the scene when a three-strip buck sergeant told a captain and company commander to go get the sergeant's tool kit. The two of us fetched it and returned it to the kid.

A Humvee wheel weighs 120 pounds, 55 kilos. A wheel stands about one meter high, and it comes apart into several pieces. Brian and I rebuilt a wheel following the incomplete, unsafe, and inconsistent instructions provided by a set of idiots.

The answer to how long it takes an operator to rebuild a Humvee wheel approximates two hours. When we were done, we presented the wheel to Staff Sergeant Rizzo for it to be inflated. When air wouldn't go in, it took two mechanics to take apart the wheel then re-assemble it. Our instructor failed at providing the right instructions in the right sequence. The new team building our wheel availed themselves of the opportunity to train our trainer. The entire effort demonstrated the worst of Army efficiency and classic waste-of-time shenanigans for which my Army has occasionally gained notoriety.

Would you like to know how to remove the tire from the rim of a Humvee? First, you unbolt the twelve bolts that hold the two sides of the rim together. You remove the smaller (outer) side of the rim. Then, you balance the wheel up on two blocks of wood. Then, two tall, healthy, strong sergeants climb up on top of the metal rim. They lock arms, and step back onto the rubber tire. Then, they jump. And jump, and jump, until the tire falls from the rim. This technique typically involves injury to one or both mechanics. This time, it was Staff Sergeant Bridgewater's turn. He streamed blood from his thigh and tore his trousers. The other fellow got hurt last time. They alternate injuries, when possible. That's how a tire is removed from a wheel.

The team disassembled the wheel again—their second time, the wheel's third time. The newly built wheel would not let air go in. Staff Sergeant Bridgewater drilled a hole through the solid rubber runs-flat, creating a tunnel for air to reach the hollow space.

A runs-flat is a heavy tire of solid rubber, like the small donut tire car makers use as spares these days. But instead of putting it in the trunk, the Humvee puts the donut within the original pneumatic tire. Putting the runs-flat into the tire was the most dangerous part of the mission. The mechanics employed a winch to compress the runs flat. Once compressed, mechanics use two crowbars to lever it into the tire. Fingers, crowbars, and hundreds of pounds of pressure is a bad mix if you own one of the fingers involved.

When the tire wouldn't hold air after the drilling effort, it was disassembled again, now starting the third effort for the trained mechanics, and the fourth effort for my unfortunate wheel. The mechanics added yucky-sticky black goo to the bead of the tire. When that wouldn't hold air, I poured part of my drinking water on the rim and found the leak came from the valve stem. The wheel was disassembled again, now the team's fourth effort and the wheel's fifth effort.

Another staff sergeant arrived on scene. This staff sergeant greeted me and Brian with appropriate military courtesy. Then he immediately observed that the poorly assembled mess failed to include an O-ring that sealed the valve stem to the steel wheel rim. We had crossed the three-hour mark. Brian was sweating, dropping about a liter of fluid onto the concrete floor of the repair bay, the wheel, and rim.

There are two kinds of officers. Some officers will tear apart a young soldier on the spot for being a disrespectful, lazy idiot. Brian opted for the quieter route. He rolled with the flow, achieving the objectives of the mission. In the end, we had an operational Humvee and thanked the soldiers involved.

After the mission, Brian briefed his boss's boss, a lieutenant colonel. Together, the lieutenant colonel, Brian, and I called the motor pool's commanding officer, a captain. The colonel wrought the wrath of rank down on the entire unit, including Staff Sergeant Rizzo. The work, which should have been done by a junior NCO or private, required the presence and active participation of a military intelligence company commander and a platoon leader.

Still driven by spite, Brian found the citation in an Army field manual that identifies tasks that are "operator executed" and those that require a mechanic. An operator is permitted to change a tire as one might do on the side of a road. An operator may use a jack to lift the vehicle, remove the lugs, replace the wheel assembly, then return the vehicle to the ground. The manual states that the repair of a wheel or the replacement of a tire plus the run-flat requires a trained mechanic. Had the staff sergeant pointed at a replacement wheel then said something such as, "Go for it, girlie," I could have replaced the tire. Though I might have had his balls for calling me "girlie" or failing to afford me the required, "Ma'am."

On another Monday in another hot week, Brian and I took advantage of Double Pog Day. I stood in line waiting to get Brian's pogs counted. A pog is a plastic coin given at the Post Exchange in lieu of real coins. Real coins are so rare here that I saw a Malaysian checkout girl ask a Malaysian checkout guy, "How many pog is this worth?" while holding up a U.S. quarter. A few months ago, I was on a C-130 that had been hit by lightning. An airman asked the passengers for a U.S. quarter to help repair a hole in the wing. Of fifteen passengers in full battle kit, we found exactly three real quarters.

Pogs have cute colorful pictures. My favorite is a scantily clad JFK on PT 109. The most offensive one is a picture of three blue-tipped Iraqi fingers. Pictures of blue-tipped fingers offered boldly just doesn't translate well.

People don't carry pogs because people don't carry purses or backpacks. Pogs are issued by the PX, then never returned. In response, the PX instituted Double Pog Day. Soldiers, civilians, Third-Country Nationals, Kellogg-Brown-Root civilians, Aussies, Poles, Georgians, Macedonians, Koreans, Marines, Sailors, Airmen, Brits, and everyone else gathers their pogs. We spend them at the PX on Double Pog Day.

I tend to give my pog change to the youngest, most junior soldier in my eyesight. I do keep a few buried in a pocket.

On this day, Brian possessed almost eleven Dollars in pogs. The first line is for counting the pogs. That is where I stand. Brian was shopping. The optimal unit size on Double–Pog Day is three. One member stands in pog-counting line. One stands in the massive checkout line. The third member does the shopping. Brian and I formed a team of two. Therefore, we would have to stand in the checkout line together.

The woman behind me in line smiled at me with your smile, Brie. Her eyes were pale blue. She was as tall as you are. She spoke to the sergeant she is traveling with. I listened to an accent that clearly came from a fellow New Englander.

I turned. "You're not from Texas, are you?" Ah, diversity! When traveling with a Texas-based division of twenty-thousand soldiers, one does not hear a lot of northern accents.

"Pennsylvania." Technically not New England, but kindred.

After we established the basics (unit, duty, home, common friends, etc.), she asked me what I thought about Iraqi food. I admitted that I had fallen in love with the triangular-shaped fresh bread, the great use of spices, and the lamb.

"Tell me what Iraqi men think of you?" I asked. "What has been your best offer?"

"Habibi! Habibi, photo you? Habibi, you want. Habibi, want home with me?"

"What do you do when you are being solicited?"

"I laugh. I'll pose for any picture."

"Really?"

"Yeah, what do I care? They're fun and harmless. And so bold."

"I was offered five hundred dinars," I said. "That's my best so far. He was a street sweeper. I was at dinner when an Iraqi Special Forces soldier started trying to pick up a friend. His first question was, 'How old you?'"

"They touch you anywhere and smile while doing it." She was a military police officer, standard issue a pistol and a rifle. She had the body of a long-time athlete. No American male would just touch her anywhere or be so playful with her. "I have come home from missions with my pockets full of silly little gifts from these guys," she finished.

This woman resembled a Nordic goddess upon which Iraqi men paid homage with trinkets, proposals, and photographs. I know from my own experiences that not one of these guys gives a name, an address, or a phone number.

Unlike Vietnam, it is men lining the streets looking for American women to marry. Single Iraqi men looking for a way of being transported from Iraq, hoping someone will tote them home as war trophies. I have met young Iraqi men who behave like three-year-old children in a candy store. Their inhibitions and manners disappear when they interact with American women. Each and every American woman knows that she is a passport and a plane ticket to the States. Listen, Mister Baghdadi, you need something more than a brass camel, small rugs, and earrings to land a woman like this military police officer.

Brian bought four bags of Twizzlers, a movie, and two cold drinks for eleven dollars in pogs. The actual value approached twenty-two dollars. We walked the two kilometers back along the base of Signal Hill (our beloved red blinking light now dark), sharing Twizzlers, drinks, and a story.

13 | Mid-Tour Break

BRIGHID, MAY/JUNE 2006

I arrive in Frankfurt, Germany two days before Sam's anticipated arrival. She is flying from Iraq on various military transport flights. The scheduling of those flights remains mysterious and unpredictable. I sleep one night in Frankfurt near the international airport, thus bringing me one day closer to Sam.

Sam will arrive at Ramstein Air Base near Landstuhl. I take a train from Frankfurt. From the station, I walk, wandering the town with my backpack. My civilian-style backpack resembles a hybrid of Sam's packs and those used during long-distance hikes. I have Velcro sandals hanging, a water bottle, and a fleece blanket rolled into a waterproof sheet. I have tied an anorak to the top and a small ditty bag filled with dried fruits, jerked meats, and hard lemon drop candies. On the train and on the streets of Germany, I look like so many others on holiday. Though unlike my fellow American tourists, I wear long, loose skirts. I find these cooler, more comfortable, and offering more freedom to move. They pack well, too. Rolling the linen, cotton, and hemp fabrics tightly only enhances the lived-in look.

I feel free. No bosses, no crises, no deadlines, no meetings, no exam to prepare for; none of the freneticism that makes up my days. I have to miss a few days of EMT classes, but I worked out a deal with the help of Alex to make up the hours and keep it all legal.

I walk from the train depot down Bahnstrasse to Von-Richthofen Strasse, then to a café called the Old Firehouse, or so translated from German.

Landstuhl stands in a region of Germany that hosts United States Armed Forces. Sam and I picked this dot on the map because Ramstein Air Base has direct military flights in and out of the conflict zones. Sam said: "Let's go where the planes go." With proximity to Frankfurt, I had ready access to flights from Boston and New York.

If returning to Iraq on a military transport proved problematic for Sam, she could fly commercial to Kuwait, then wend her way back into Baghdad.

We discussed using the mid-tour break to return to Vermont, but decided that by splitting the travel effort, we could maximize our time together, and in vacation mode. I booked two nights at a hotel on a hill that looked interesting. The facility ticked boxes for required services: bed, restaurant, spa. The fact that it resembled a castle and stood two kilometers from the train station was merely a bonus.

I explore Landstuhl, enjoying how entirely it does not resemble New England. The influence of American military means that nearly everything is presented in both English and German, providing me with my own subtitles. It takes only a few encounters to understand that no street was actually named *Einbahnstraße*. I thought I was pretty clever to riddle out that *straße* or *strasse* equaled street. I walk Railroad Street, *Von Richthofen* street, *Kaiser* or King Street, and *haupstrasse* or Main Street. *Einbahnstrasse* eventually resolves itself in my mind into instructions telling cars that the street is one-way. My education in the German language thus begins.

I have no map, but I see a hill. *Burg* and *Schloss* resolve into words for castles, so when I come to Castle Street and Castle Way, I continue walking. The walk takes me up the backside of the hill.

Ramstein Air Base serves as the European entry point to flights into Iraq and Afghanistan. The flights have three missions: personnel, materiel, and medical. Additionally, Landstuhl Regional Medical Center serves as the primary evacuation and trauma hospital for both wars. Wounded soldiers arrive daily from combat. The medical planes leave Germany nearly empty, kitted out as intensive care units, the staff and gear returning to combat zones to carry the next load. Ramstein Air Base follows American rules for access; therefore, I cannot enter the base without an appointment, an escort, or a military-issued ID.

As I cannot go to the base to await my soldier, I check into our hotel with all-too-explicit instructions that my traveling companion may arrive at any time in the next days, and that upon her arrival she is to be given the key to the room.

"Please send her up without a phone call or any other fuss," I say to the staff

When I leave the hotel for a walk to the castle ruins, I feel anxiety about leaving the room empty. The phrase *what if* echoes. *What if* Sam comes and I am not there? *What if* Sam gets delayed, how will I know? My mobile phone does not have the correct chipset for Europe. I debated buying a local phone with pre-paid minutes, but then I would not know how to get this new number to Sam. Then what would I need it for after this brief moment of anxiety? I rapidly dismiss the idea of buying a local phone. And I dismiss the idea of waiting in the room. Whatever adventure—or misadventure—Sam finds during her travels from metropolitan Baghdad to Germany will entitle her to a shower and a nap. Sam does not need to find me sitting in the room waiting when I could be or should be doing something out-of-doors. I feel altogether tempted to sit and wait, but I am no loving pup awaiting her mistress. She'll find me. I'll find her. That's the only answer, as it has been for years. We'll find each other.

Most families, when meeting their soldier returning from combat, would meet them at the airport with signs and hugs and kisses and yellow roses. Sarah and I are not permitted that freedom. I do not have a military dependent card, nor access to any family benefits. If I were granted a military dependent identification card, I could enter the base, use the Post Exchange, and meet Sam's flight. All of the things! Yet, those privileges remain reserved for other military families. Sam already lives in the secretive world of military intelligence. Within that bubble, Sam lives with another secret: me.

I follow signs and a trail map I pinched in the hotel's lobby. My objective involves a castle ruin at the top of the hill, a scar from an ancient war.

New England has so few castles.

Lieutenant Sarah Ann Musgrave enters our room at one o'clock in the morning. I am asleep until I feel her moving about the room. She has found me. I was sleeping soundly in a hotel snugged into a German hill below a five-hundred-year-old castle, awaiting my soldier woman.

At breakfast, I see her for the first time since her departure from

Texas in October. Her face carries new lines, new shadows. Her skin looks leather-tough; her eyes are tired and obscured by crow's feet at both sides. The regions at the edge of her nose look irritated and red. One ear lobe is swollen and annoyed. Her hands feel like sandpaper. I see that she has been trying to grow her hair out in anticipation of our visit. I'd guess that she shares electric shears with others in her unit.

I have never seen her eyes look so dull. And unlike the Sam I've known for almost six years, her alertness seems out of place and ill-timed. She has always been aware of everything. She can watch without moving, like a hunter or a bird-of-prey. Today, her movements seem furtive, twitchy. She has lost weight during the six months she's been in the desert.

I touch Sam's face above the mouth where the skin folds. It looks red. She almost flinches, then lets my hand come up. Once there, she ensconces my hand with her own. I did not know what I was seeing on her face, on her ears, through her skin except that the desert had left several marks on this woman.

I rise from the table. In the lobby, I book two of the longest and most extravagant spa appointments possible.

Returning to our room after an early supper, I feel Sam's face again.

"I am sorry, Brie."

"Nothing to apologize for. You are the same and yet different. It is the same face but..." I leave the comment unfinished. You don't tell your girlfriend that her skin resembles the dried and neglected leather of a long-forgotten handbag.

"You don't need to know this, but I am putting athlete's foot cream here, on my ear, under my nose, in my belly button, and here, on my cheek."

"Really."

"I think I am pretty worn down."

I guess I can tease her about the worn-out-leather comment in a few years.

"Toe-cheese cream? On your face?"

She nods in acknowledgement. "And other places too."

"Toes."

"And other places, too."

Both of her feet have a mild purple color that has not soaked away during the day, though less purple than what I witnessed before breakfast when I watched her dress. I wrote the color off as bad lighting. In the morning, after her first shower of the day, she sits on the edge of the bed naked. She brings one foot up and covers it in white cream and thick tea-tree-oil-based lotion. She then puts on socks. She reaches for her backpack to get something out, then instead walks to the bathroom, washing her hands in hot, soapy water. She returns to the bed to pull on the white cotton underwear I had mailed to her. After the underwear, she pulls on the blue jeans. The blue jeans, clearly not worn since Texas, need a belt. She retrieves one from her uniform, then ties her feet back into the desert-colored boots she traveled in.

After a day of soaking, picking, cleaning, and professional care, her feet remain mildly purple.

"Sam, I am not happy with those purple feet."

"Oh, now that you are an EMT, you're the boss?" I am certain she is trying to be funny, but she sounds so pathetic and tired that the comment misses the mark.

"Your feet need sunlight and air. That's what Doc Doran says."

We shop for a pair of sandals which Sam does with her grab-and-go flair.

"No, we didn't buy those so you could keep walking in those boots. Take them off." I sound like my own grandmother, so very brusque.

She plants her ass down on the curb. She folds one leg up, strips it to the purple. On goes one sandal, then the other. She ties the laces of her ugly, heavy, filthy boots together and swings them over her shoulder. She stuffs the socks into the pockets of her jeans.

Her feet need to see sunlight, beach sand, and soak in the ocean, I think. They look as if they had been poorly pickled. Frankly, they smelled like pickled human feet, too. *Sauerfüßen. Sauer-feet.*

Her clothing smells of Baghdad and jet fuel and dust.

On day two, we schlep to the Ramstein Base Exchange. As herself, being herself, she gets excited about a full set of new uniforms and new soft combat boots. And that is what she carries to the counter:

uniforms, socks, undies, bras, uniform T-shirts, and boots. She also adds several large tubes of toe cream.

She orders new Velcro name tapes: MUSGRAVE. She wants the name tapes sewn on her trousers and a few centimeters of the sleeves removed.

"We'll have them for you tomorrow, Ma'am."

I'll have to get use to people calling my Sam "Ma'am" again. At the hotel in Killeen, courtesy was a bit more informal. We were off-post and gathering off-hours and hosted by a civilian hotel. Here, we are on a U.S. military base in Germany.

"Don't worry about it. I'll pick them up in two weeks and no sooner." She smiles. She actually smiles. I didn't know she could anymore. That face would crack like an old Dutch master's painting.

Outside the PX, we buy a rail pass, the kind you can only get in the United States before you travel. But, we are in the United States. So, the European government lets us buy these passes.

Train passes and backpacks. That's freedom.

Train passes and backpacks. Isn't that the American picture of a gap-year? Teenagers and young people on a grand tour?

We soak. We nap. We don't nap, as it were. I push fluids into my prune-like Sarah.

At dawn of the third day, we rise, check out, and catch the TGV to Paris.

In Paris, we step off the train and walk. A bit of a busman's holiday for Sam, but the sun is filtered by cloud and there is moisture in the air. There is food within every eyeline.

The color of Sam's feet improves, an observation I make by looking at her sandals.

I can tell she is unhappy walking. Her toes and skin bring discomfort. Even a slow amble presents problems. Body and soul, she walks in Iraq with mission-focus. A goal, an objective, a distance to cover, all while being exposed to IEDs, small arms fire, and other horrors of war. From bases and camps around Baghdad, she goes into the streets to collect information, talk with people, and walk. She walks Iraq through every weather, from baking heat to flooding rains. In her boots, her feet swell and sweat. When outside-the-wire, she wears over sixty pounds of battle gear, weapons, ammo, water, food, and communications equipment in addition to her flak-vest with ceramic inserts. She wears a Kevlar helmet with an earpiece that permits her to hear other soldiers. Any place, every place where the uniform or gear wears on her skin, she develops hot-spots. In the folds of skin such as near her nose, eyes, and ears, she develops fungal infections.

I can now understand how she battles the nearly constant dehydration. Drinking water requires peeing. When in the field, peeing proves to be a logistical nightmare. She cannot put her weapons down, therefore needs a soldier to hold them. A pistol hangs from her belt and is strapped tight to her left thigh. Her carbine rifle clips to her vest with a carabiner that allows for easy and ready access. Preparing to pee means removing the pistol and the rifle, loosening the thigh straps that hold her pistol to her thigh, and loosening the waist belt. When using the standard toilet found in Iraq, she plants her feet on the sides of a small hole in the floor, a technology that works well for women in skirts. She squats over the hole keeping uniform trousers, holster, belt, and all other kit off of the floor and out of the stream of pee. Cleaning herself after the effort involves similar complexity. As a result, my Sam says that she often decides to not pee during missions unless she knows she can find a place outside to "pop-a-squat." The ladies' toilets of Iraq were not designed for a fully armed woman wearing long pants, boots, and sixty pounds of battle gear. Iraqi ladies do not like seeing, nor do they understand, how some American female soldiers pee while standing using bottles.

I pledge to myself that I shall return Sam to Iraq clean, healthy, and hydrated.

Entering the Paris streets, we feel exactly like tourists. I ought to say that I feel exactly like a tourist on a summer holiday. It takes me a beat to understand that Sam silently suffers in order to bring me the pleasure I desire. I buy a paper map, a tourist map, from a street vendor. We (I) decide to navigate towards the famous sites, starting with Notre Dame and the Seine. Sam just nods and says, "Yes," to my questions.

CHAPTER 13

Walking the Seine, looking at the artists and fellow tourists, we hold hands like lovers and friends do. Through her hand, I understand Sam in new ways. She startles, flinches; she feels ill at ease with the movement and people around us. Normally, my Sam sees all, hears all, while remaining aloof. This Sam, holding my hand, responds to the runner approaching from behind—was she preparing to drop to a crouch and draw her pistol in defense? She navigates around people, giving more distance than most urban Europeans. She steers us away from clusters of humans. My hunter has adopted prey-like responses to the environment. Like the deer who feeds in her Vermont fields and the squirrels that play on the stone walls and trees, Sam assesses every movement as a threat. Thus, she should. A military intelligence officer working in and around Baghdad during a civil war must react to every sound and every movement. On her property in Trowbridge, bears act like bears, porcupines are always porcupines, and stone walls do not explode. Movement falls within the predictable norms of a Vermont forest.

I start the next conversation in my head. I think of saying: *Let's leave Paris and find a beach or a mountain.*

She would then say to me: *You have wanted a Paris vacation for a long time. We're here. Let's enjoy this.*

Another startle, another skipped heartbeat, then I would plow on: *You are not conformable here. We need to get you somewhere where you feel safe.*

The argument and my tears lay beyond the next sentence. Also, my joy of Paris involves walking. Sam's days in Iraq involve walking and talking with strangers. Time to substitute this bad idea for one that involves nearly zero people, sunlight, good food, and less walking.

I ask a lady with a fabric shopping bag on her arm, *"Où est la librairie?"*

Ok, let's admit I could riddle out the question. I didn't plan for the answer which came in rapid-fire Parisian French. It was like being in one of Sam's Blackhawk helicopters. All acceleration and noise. I hear *"sur la gouche"* which I do know means "on the left." I understand the name of a street because it started with *"rue de."*

I vector us towards the left, looking for a rue-de-something-incomprehensible. Likely a famous Parisian artist or hero or saint or some mother's son who died in a forgotten war.

I ask another stranger, *"Où est la librairie?"*

The fellow answers in British English. He does some handwaving and muttering. I infer that we likely remain on this path.

The third person I ask simply points, *"La!"* She indicates that we stand across the street from our mission objective.

Entering the store, the host greets us warmly. I can't find sufficient French for the question: *Where are your travel guides?* I am certain that if I deliver the phrase I crafted, it would have translated to, *Where are your guides for work?*The clerk asks me in English, "What are you looking for?"

"A beach with few people on it where we can be alone and hear no one."

"Naturist?"

Not really knowing the full European use of the word, I say, *"Oui."*

"No better place for naturism than can be found on the beaches south of Montpellier," she adds, well expounded on the values of naturism. During this conversation, I am thinking of a geeky person in an anorak with spy glasses chasing shore birds. I admit to being slow to accept the non-U.S. version of the word. Good word, but not my word, our word.

The bookseller guides us to a selection of blue and white books about the region she advocates for. Even with classroom French, I adjusted my understanding of the phrase. We are, clearly, talking about nudist beaches and such.

Leaving the store, I ask, "Shall we? Should we? You are from Vermont and the capital of Vermont is Montpelier. Here we are in France with a rail pass. We should go see Montpellier then head to the beaches near *Le Grau-du-Roi.*"

We walk slowly towards our hotel, stopping for three benches and one afternoon tea. Sam follows like a tired and hot dog who would rather be sleeping on a rug in front of a rustic fireplace. With the travel guide and my train map, I plot a course towards the beach and away from the crowds of Paris. From our Paris hotel, I call *Le Page* in *Grande-Motte*, making both room and spa reservations.

In the room, Sam falls asleep on my lap. I read. At six, I embrace Sam's shoulder with my hand, giving a gentle squeeze and shake.

"Sam?"

She wakes, but not in her old way. I feel the startle response ricochet down her spine then back up it. I had dreaded stirring her, but I need to move. My toes tingle with numbness. The bladder reports full. The belly whines for food.

"Sam, let's find a nice meal for our last night in Paris."

She rouses quickly, showers, then slips into her jeans. She pulls on yet another black cotton t-shirt. She explains that these were the t-shirts worn under Air Force uniforms. The Army folks wear the khaki/brown version of this same shirt. She tells me that the PX also sells the same t-shirt in a plain white. She doesn't buy the white shirts because the weight of the plain white one is heavier and requires more space in her pack.

It is a classically sexy look. The black nylon uniform belt knocks it down a notch. Without the belt (and improved skin), she could be shown on LED billboards in Times Square. Her short hair, muscular physique, and desert-starved body would make her popular on some modeling runways. The haircut from Landstuhl resulted in a uniformly short crop that now stood in a spiky array. Months in combat, dehydration, and frayed nerves converted my warrior into a waifish runway model—except Sam was too short for that work.

If I say, "Honey, take that belt off," the belt would fall first, then the rest of the clothing. Instead, I vow to find a new belt that augments the look. Even a bit of string would look better than the webbed nylon belt she wears every day.

The *maître d'* seats us in the window near the door. "Here, please," he says, holding the chairs for each of us. He whisks away the white card that read: *Reservé*. The waiter also remove the vase of flowers, returning with a smaller bouquet of freshly cut irises and a small yellow flower that accentuates the hint of yellow found buried low in the deep blue.

"For you," he says, flirting with me. "It brings out the blue of those eyes and that scarf." Yes, I did just buy the silk scarf. I grabbed it on impulse after finding a thin brown leather belt for Sam. It brought the sexy back.

He fusses at the symmetry of the flowers.

"Merci, mon ami." I touch him on the upper arm. I can flirt, too.

Within a minute, two glasses of chilled white wine appear on our table.

The sommelier says: "Delano asked that I bring you something to enjoy while you relax and study the menu." Bread follows, as did bits of aged cheese, and a couple of olives.

"Merci."

We clink then taste. I smile at the sommelier and say: "Wha-zoo. *C'est parfait.*" Then, in English, I continue, "This wine tastes exactly like a summer afternoon in the country. It reminds me of the moment the sun relaxes its heat and turns the horizon to gold. That is the flavor of this wine." The wine reminds me of a Tuscan hillside, but of course, I would not and could not say that to a sommelier in Paris.

He smiles. So, I offer my hand, "*Je m'appelle Brie et la, elle est Sam.*" Sam forms a polite smile and returns the greeting, *"Salut."*

The crow's feet at the edges of Sam's eyes have softened during the recent days. The ladies at the spa got the baked-in Iraqi dust out from the tiny folds. The creams, moisturizers, and several liters of water per day have brought Sam's level of hydration up to near normal. Sam and her skin fit better. Another day of water, wine, and rich foods, and her skin may return to luster. A real improvement from old leather.

"My friend, tell me about this wine. Where does it come from?" We learn of a tiny vineyard that grows grapes on the north side of a Pyrenean mountain, started by the son of a cheese-making family. He paints the image for us both with dairy goats, green summer pastures, ancient stone huts, and an old man with skin the color of Sam's.

We do not order our own food. When the men arrive to discuss options, I suggest that they serve us whatever they recommended, whatever is freshest, whatever has the best story, whatever the chef wants to. Our trust is repaid with mussels and escargot with garlic and olive oil with fresh herbs, including familiar lemon thyme similar to what Sam had growing near the kitchen door. Sam and I share slices of a perfectly grilled duck. Dessert involves a few berries grown in Alsace with fermented cream and mint.

Delano, the *maître d'*, returns to check on us. As we finish the dessert wine and the last bit of cheese from the berry plate, he asks, "Where are you from?" I strove to answer: "*Nous habitons dan le* Vermont."

I get a curious look from the man.

I say in English, "Is my accent that bad? I think I said: *We live in Vermont.*"

"You did. Your accent is not too bad, though you must spend more time in Paris, of course. I heard you say that you live in the Green Mountain." Vermont means "green mountain" no matter how you slice it. The spelling is slightly wrong, but spelling is arbitrary. Look at how badly we did with our Montpelier compared to the original one.

In English, I offer the correction. "We live in the state called Vermont, it is named for our green mountains. It is below Quebec and near Massachusetts." The confusion of my statement resolves. I continue, "The capital city of our state is Montpellier, named for your city, I believe." Sam does not look at the bill; instead, she slides her credit card into the leather folio.

As we leave, both Delano and our sommelier walk us to the door. On the street, we part with rounds of embraces and Gallic kisses, as if old friends long parted. We enjoyed that restaurant for three hours sitting in that window sweat. Sam grabs my hand. She kisses me warmly and properly, which brings joy to our hosts.

We catch the first morning train to Montpellier, then hop the train to *Le Grand-du-Roi*. As we approach the Mediterranean coast, I think of beaches. I envision laying on the beach with my Sarah and our frolicking in the water.

Days later on the train north to Lyon, I feel the guilty pleasure of having sunburned parts of my body that had never seen the sun. On the train to Geneva, my butt gets itchy. So do my breasts. Thankfully, the purple hue of Sam's feet has disappeared entirely. Her skin looks pink. Her entire body has softened by walking in the sand. The various fungal infections on her face, belly button, feet, ears, and in the folds next to her nose have cleared up.

On day eleven, the internal alarms ring. We need to return to Germany and check in at Ramstein. Leaving the beach served as the end of our leisure. We have days to travel and meals to enjoy, yet we both know we must part.

I think about the massively large base exchange at Ramstein that resembles an American mall. I think about the signs around Landstuhl that catered to American service members. I think about the grey cargo plane that will transport my Sam back to Iraq for the rest of the year. Instead of a lithe, sexy woman wearing t-shirts and the same pair of too-large jeans every day, I bring to mind the photos of Lieutenant Sarah Ann Musgrave standing next to a building or a Blackhawk helicopter in her battle uniform. A pistol mounted to her left thigh and rifle slung around her armored vest, a vest laden with ammo, medical kit, food, and a head scarf. I think about those feet back inside of desert combat boots. Although we bought lighter weight and more breathable shoes, no doubt that the heat, sweat, and hours of walking will turn her feet purple and welcome a host of nasty fungi back to her toes.

On Saturday afternoon, our train pulls into Strasbourg Station. Here, we change trains so that we can work our way northwest. This train will continue to follow the Rhine north to Mannheim. We gather our packs. wait at the designated door, and step onto the platform.

Sam freezes.

I walk into her backside because I am not looking and I do not expect the abrupt stop. The people behind us don't stop. They bump into me. I give Sam a push to the left so I can get by and the others can wiggle their way around us.

Sam's eyes are glued down the platform that we must walk to leave this part of the station. I follow her eyes down the platform. Like her, I see the massive crowd.

When the crowd sees the train unload its passengers, they erupt in chaotic and excruciating screams. The glass arching windows overhead echo the roar. The crowd surges forward. The three carriages measure the distance between us and the roaring, pushing crowd.

I grab Sam, turning her away from the stream of humans. She remains immobile. I assess the situation. I see that a local sports team has alighted from the train. The crowd holds banners and wears team colors. Police form a barrier between the athletes and fans.

Sam starts to breathe.

I watch Sam gauge the threat that we both faced from futball fans. I know I cannot understand the impact of this crowd on my mildly broken warrior. She had been gradually relaxing. Bhe deer-version, squirrel-version of Sam returned the second she heard the crowd. My Sam would normally react to a threat by running or preparing for a fight. Instead, she freezes. She did not—could not—move.

I coax and pull her towards the least-peopled area of the station. I find a bench upon which we sit and breathe.

We sit. We breathe.

I hold her right hand with my left and loop my right arm over her shoulders. I have never been in a position of having to care for my Sam in this way. She's my rock. I am Fidget Brighid. I wear the goofy skirts and such. She's the one who can put a hole in the center of a piece of paper at one hundred meters.

The futball fans disappear like a wave does after landing on the beach.

Sam breathes. And breathes again, eventually saying, "I'm ok."

I listen while still wrapped around her protectively.

A minute later, she exhales, saying, "Let's go, we'll miss our train."

We stand in the lobby, seeking the information board. The board confirms what our eyes tell us: our train is in the process of leaving the station. Unlike Western movies, and World War II movies, or my ancestor Private Henry McDonald, one cannot chase a train then step up to the moving carriage. The train's exterior has been designed with the aerodynamics of an airplane.

The ninety-minute interval between trains gives the opportunity to explore Strasbourg. We leave the glass enclosure, then promptly lay down on the grass in a park across the street. Thousands of bicycles have been locked and stand sentry around the park. Long stretches of buses and electric street trolleys form the traffic in the circle around us. The locals walk, peddle, or sit. Sam and I are the only two who lay on the grass.

Like Sam, I form a pillow of my backpack. Two pigeons bop over to inspect the unusual sight, likely expecting us to offer something delicious to nibble on. Sorry, fellas.

Sam falls asleep. I listen to music on my portable MP3 player.

We return to the castle on the hill in Landstuhl. Unlike the first stay, the focus of this stay is Ramstein Air Base. Sam has to check in. She has to coordinate flights. She has uniforms to pick up. Sam must transform back to soldier. She needs the extra time because she will return to Iraq "Space-A," or "space available." Some flights go to Balad, some to Baghdad, and some to Kuwait. Finding a seat to a destination as a young lieutenant returning from leave requires flexibility and time. On the air base and around the military nexus of Landstuhl Regional Medical Center, we cease being a couple. No nudist beaches casually touching hands. We leave that behind when we cross the line from Paris to Germany.

Our *maître d'* in Paris could never have known about our first date. On that night, our server had been named Monica. Sam asked me to dine with her. I did not know if I had said yes to a date or yes to an evening that was not a date. Never before had a woman asked me out like that. Not knowing, I dressed and prepared for a date in a blue dress that I loved. Our date was on the 10th of September, 2000. We were both under the legal drinking age. Monica asked us for our identification and asked if we had walked to the restaurant. She returned with two glasses of red wine. Monica, smiling at us both, asked, "Is this a date?" I responded with an immediate, "Yes." Monica winked, likely guessing it was our first date.

On the day of her enlistment, I dropped Sam at the Military Entrance Processing Station near Springfield, Massachusetts. She disappeared into a labyrinth that involved bootcamp, then specialized trainings thereafter. I saw her off when Sergeant Musgrave deployed to Iraq in 2003. In the fall of 2005, we spent two weeks together at Fort Hood before Lieutenant Musgrave flew to Kuwait, then Iraq.

Now, in the summer of 2006, Sam disappears into a U.S. military base in Germany. I'll catch my planned flight to Boston and head home to Trowbridge.

14 | Media

SAM'S JOURNAL, JUNE 2006

My division has lost 107 soldiers in combat. As of writing this, we have two soldiers missing in action. We have lost fifteen legs, and fifteen arms. One of our soldiers has lost both legs. Several of our soldiers have suffered third degree burns. We have had suicides, suicide attempts, and rape.

I am starting to recognize that nobody but you, Brie, will read these journals. Maybe I will read them on some stormy winter's night in our Vermont living room. I don't even know why I'd go back to read this shit. I'm living it now. Why would I go back to visit this time? This year shall not be the foundation of The Great American War Memoir. *Who'd want to read: We have no fucking idea what the fuck is going on. Hey, I am an American Soldier, a hero of the day who responded to the call of 9/11 (even though I enlisted before September 2001). And what did I do? I went to Iraq once, then again, and never understood the point. Yay team. Me: hero. The End, huh? No.* You can't make a narrative of a plotless pile of spaghetti. We go on. Brie, you get up for medical calls and fires when called, and I am here, wherever the fuck here is today.

This ceased to be an American war months ago. During the month of May, there were 1,200 Iraqis killed by non-allied forces—either Iraqis or foreign fighters. Each day, twenty—thirty, forty—people are killed on the streets of Baghdad. They are not killed by bullets. They are not sliced by sword. They are cut and torn by shards of metal, pieces of cars, nails, glass, concrete strewn from bombs. Mosques and cafes are unsafe in this beautiful city.

I was asked the other day, "Why do the locals let us drive into a bomb when they all know it is there? Does that not make them as guilty as those who laid the bomb?"

Who will be there tomorrow?" I respond. "If they protect us today, will we protect them tomorrow? Are we not leaving here? Can we make a promise to protect them tomorrow? Every house has two satellite dishes, or more. Every man has a cell phone. Don't you think that they know as much about our politics as you do? They know that I will leave and every officer like me will leave at the end of a tour of duty. Who are they to trust? The U.S. Army, but that's not really possible, is it? They can learn to trust specific soldiers, but if we're not here tomorrow, then we cannot be their friend today."

When an American officer asked an Iraqi officer, "What are you going to do to make sure that forces are mixed Sunni and Shi'a?", the Iraqi officer answered, "I am Sunni. He is Shi'a. We, both, were imprisoned by Saddam. He is Sunni and he is Shi'a." The officer pointed around the table. The prison to which he referred is Abu Ghraib. The U.S. Army had taken over the Abu Ghraib prison, a symbol of Saddam's rule, which now serves as a U.S. prison and apparent torture chamber. Both Saddam and America created the world's most notorious prison.

A war is fought over dirt. Chunks of dirt are owned by forces, patrolled by forces. Each week, here, more dirt is patrolled by Iraqi forces. Iraqis patrol the area near Karbala (near my next deployment). This decision may impact my safety and the safety of my team. The Iraqi police patrol the region to the west of the International Zone in downtown Baghdad. Regrettably, the region earned the nickname "the great phallus of Baghdad" due to the shape of the river on the map. An American teenage boy would be punished for drawing this map on his schoolwork.

The conflict revolves around the long-term government for Iraq. Some desire clerics in charge and stronger adherence to Sharia Law, thereby resembling Iran. Others recognize the long history of Baghdad and Iraq as a commercial center. Baghdad, the home of Sinbad and Scheherazade, is a green city of eight million people around a winding river. It is an ancient city. Surrounded by desert, Iraqi gardens thrive. Even in war, the fields are green.

This region can break the mind of the scholar, the heart of the hopeful, and the soul of a noble. Palestinian kills Palestinian. Arab kills Kurd. Kurd kills Turk. Persian kills Arab. And Baghdad is a city with Kurds, Arabs, Persians, Christian, Jews, Sunnis, and Shi'ah. There are those that want to live by the rule of law, and those who want to be ruled by the law of clerics. I have no answers to give to my command and no answer to give to the American people. And for you, Brie, I give love. 1-4-3, babe.

Fuck the *New York Times* rule.

I am here facing conflict on behalf of the will of Americans and our government. I chose to be here. But reading how we are being treated hurts...

We are being hurt by our government's recklessness. Let me explore secrets and truth. A secret protects lives. If secret information becomes known, then our people may get killed. As secrets become more sensitive, the number of lives at risk increases. Certainly, we also classify technology as secret, yet at the core, we equate secrecy with human lives. Keeping secrets saves lives. Revealing secrets puts lives at risk: a classic definition, albeit naive. Nations, including my own, abuse this definition.

The exact time, location, and size of force attacking the Normandy Coast on June 6, 1945 was a secret. A secret called: Operation Overlord. It isn't a secret anymore, by the way. Secrets get declassified with time and as the risks to human life reduce to nil.

Are the names of the members of the Armed Forces, their home phone numbers, social security numbers, and other personal information a secret? I would have thought so. Regrettably, this information is not classified as secret. This information is public. When we aggregate information about our military personnel, do we classify this large data set as secret? Still no. We do not. Given all of the elements of the information are public, then the entire set of data is public.

This month, the soldiers in Iraq and Afghanistan learned that a copy of confidential information about American veterans disappeared from the Veterans Administration. The information is not secret in the legal sense, but it contains the personal data of veterans. *The New York Times* used the word "leaked" when they described the disappearance of the copy, as if there were a hole in a bucket and soldiers' names dribbled out onto the ground.

The Department of Defense issued warnings to everyone. Soldiers have been instructed to review our credit information and guard against identity theft. On top of being deployed into Iraq and Afghanistan, the leadership has said: "We're awfully sorry." They then provided each of us with a pathway for a free credit check. Interestingly (confusingly), the Veterans Administration becomes available to a soldier only after active service. Given the Department of Defense publicly offered support to active-duty soldiers, I think there is whisper that the leak may not be limited to those within the VA's domain. Possibly, the DOD admits a leak exists within their own systems. Otherwise, they would not offer free credit check services and issue warnings to active-duty soldiers. The DOD pays me and my military intelligence company to discover personal information about our allies and enemies and nearly everyone in between those extremes. We gather phone numbers and addresses; we create network diagrams of people and their relationships. We have teams that occasionally hack into the lives of our adversaries using their personal data such as birthnames, dates of birth, and family names. As a military intelligence officer, I have been trained to recognize intelligence-grade data.

My bosses, our bosses, informed us that we can mitigate risks with... a credit check? As if the enemy, if he got his hands on this data, would spontaneously start buying expensive televisions and order new credit cards with our identities. I think not. They would use these data to understand their adversary, just as we do. When we examine the online data of an adversary, we study patterns, tastes, preferences, and movements. We strive to find vulnerabilities we can exploit for more information. Classically, spies used information to blackmail targets to bring forth documents, photographs, and other data. We play the same game.

When a soldier's personal data has been exposed, that soldier may find herself subject to blackmail and exploitation by an enemy.

I wonder who stole this data? And why? Who would want this data about soldiers and their families?

An American soldier serves publicly. Many records about a soldier's service remain public. Many soldiers and their families live on, or near, large military bases. Finding American soldiers at home does not present a significant technical nor logistic challenge. Regardless, these massive databases have aggregated our personal data. Then our government failed to provide sufficient safeguards to protect us. Because the VA data falls below the legal threshold for secret, this data get protected by weak laws.

On the June 9th, *The New York Times* reported that there was a theft of 1,500 names from the Department of Energy. Hackers stole into the databases of the National Nuclear Administration Center in Albuquerque, New Mexico and stole information about the people working for the nuclear weapons sections of the DOE. The information stolen included names, birthdates, social security numbers, security clearance level, and employment location. It took the DOE nine months to reveal this theft. It didn't tell the impacted employees and it didn't tell senior managers. They chose to shield this theft from senior management and those impacted. The Chinese demonstrated a past interest in this data, haven't they? And now it was cleverly stolen? *Really.* The people who stole these 1,500 records about 1,500 people may have used the data to explore means of exploiting nuclear physicists who serve in a national research lab. Instead of preventing possible blackmail or warning staff about vulnerabilities, the technical team kept the hack quiet.

One of the many reasons for starting this war in Iraq involved preventing the expansion of weapons-of-mass destruction. Still, three years into this war, military intelligence units continue to investigate chemical, biological, and nuclear weapons information. Had we been able to steal digital data from Iraq or Iran about their nuclear engineers, we would have done so. Imagine the smiles if we captured data of every scientist that included their names, financial identification numbers, birthdays, and addresses? We would explore these data to better understand the nuclear programs in Iraq and Iran and elsewhere.

The treatment of our scientists and our veterans exceeds the risks of identity theft. It involves the world of global espionage. Who wants personal data about our nuclear scientists? Who wants the personal data of our past and current soldiers? Our adversaries, even our allies, would find value in possessing this data. Theses data provides leverage over individual Americans who operate in positions of trust. Most people can be moved if the lever rests on the right fulcrum. You, you are gay, and that is illegal in your Army. Tell me secrets or I'll get you discharged. You, you have a gambling problem and mounting debt. Tell me things or I'll make your life miserable.

Data describing who does what with our nuclear weapons got stolen or leaked. The bad guys knew this before the victims and the agency bosses did. I am confident that the lives of our nuclear weapons scientists have been exposed to more risks due to this theft of data. A clever, patient spy waits years before using elements from it. Yes, well, the DOE has now issued warnings to their employees to be on guard against identity theft. They should also issue warnings such as: do not get sick! Do not get in debt! Do not gamble! Do not talk with strangers! Do not have clandestine sexual liaisons!

The last line of the *NYT* article reads: "'Somebody's ID has a real value, a monetary value,' Mr. Ansanelli said." Certainly, the personal data of those who safeguard our nuclear weapons secrets has real value. The list of organizations wanting that data is a long, long list. Remember that these lists of secret-keepers technically fall short of our nation's legal definition of secret.

Take another step with me down this path of secrets, secret-keepers, and information that is not legally secret. In July 2003, we learned the story of Valorie Plame. Valorie Plame served our nation as a CIA officer, a spy who was married to a senior member of our foreign service. This information was secret. Plame's status as a CIA officer was a secret and afforded legal protection of secret information. In 2003, a government official informed the world that she is an intelligence officer. Plame served our nation as a spy while married to a diplomat. One might explore a pattern of using those who traveled with diplomats as spies. Is this a pattern that intelligence agencies use? One might ask if other spouses of foreign service officials serve as agents in our intelligence agencies. Not only did our government put Ms. Plame's life at risk and end her chosen career, our government told the world where we hide our intelligence officers. We decided not to safeguard these data. We failed to provide the protection that this person needed.

Unlike the release of Department of Energy employees or the release of Veterans Administration data, the exposure of Valorie Plame as a spy met the criteria for being a criminal act. Our government promised prosecution for those involved. The government has the responsibility to protect those of us who serve our nation. These incidents involving the VA, the DOE, and Valorie Plame illustrate issues at three levels. In every case, we (the soldiers, spies, and scientists) carry the greatest risk.

The theft or loss of VA data appears to be an act of stupidity. The DOE theft appears to be the work of foreign agents who were then aided by nine months of silence. The third breach of trust involves the malicious conduct of a member of the executive branch who appears to have used the secret information as blackmail and leverage for political gain.

This week, the U.S. Government killed a human being; albeit a bad guy, a very bad guy. The decision to kill him was result of failed attempts at capturing him. The Iraqi Police captured Al-Zarqawi once. They let him go because they didn't know who he was. Al-Zarqawi was almost captured a few months ago but escaped during a short gun battle.

This time, our government decided to kill him instead of capturing him.

Given my months here, it is very, very clear how averse we are to the use of violence in this war. It is a particularly confusing situation for the soldiers here. Their rules of engagement (ROE) are so strict that senior officers investigate every discharge of a weapon. And as you'll notice from the upcoming investigations about the incident at Hadith, fault will likely be placed on the officers for failing to investigate aggressively and immediately. I'll come back to Hadith and the U.S. Marines in a bit.

There are no aerial bombings here, as a rule. They are indiscriminate. You can't bomb people and expect them to love you. It doesn't work that way.

I have been watching the information about the killing of Al-Zarqawi unfold in the news. I am primarily reading *CNN, BBC, NYT,* and *Al-Jazeera*. My captain, Brian, reads the Seattle papers and Google News. We sit in our office and pass links back and forth via email (it is too damn hot outside to do much at the peak of day anyway).

Brian was the first to trigger on inconsistencies in the facts as they were being reported by various sources. He pointed out flaws in the timeline. I, too, was picking through the information, although my focus was more on the revelation of tactics, techniques, and technology.

One article announced that Al-Zarqawi understood that the Americans have an easy time tracking cell phones.

I will digress about our local-market mobile phones. The local phone company is called Iraqna. I, too, have an Iraqna phone. Mine is a super cheap phone bought by the government and it uses pre-paid calling cards that cannot be traced to the owner. I can buy Iraqna calling cards from the rug merchant, the tailor, and the tool store. The calling cards are sold in denominations of U.S. dollars. The $40 card is good for six months and hundreds of local minutes. To use a calling card, you simply key in the digits you see when you rub off a silver film. The electronic signature or identity of the phone changes when you change the SIM card which can be bought on the street from any number of people for $30. All modern phones use GPS. They transmit their location, always. This business you see on *CSI* and *Law and Order* about triangulating cell phone calls is history. Every element of data is transmitted with a precise location and universal coordinated time.

There was a situation about a year ago with eighteen CIA agents snatching a Muslim cleric off the streets of Milan, Italy. These idiot agents undertook their entire secret operation using modern cell phones.

The Italian government monitored the movements of our guys, listened to their conversations, and eventually issued warrants for their arrest. The Italians were able to provide our government with details about our operations. Where they did their stakeouts, where they slept, where they met, where they ate. The Italians had everything but the actual identities of our operatives.

Another issue with mobile phones has become clear with the recent wiretapping case of a mobster. A mobile phone is a two-way radio, with a microphone and speaker on it. A mobile phone is also a computer. It is hardware with a processing chip, memory, and it runs software. Most cell phones have databases of phone numbers, missed calls, and even a calculator. Those are all software applications. It is possible to download software to many types of cell phones that allows them to capture sounds and transmit sounds with GPS coordinates. With this trick, your cell phone would appear off and still be transmitting everything that is being said nearby. With a little amplification and digital surgery on the background noises, the quality is really pretty good. This is called a listening device or a bug. A cell phone can be programmed or modified to be a bugging device, as well as a location tracker.

As an aside: cell phones are not permitted in most locations classified as secret.

Returning to my thread about Al-Zarqawi: the article told me that Al-Zarqawi started using a Thuraya phone. The article said that Al-Zarqawi knew that tracking Thuraya phones is much more difficult for the U.S. government. How true, I said. Interesting that he knew this information. We kept that information secret. Secret-ish, I guess.

What do I know about Thuraya phones, you ask? I have one. I have a Thuraya phone. It is a small, satellite phone that is about twice the size of a normal cell phone. My Thuraya phone uses untraceable prepaid calling cards. My Thuraya phone does not transmit GPS coordinates. When it is off, it can't really be of value to the opposing team.

As long as one keeps changing phones, these phones can be anonymous. Granted, there are people listening, but conversations often don't make sense if one speaks obtusely about their subject. There are times when I have used my Iraqna phone to call Brian and said: "Hey, the time is 0615." Then I hung up. He knows that we are flying, and he'll figure out that I communicated the flight time which is secret. We'll both know the location and the rest.

You'll note, a day or two later, that the media is reporting that cell phones lent to the tracking and identification of Al-Zarqawi. It is regrettable that an early report showed a vulnerability in our sophisticated technology. Regrettable, but not criminal. The *NYT* would have gotten that information from a military officer. It is too bad that this officer talked about a blind spot, a vulnerability in our data-gathering efforts. Instead of using the formal word secret, I called it a blind spot. I cannot call it secret because Al-Zarqawi was not supposed to know our secrets, nor much about our vulnerabilities. Nor should *The New York Times*. If both knew, then the information is not legally secret. Right?

Anyone who has read suspense books in the last decades or seen a movie about this sort of stuff understands the technology of a precision attack. Someone sits very near the target and lights up the target with a laser. The operatives watch the target move and continue to confirm that he is alive and that he is the right guy.

We are trying to stand up a security force here in Iraq, so we'd want them to get affirmation and recognition as good people from Iraqis. When the Iraq forces engage, we don't want too many casualties, so we have ambulances standing by for military and civilian casualties. After the Iraqis get credit for being first on site, we send in American forces to help. We want the Iraqi forces to be first.

Here we are with the *NYT* telling us exactly what type of bomb was used. They report that it is laser-guided. This information tells us that a forward observer was very, very close to the building. Given our Rules of Engagement, you now know that this forward observer was also confirming the guy's identity and movement while the bomb fell. We know all of this. We know that tracking this guy was a complicated bit of intelligence work using technology, double agents, and long stakeouts.

We now need to tell the world that the Iraqi and U.S. governments correctly identified one of the worst people involved in this war.

We need credibility when we do this.

It is absolutely forbidden to photograph prisons, prisoners, dead bodies, and the like. But someone makes the decision to publish a photograph of the dead Al-Zarqawi. I can see why. We need to prove Al-Zarqawi is dead. We need credible proof that he is dead.

Then the media outlets start pointing out flaws in the timelines. How could the now-famous Al-Zarqawi photograph have a time stamp two minutes after the bombing? His dead face has been washed, they accurately point out.

Then the media outlets start pointing out flaws in the personnel involved. One group denies the involvement of Special Forces and another group announces that the president called the Joint Special Operations Command (JSOC) commander to congratulate him. Brian and I, both military intelligence officers, have the training that allows us to understand the mission. We read in the news media that the United States wants to crow about the death of this bad guy. Our leaders invented a cover story, then released data and timelines that contradict their own fiction. Within a day, everyone knew that our government, again, had lied. The most likely scenario involved proper and long-term intelligence efforts, blending human intelligence, signals intelligence, and a bit of luck. Given the weapons used, the DOD sent in a small team of special operators who executed the mission with precision. Then, to protect various secrets such as the units involved, the technology involved, and the vulnerabilities exploited, the government released a cover story. With stupid, careless recklessness, the authors of the fiction failed to align the fiction with the facts. A little lie often obscures the bigger lie. Now we are chasing dozens of bogus reports.

Today, I read in the news media details about conflicting facts: Al-Zarqawi was killed immediately; Al-Zarqawi lived for a moment; Al-Zarqawi was beaten; Al-Zarqawi was shot; Al-Zarqawi tried to escape; Al-Zarqawi died on the stretcher of wounds from the bombing; Al-Zarqawi's death and the bombing were two hours apart; Al-Zarqawi was not shot.

Furthermore, the incident yielded such a trove of intelligence that 120 arrests have been made. Where did this intelligence come from, someone asks? Clearly if the killing of a bad guy is followed by 120 related arrests, then intelligence has been gathered by a variety of means, and some during the incident in which Al-Zarqawi was killed. Otherwise, it isn't possible to tie 120 arrests to the capture and killing of Al-Zarqawi. This follows the precise pattern of our work, although my efforts tend to be limited to people within a neighborhood or a small-time operator.

I, too, am in the secret-keeping business. My chosen career is the harvester of secrets. In the olden days, one might have called me a spy, a word that has fallen out of favor. To you, Brie, I tell the truth even when obliged to lie. We both know I am lying and that is part of our relationship. Like the edge of an old-timey map where the legend reads: "Beyond here, there be dragons." In my non-military life, we know I keep a line and the map reads: "Beyond here, there be secrets."

Let me just offer this to my government. If credibility is an objective, then telling the truth is a required path to that goal. Another path that we must take is that we cannot have the appearance of lying. Do not get caught lying. Every undercover cop, every clandestine CIA operator, every military special operator knows that rule. Either tell the truth, do not talk, or do not get caught telling a lie. Death awaits us all.

Now, if there are secrets to keep (and there are), then before we release information (which is public and must be released), we must clearly identify the secrets. Pull the secrets out of frame, then tell the truth.

Let's say, for example, that information gathered during the killing of Al-Zarqawi lent to the capture of 120 other people. But you don't want to reveal what the information was or who provided that information. So, do not publish to anyone that the subsequent arrests were tied to the capture of Al-Zarqawi. Let the gap exist. Announce those arrests from another command, from another location, in another week. Let the historian make the connection, not the enemy. This gap will protect sources and technologies for a short while.

As a person who drives and walks the streets of Iraq during a war, I need protection. I do not need the government to release my private data. I do not need my government to reveal my name. I do not need people to doubt my ability to protect my sources. I never want to be part of an operation like the one in Milan, Italy with eighteen operators who now face criminal charges by the Italian government. I need my government to keep my secrets with the same integrity that I use to keep their secrets.

Let's say you don't want people to know about techniques used by the Special Forces guys. Then look the media in the face and say, "I am not going to talk about the protocols used by our intelligence and Special Forces units. I won't admit they were involved, and I won't deny it. Stop asking." If you pull this off, don't then subsequently tell the world that the president called the JSOC commander to congratulate him. Keep that conversation quiet. Release that information and you'll have people confirming the obvious link.

Now, if you don't have the whole truth at the moment, tell the truth you've got. And admit that during the next twenty-four to forty-eight hours, additional information will be available.

One must tell the truth, even in a war started by a lie. If we don't have the credibility and the skills to tell how we captured then killed Al-Zarqawi, then we won't have the trust required to investigate and report on the apparent massacre at Hadith. Hadith and the U.S. Marine Corps will be tainted by the facts surrounding Al-Zarqawi's capture.

One can tell the truth and still keep necessary secrets. It takes skill and thought. It takes courage. The value of a secret is measured in the lives it protects from our adversaries. We must protect those who have decided to become intelligence operatives for our nation. We must not allow the Chinese to have the names, social security numbers, addresses, clearance level, and occupation of those who safeguard our nuclear weapons technology. And if we are going to have an effective special operations command, we must protect some of the tactics, techniques, and procedures from general knowledge while still acknowledging that they exist and operate.

This war is public property. It is the property of every American. Every member of the armed forces, every civilian, and every foreign worker here serves the citizens of the United States. There must be great transparency, and great credibility, with every step we take.

Regardless of the reasons that got us here, our every action here must speak to our honor, our ethics, and our value of human life. One must tell the truth. It is our duty. When I talk with a schoolteacher, a mother, a nurse, a doctor, I need their trust. I am a dark-haired woman with brown eyes and slightly olive-colored skin after months now in Iraq. I speak Arabic poorly, but everyone knows that I am an American officer seeking information. Please, I say, *tell me information you know, and I will keep you safe.* This is the same line used by police detectives. Please tell me what you know, and I will keep you safe. I can only make that promise if the promises around me are being kept.

If someone knew about my relationship with you, I'd lose my career and possibly face criminal charges through the UCMJ. I am vulnerable to blackmail because of this information. And yet, I enter people's homes asking them to trust me. I, the American Soldier, share coffee and lamb and soft bread with women, telling them that I am an open book and worthy of their trust. If you share with me what you know, I will try to keep you safe.

Reading these articles in the news, I begin to doubt if my own government will keep me safe.

I am going near Karbala for a lengthy assignment. I have known this for a while. I'll miss Baghdad. Baghdad is a beautiful city and an ancient city. I'll commute here for mail and meetings. This assignment may last a couple of months.

15 | Arkansas

HENRY, SPRING 1872

Sergeant Porter enters the private's barracks as the buglers play "Retreat," the post's traditional tribute to sunset. Wordlessly, the sergeant points to Corporal Henry McDonald. The sergeant waggles him forward with two fingers. Henry climbs into his new dark blue tunic, a pair of bright yellow chevrons stitched on his upper arms providing a striking visual contrast. On a Friday evening, Henry wears sun-faded trousers that resembles a summer's sky, but the tunic—the tunic makes a bold statement.

The sergeant waits on the parade ground, a discreet distance and out of earshot of the barracks. As Henry approaches his sergeant, he snaps to attention. The sergeant says, "Enough of that, Henry. Come, we'll wet you in."

The two men walk to the officer's stables and the sergeants' unofficial NCO club. As Henry opens the door, the sergeant says, "You cannot really be a member until you earn that third stripe, but you've done well."

The post sergeants turned their attention to Henry. They stand when Sergeant Porter and Corporal McDonald enter the smokey room. The men, ranging in ages from near sixty to twenty-five, form a loose line.

The post command sergeant major approaches Henry. The CSM punches Henry hard on the new stripes. The sergeant major then grabs Henry's now limp and numb hand to shake it. Then Sergeant Porter hands both men a short glass of bourbon. Henry comprehends the scope and duty of the mission. The CSM toasts the new non-commissioned officer and pours the bourbon down his gullet. Henry follows, assuming he is following an ancient and secret custom. The CSM and Henry hand their glasses back to Sergeant Porter.

The C company first sergeant, with the gold diamond embroidered below his chevrons, punches Henry hard in the exact same place that the CSM just hit. The first sergeant grabs Henry's hand for an aggressively manly shake. These two now raise full glasses as a toast. Henry drinks it down in one gulp. He counts the men standing there: the quartermaster sergeant, the headquarters staff sergeant, and on through the list of post NCOs. Eight more punches, eight more drinks, and eight more hale handshakes. Eight becomes nine when Henry discovers that his own sergeant reserved the final toast for himself.

"What do you think, lads? We've got those stripes well attached. Welcome, my boy. You've done well. I have a feeling you are going places." The other sergeants give a laugh at this comment. Henry staggers under the influence of both the assault of the bourbon and the fists, missing the joke others heard.

"To Corporal Henry McDonald."

Sergeant Porter placed a gentle punch to his tender arm then presents Henry with a rather full pour of the bourbon.

Henry finds a barrel upon which to rest his backside. His left arm gripes the table. His feet form a solid triangular base, yet the room swims. The sergeants treat the new initiate with polite disregard. Men relate stories of past promotions. The CSM earned his first stripes at the first battle of Bull Run by being the sole member of his patrol to have returned. He tells stories of bloody days and nights when there was no time, or bourbon, to christen promotions. By the time he had sewed on the stripes, he had been promoted again to sergeant.

Henry loses track of the banter, fading. Two thoughts kept him focused. First, do not vomit. Second, do not fall.

The room continues to get warm. When the left-handed quartermaster sergeant, the only man in the room to punch his right arm left to urinate, Henry sneaks out on his heels.

Shortly after "Reveille," the post's daily greeting to the sun, Private Paul Abrams discovers Henry curled on the ground with his back against the stable wall, covered with two U.S. Army horse blankets. He rouses his friend. Paul steps back from the unfamiliar sour reek that came from Henry.

"Come on, Henry, you've got to get up."

Henry winces, recoiling from Paul's supportive hands.

"Get up. That's the boy."

Cajoling, Paul gets the new corporal into the stables. The corporal's adjutant unbuttons the tunic and pulls it off. Henry fights the movement with ineffectual resistance. Paul succeeds, unbuttoning the white shirt. It is then that Paul sees Henry's arms. Both are bright purple. The left shoulder is significantly more abused than the right.

"Jeez, Henry, what happened?"

"They needed to make sure my stripes were attached." Henry gets the words out. He immediately regrets speaking. "Oh, I feel horrible." Then he bends and vomits into the straw at his feet.

Paul returns to the stables minutes later with Belville, Donovan, and Mueller. They carry a couple of buckets, Henry's older faded tunic, and a few linens. The squad cleans up their corporal, all while admiring the beating he took at the hands of the sergeants. When the bugle calls for breakfast, the soldiers walk out into the breaking day, Mueller and Donovan flanking Henry, keeping him upright. Henry's own will forces a smile on everyone's face.

The cadre of non-commissioned officers communicated, during the initiation, that they offer their own justice as well. The message was a mixture of welcoming and warning. With greater rank comes greater responsibilities. With greater responsibilities comes greater risks. Stories informed Henry of corporals and sergeants who failed at their duties and faced the unofficial tribunal of their own peers, the post's NCOs, before formal charges could get written. Drunk, bruised, and barely able to sit upright on his barrel, he faces the duty with the frankness of a new day. His superiors accept Henry as a warrior and a leader.

After lunch, Sergeant Porter informs Corporal McDonald that he is to take five soldiers and five horses for a training ride to work on "horsemanship," as he called it.

"Mac, draw enough food and supplies from the quartermaster for two days. Just be back before stable call on Sunday."

Henry comes to attention. "Yes, Sergeant."

The quartermaster sergeant presents five rucksacks, feed for animals, and everything ready on the docks behind the warehouse. Corporal McDonald rides from the garrison with Privates Belville, Donovan, Mueller, and Abrams in tow. They ride with straight backs and in neat order. They walk their horses east to the battlefields along the Chickamauga, then stop. The men hobble the horses and rest.

Henry sits with his back on a tree, feeling mildly better but needing a nap. Within a few minutes, he grabs his pack and a blanket. At the stream's edge, he lays down and falls asleep.

At 3:30 on Sunday afternoon, the patrol returns to the garrison looking fresh. Henry carries a proud smile. The squad returns the packs and blankets to the quartermaster.

The sergeant says, "You did alright, boy."

When Henry check in with Sergeant Porter, Porter asks, "Feeling any better?"

"Oh, I feel grand, Sergeant."

"Henry, you looked like the dog's breakfast before you left. How's the arm?"

"I can move it."

"Show me." Porter winks.

"Maybe later, Sergeant." Henry winks back.

"And Henry, when we're in private, you can call me Bill or Billy. You are a non-commissioned officer now. Let your guys know that they are going out tomorrow. The trip will be a bit longer than prior trips."

"Yes, Sergeant."

Standing at attention in front of Lieutenant William Wolfe, the post adjutant, Henry listens to orders then accepts the handwritten copy on behalf of he and Sergeant Porter. Ten men of C Company of the Second Infantry Regiment garrisoned at Chattanooga will be detached for service in support of the railroad in Arkansas and the Indian Territory. The men will be issued horses and pack animals in Little Rock.

Throughout the day, the detachment prepares for an extended trip. Men write letters to loved ones saying explaining that they are headed into Indian Territory. Men spend time with the quartermasters, making sure that their kit would meet the demands of extended separation from the garrison. At the afternoon stables call, Henry and Sergeant Porter return to the headquarters building, where Lieutenant Wolfe presents them with a ledger book plus a leather purse of cash and coin. The leather purse also includes a draft the soldiers can use for additional money at banks or military posts as needed.

Before dawn, the squad of soldiers gather at the depot awaiting the train that will carry them to Decatur, Alabama. They stand next to their five wooden crates and a series of small cloth travel bags. Their rucksacks carry what they need for three days of train travel. Each man has a few coins. The bags and chest carry tinned food, dry goods, ammunition, ledger books, order books, cooking pots, blankets, tents, and the sundry items that a patrol may require during a month or two of service removed from their home garrison. Their carbine rifles lay in wooden crates. Only Sergeant Porter and Henry wear side arms boarding the train in Chattanooga. Unlike any recent mission, the men demonstrate excitement about traveling west. They look forward to the days on the train and an overnight stay in Memphis.

The train terminates in Memphis. The railroads travel north, northeast, east, and south from the city. They do not travel west. The Mississippi River prevents the trains and tracks from crossing. The Memphis and Little Rock Railroad originates in West Memphis, Arkansas, on the other side of the river.

Bellville asks the most obvious question. "How do they get the train across?"

Mueller responds. "They don't. There is a separate train on that side."

To which Bellville asks, "Right. So how did that train get over there? It didn't float over, did it?"

Paul Abrams, studying the river and the traffic, says, "Maybe it did. You could if the boat is big enough."

Within the hour, the ten soldiers wrestle with the crowds on the dock. Two porters with hand carts transport the crates and soft luggage. The soldiers wear their rucksacks and gawk at the mighty river. The porters, who know the routine and time frame, push on, not waiting for their clients. The porters get paid by the trip from depot to depot. They need to hustle. They pull the crates, goods, luggage, trunks and everything that people pack. They load it then guide their clients from the depot down to the ferry docks. Several of the ferrymen who approach the porters bolt when they see ten uniformed soldiers following the hand cart. The porters lead them to an empty portion of dock.

"There, sir, that is your ferry. Don't listen to the others."

"When will it be back?"

"Oh, directly, sir. Directly."

The crush of crowds and the soldiers do not blend well, like oil and water. The people give space to the soldiers and the soldiers form a cordon around their cart. In every other place on the docks, people bump and jostle. Ferrymen hock their services. Men sell fruit and sausages from hand carts. And a man with a fiddle plays for coins.

Henry approaches the fiddler. In a few words, he requests the fiddler to step into the soldier's circle. Donovan advances closer. Donovan lays a coin on the crate of rifles, saying, "Henry, how about 'Wild Mountain Thyme'?"

"Do you know it?" Henry asks the fiddler.

"Of course." The fiddler disappears the coin behind his belt, then jumps into the melody fast and high.

Donovan calls out, "A bit slower, will ya, mate. And bring it down."

Donovan starts singing acapella. The fiddler joins. Henry joins. With their backs to the crowd on the docks, the three discover their rhythm, then their harmonies. Another coin, and the trio launches into a moderately paced version of "Barbara Allan." Belville opens up. Private O'Conner, new to the traveling team, fills in with a fine baritone. Private Griffin fetches a tin whistle from his rucksack.

The fiddler turns to the growing crowd. He places his hat upon the ground. While still taking coins from the soldiers, passersby start to contribute.

Henry puts his hand in the air, offering the opening notes to Stephen Foster's "Hard Times" acapella and solo until the others join him.

Seeing coins on the rifle crate, people on the docks present the soldiers with coins as well. A few people listen and come closer while they too await for ferries that will take them across the Mississippi. The food vendors, spying the attentive crowd, push their carts towards the money.

Henry catches the furtive movement of one cutpurse. He continues his singing, turning to the audience as if making a solo. With the speed of a lizard's tongue, Henry snags the urchin by the wrist. Without missing a beat, or a note, Henry places the boy on the ground near the cart and inside the circle of soldiers.

"Hey, Paul, find a city marshal or someone."

The steam-powered ferry has begun its return journey. Paul returns to the circle without support. Henry cuffs the kid on the head, pushing him out of the circle and letting him go.

The ferry slows.

Henry put his hands out to the other singers. They pool their money, then divide it evenly between the singing soldiers and the fiddler.

Arriving on the Arkansas side of the Mississippi River, Henry sends Paul to look for lodging or a military post. Paul returns with an old and grey-bearded staff sergeant, who represents the entire staff and contingency of the West Memphis Army post, or more specifically, outpost.

He offers instructions to Sergeant Porter. "Hotel there, check in, they will bill the Army. Gear to the small warehouse."

Sergeant Porter addresses the soldiers. "There is no way we are leaving our kit in that storeroom unguarded. We're here until the train comes. So, from now 'til then, you eight will rotate guard duty in three-hour shifts. And no! I don't know when the train is coming. It will be here after you see steam coming from the west."

In Little Rock, the solders unload supplies from the train's baggage car, placing the materiel on a hand cart next to the depot. Once again, they are greeted by a staff sergeant, another old veteran of the recent war and maybe the wars in Texas and Mexico. He walks uncomfortably on stiff knees and with a reversed arch in his back. He wears a pistol at his right hip in an Army-issued holster that had not seen blacking in months.

"I've got a telegram for you. Sergeant. You'll be establishing a camp near the bridge at Baring Cross. And when you can, in the morning, please introduce yourselves to the city marshal and the federal marshal."

Knowing the routine of moving baggage and walking further, the soldiers each disappear behind building corners, and trees, though not many trees yet stand on the riverbank.

The resident staff sergeant regards the soldiers' liberal use of the hand cart in Bellville's hands. "You are not to take that," he says to Sergeant Porter. "The Army has our own."

"And Sergeant O'Rourke, where is that cart?"

"It's near your camp and next to our warehouse."

"We have a warehouse?"

"Not really. It belongs to the Army and Fort Smith."

"Corp, I want you to accompany Staff Sergeant O'Rourke to our new camp, then send back the hand cart." Henry can feel the resentment, anger, and aggression brewing in Sergeant Porter.

"Got it, Sergeant."

Without a word, Belville, Mueller, Abrams, Donovan, and Sturtevant fall in. The team of young men—each of whom lied to the Army recruiting sergeants about their age—move with the speed and vigor of eighteen- and nineteen-year-old athletes.

Sergeant O'Rourke posts alone, lives alone, and patrols alone in Little Rock, Arkansas. O'Rourke had been unofficially retired from active duty and was given a post next to a train depot and a telegraph line. He will remain at this post, or another identical post, until achieving the years of service and age to retire. The squad slows to accommodate the pace of the elderly soldier. They pass a few warehouses including two other hand carts, as well as several stables.

Eventually, they come upon a flat field. The packed soil hosts broadleaved weeds and shows cracks in the bare earth. The field does not support the growth of the native tall grasses visible elsewhere on the plain.

"Corporal, here is your camp."

"And the hand cart?"

"We already passed that," the aging staff sergeant says.

"Abrams, Belville, remain here. Discover what you can. Water, latrines, etc. The rest with me." Then to the staff sergeant, he says, "Do you mind taking us to the hand cart?"

"As I said, we already passed it, but I am going that way now."

Sergeant O'Rourke ignores the squad, turning his back on them.

The soldiers shuffle towards the main road. They walk between the Army-style stables and what Henry now recognizes as an Army-style warehouse.

"There, that's the hand cart. Make sure you return it when you are done."

Sergeant Porter surveys their campground. "This was a camp," he says, "or a fort, at one point oriented east to west. The camp held a bit of high ground between the river and the train behind it."

Henry, too, can see that the stables and warehouse once stood within the square compound. The front door to both buildings face this now-empty bit of dirt. The town forms at the edge of the post, resembling the vicus that formed outside of ancient Roman forts in Europe and North Africa. With the camp gone, the town has yet to encroach on this patch of dirt.

Paul briefs the returning soldiers, having identified a working well and the remains of forgotten latrines and latrine trenches.

Sergeant Porter announces, "Men, this is home, at least for a while. Tents, firewood, cooking fires, water. Let's get going."

They use the cart as a worktable, cook table, dining table, and occasionally, as a cart. O'Conner and Belville drag it down towards the river to pick up wood for fires. Sergeant Porter slips into the warehouse. And just like that, the men of C Company of the Second Infantry Regiment join the long parade of soldiers sent to the Wild West to settle disputes, enforce laws, prevent banditry, and quell unrest by native peoples.

Arkansas was admitted to the union in 1836, followed by Michigan and Florida. Texas joined in 1845. In rapid order, Iowa, Wisconsin, California, Minnesota, and Oregon all joined the union. The admissions of West Virginia, once part of Virginia, and Nevada happened during the Civil War. Now, western lands were being divided by farmers, ranchers, businesses, railroads, and others into territories, each vying for the opportunity to join the United States with formal recognition as a state. Lewis and Clark followed the land west in their Corps of Discovery Expedition barely seventy years prior.

Approximately one year prior to Henry's enlistment, the ceremonial linking of the east and west happened at Promontory Point in Utah. As of September 1869, a person could take a train from San Francisco Bay to New York City.

Henry enlisted in March 1870. And in the warming months of 1872, Corporal Henry McDonald stands on the banks of the Arkansas River, looking west.

The United States drew official maps of North America that described lands with neat solid borders that went east-west and north-south, placing the Choctaw, Cherokee, Chickasaws, and Seminoles within these boxes. Maps included notes such as: *Cherokee Reservation, Treaty July 1865.* Then immediately to the west, in lands that included the Cimarron and Arkansas Rivers, the note *Ceded to U.S. by Cherokees, Article 15 and 16, July 19, 1866.*

The notation on the map fails to tell this history behind these blocks of land. It does not inform the reader that the United States Army forced the Cherokee, Chickasaw, Choctaw, Seminole and others to this land from their own homes along the Appalachian Mountains and the eastern seacoast. The original homes for these peoples were in the lush lands along the Atlantic and the mountains. The Army herded the people west, leaving a trail of tears. The United States government deeded lands in the prairies to these eastern and coastal peoples. Of course, the land that the government deeded had already belonged to others. Within two decades, the United States government was already taking the deeded lands back.

As darkness settles, O'Conner pulls a small bottle of bourbon from his boot, passing it to his left. When Sergeant Porter approaches the circle, Mueller rapidly hides the bottle behind his knee. William Porter makes a seat for himself, then looks at Mueller, waiting.

"Private, you are going to horde that bottle for yourself or continue to pass it?"

"What..."

The phrase *what bottle?* was about to escape Mueller's lips when Henry gestures with a thumb, suggesting that the bottle continue its circuit. Those watching closely might have observed that Henry does not take a sip on his turn. The sergeant takes a polite sip, wipes the rim with this sleeve, then passes it to his left.

In a soft tone while leaning towards Henry, the sergeant says, "That old guy has built himself a castle in there, even has a feather bed on a proper bedstead. He has an iron cook stove and, given how neat and tidy it looks in there, I expect he keeps a woman in there to help with the cooking, cleaning, and everything else. He does not want us here. Not one bit."

"What should we do?"

"For now, let him alone. And tell the boys to let him alone. We're better off without him in our business, but we are not welcome here. This is a place where the army lets people retire on active duty and dispose of damned effective soldiers.

"Men, I am just so proud of each of you. In my day, we went through the meat grinder in the war. You all proved yourselves as warriors and a great bunch to work with. If I'm to be rusticated to the West, I guess I can do it with you ugly mutts. I'd rather be in it than readin' about it. But in a way, I am sorry we all landed here."

The squad offers overlapping and banal comments to their boss.

Henry, using his forge-trained voice in the growing dark, says, "I don't know how many times I went to arrest KKK thugs then watched them walk out of jails because someone somewhere believes these men have the right to lynch people, steal lands, and chain men to their work."

"Yeah, they sure didn't like us catchin' 'em," offers Belville.

"Nothing will change for the good there," adds Paul.

"Well," Sergeant Porter jumps back in, "pass that bottle and let's put this behind us for the night."

The bottle makes another round. Sergeant Porter tips the last of it in a final, satisfying gulp that is a bit larger than polite. He places the bottle on the ground, then, finding a tone between command and parental, he says, "Men, we are on our own. We do not have buglers nor officers telling us what to do each minute of the day. We are still soldiers and we will keep the discipline. Without a wall and a locking warehouse, we will have to post two sentries at all times."

Using the circle of men, he points to pairs of soldiers and gives each group two-hour assignments. "Drinking or sleeping on sentry duty will get you in trouble either by me here or back in Chattanooga by our command. I can't mind a little sip after a long trip, but that ends here. Let's open the crates so that each of you can be issued a sidearm and ammunition. We will then remove two carbines from the crate of rifles. Just pass the rifle to the next pair as you hand off. Tomorrow, we start at sun-up, Reveille. Everybody is up. Divide the morning duties amongst yourselves. We'll need fire, coffee, and breakfast."

With these words said, Sergeant Porter stands, bringing the rest of the detachment to their feet. "And men, if there is trouble, you know where to bring that." All of the men give a chuckle, a couple poking Henry in the ribs with their elbows.

As the soldiers disburse, the sergeant asks, "Henry, how are those arms of yours?"

"Perfect. They're fine, why do you ask?"

"Good for you, young man. I heard through the garrison that the bruising was pretty extensive."

The color has drifted downhill towards Henry's forearms, yellow creeping into the margins. The embarrassment of having been sick on himself brings a blush of shame that Sergeant Porter does not see in the growing darkness of the evening.

As the soldiers lever the tops of crates, Henry digs through to retrieve his favorite rifle he had wrapped carefully in linen. He removes it. Then, from the crate of ammunition, he issues himself rounds. He loads his rifle, then lays it in his tent next to the wall. The eight privates boisterously rearrange their sleeping quarters to correspond with their sentry duty.

The adjutant, Paul, offers a suggestion that would be easiest if men on sentry duty together slept in the same tent. Then Paul points each pair to their tent in sequence: eight to ten here, ten to midnight, and thus through the nighttime hours. This results in every man moving his kit from one tent to another.

Henry and Sergeant Porter, the only two without sentry duty, occupy the fifth tent. Sergeant Porter beds himself with a second revolver. While the camp has served decades of soldiers, Sergeant Porter, a combat veteran of the Civil War and now more recent battles on the same ground, knows he is not going to be found asleep and outgunned at the edge of the western frontier.

At eight in the morning, Sergeant Porter and Corporal McDonald sit in the hotel's restaurant at a table with the United States Deputy Marshal Joseph Blaine. The marshal introduces himself as "JB." Henry and the sergeant offer their first names. Marshal Blaine first admits that he had not been notified that ten soldiers had been sent to Little Rock to assist the railroad. Second, he admits to ongoing problems in the region with every type of crime, from the occasional murder, to vice, cutpurse thefts, armed robbery, and bands of bandits.

The federal marshal says, "The moment people come west of the river, they think the laws of the land have been lifted. And maybe once upon a time, they were. That was before the war and before the railroad. Now we have schools and churches and respectable people moving in with families. The days of whorin' and drinkin' and shootin' up the streets should have ended two decades ago. Bandits travel from the west forgetting that they are re-entering civilization. Then people outlawed in the east or chased by a mob come through here, thinking this is the Old West, ready to shoot it up. We are caught between the east and the west."

"What can we do, Marshal?"

"I don't honestly know."

At that opening, Sergeant Porter tells stories of C company and the men he brought west.

"These men have been involved in more gun battles, arrested more men, and accounted for themselves better than any troop since the recent war. They may look young, but these men are the best and have seen the worst."

Sergeant Porter and the marshal exchange stories of supporting revenue agents and other marshals in their efforts to find men wanted under federal law, many of them wanted for murder and civil rights violations.

"These guys," Sergeant Porter says, referring to the KKK they arrested, "were mostly former soldiers from the southern Army. They decided that a family had settled on land that historically belonged to one plantation or another, they would take it. Or they would want the rich river-bottom land for themselves. They would hang resisters and rape the women. And if a black man stood for election, he'd likely get shot in his bed."

Marshal Blaine listens respectfully, adding, "I had heard the stories, but often from those traveling through here. Families escaping Georgia and Alabama would cross the river, then come through Arkansas on their way to lands in Nevada, lands that they had heard they could farm. In some cases, southern sympathizers dressed as bandits harassed the travelers who wended their way out of the former slave states. In other cases, they would be met by fellow travelers who came south to provide escort and support."

Henry interrupts with his own question. "Do you ever see Buffalo Soldiers come through here?"

The conversation and coffee allow the marshal to digest the information and the presence of these soldiers. Standing, the marshal offers his hand to Henry then to William with a firm, manly grip.

"Sergeant," he says, "I could use some help with the roving bandits. They are pretty tough to catch. I do wonder, sir, if there is not a smuggling ring operating near here."

"What makes you say that?"

"I get reports from businesses, ranchers, and even the Army that materiels ordered from the east disappear along this line somewhere."

"Where does it end up?"

"I don't know. I assume back on the river heading south, then to international waters, but I do not know."

"Marshall, I'll bet me and the boys will find some way of stirring things up. Seems to be our pattern. Like other troublemakers, we got pushed from Georgia."

16 | An Itch and a Ring

BRIGHID, JULY 2006

I flew two days after you disappeared into the terminal at the air base. Sweetie, I gotta tell ya, I squirmed in my seat. What felt daring—to lay on a Mediterranean beach in the buff—resulted in mild discomfort and a profound itchiness while I sat on the Lufthansa aircraft from Frankfurt to Boston. Awkwardly, I got placed near a mid-cabin latrine. Through the day, Germans came to me asking: *Ist sie frei?*

I felt proud that I could read German signs and navigate easily. I learned to order black tea, red wine, and rather little else. I am uncertain why these passengers behaved differently than passengers on other flights. I am accustomed to people wiggling the knob and banging on the door. Many flights have small, illuminated signs with a red "X" indicating "occupied." On this flight, my fellow passengers appointed me the keeper-of-the-door. I would answer *Ja* or *Nein*, indicating if the toilet was occupied or free.

The flight attendant came by, saying something kindly in German. I answered plainly, "Do you mind speaking English? I don't speak German."

He said, "Then why…" Both the question and the flight attendant trailed off.

Yes, I wondered the same. Why were they asking me about the status of the toilet; and why were they asking me in German? The next person that came stood in the aisle next to my seat. I got hip, then butt, then front, as the person made slow, impatient circles outside of the toilet.

Assembling an incomplete sentence, I said: *"Ist frei"* which got the passenger's butt out of my shoulder space.

My itchy hours passed. One passenger leaned over, asking, *"Toilette?"* The most awkward itches radiated from my butt. My butt had never been exposed to the sun. Certainly, I have swum naked, but normally at night, offering the moon a smaller and paler rival. The other region of itchiness came from underneath my breasts. It is just wrong to lift and scratch a boob while on a crowded flight. Furthermore, in my unwanted position as the keeper-of-the-door, there was no discreet means of slipping a fingernail up under my own shirt. That would be the moment when the next passenger asked me permission to use the public toilet. I endeavored a stealthy scratch with the back of my hands. The spine of my book landed me two good and well-aimed scratches; Fidget Brighid...a nickname from childhood that I hated.

Finally, the sound of the engines dropped slightly, indicating the start of our gradual descent into Boston Logan. I pivoted around to the bathroom with a tube of lotion. I gave it all a good scratch, then applied lotion. I returned to my seat immediately in front of the toilet door, feeling mildly refreshed. I leaned back in my seat for the first time in hours and closed my eyes on the long descent into New England.

The following afternoon, I returned to our house on top of a hill in southern Vermont. See, I said it, "our house." Walking through the door, the place felt like home. Trowbridge still seems a bit of a mystery to me given I did not know many local people, yet. But the EMS squad and the few calls have opened my eyes to the hidden charm of Trowbridge.

I have been coming to this house for five years. For the last nine months, living here on the weekends and many times more often than that, I've come to know your hills and your childhood trails. Landmarks on these hills carry your names: the Douglas Tree, the Tree at the Fork, the Cellar Tree, the Ironwood Knoll, and on through the list.

The terrain surrounding our home can be described as if someone has mapped it on paper. The terrain spreads across my mind like the inside cover of *Winnie-the-Pooh*. This hill with the south face dominated by hemlocks is called Hemlock Hill. That section of exposed rock, Porcupine Bluff. Christopher Robin and his gang named the stand of six pines the "One Hundred Acre Wood." And in the low left corner is the place *Where the Woozle Wasn't*. That is my sense of this place.

I step into your childhood, and I fabricate your childhood stories. I get to know the two aunts who raised you. You simply call them "The Aunts" as if they were an undifferentiated pair of elderly ladies. But in this house, I feel and see the influence of each woman separately. The experience resembles walking into the storybook of my best friend. Unlike Christopher Robin, you shot a BB gun at a young age and a twenty-two rifle by the age of eight. Christopher Robin, raised in gentle England, could only fire cork stoppers with his gun. But, as the story tells it, the Silly Bear was saved from floating away while clinging to a blue balloon.

Since returning from Germany, I have gauged the effort it would take for me to live here, to make this my permanent home. The home sits on a hill with acres of fields and pasture lands. I lean against the barn, made of chestnut board, exploring ideas that involve chickens, a pig, a garden with tomatoes, dill, oregano, basil, and salad greens. I am the most high-tech person I know except when in one of my employer's buildings. I know and understand the physics of light bouncing within strands of fiber optic cable. I have published articles and traveled the globe giving talks on the magic that makes the internet work. Yet I am looking at this green grass, the small man-made pond, and this tumble-down grape arbor, thinking of farming on this property.

A fellow in a silver pickup truck mows the grass once per week and checks the doors, windows, and heating. The house's caretaker treats me as a guest. He never says anything, just nods and goes about his work. He plows the drive in the winter and shovels pathways to the various doors. Week after week, the house remains empty and dark, until I show up. I tend to park in his way. I feel guilty sipping tea while he works.

With hundreds of acres, I cannot dance with the naked ease we enjoyed in France. The paved road ends on this property. A dirt road wanders northeast. The land and the house are bound by two-hundred-year-old stone walls. The best of them come to my hips. Me laying out in the pasture would cause me to be eaten alive by bugs and to shock people who would surely spy me. While certainly some in Vermont do get naked, the people in these hills appear to be the sort that keep their clothes on nearly always. Although, I swear, I saw a man riding a motorcycle naked on a warm Sunday afternoon. But he had Massachusetts plates.

I debate keeping the all-over tan I started or letting it go. If I keep it, then next time we go to a beach, I might not be so damn itchy returning home on a long flight.

As plans and visions flow through my head, I struggle with the idea of earning money in these hills. Few seem to earn significant incomes while living here. A few movie stars own large properties nearby. My chosen career involves designing, setting up, and improving internet connections. I like research, too. Here in the town of Trowbridge, Vermont, people mention that when electric power was first brought over the hill to this town, the spool of wire rested on the back of a mule named Gus. While parts of New York City were electrified by Edison in the late 1800s, Trowbridge got their first reliable electric power in the decades surrounding World War II. People here remember the stories, it was that recent. Through the 1970s and 1980s, families shared telephone circuits known as party lines.

In the summer of 2006, I have ordered a satellite dish to bring me internet. This internet is good enough to send and receive email. I can watch the occasional movie, but the buffering is pretty extensive. You and I tried repeatedly to use internet-based phone calls, but the lag bouncing between earth and satellites causes the conversation to resemble a walkie-talkie. I speak. We wait, then you speak. You occasionally call my mobile phone via Hanscom Air Force Base, which is located in Massachusetts. I now know that calls from random military bases are you. I love the intrigue.

If I start a garden right here, then it seems I cannot be reached by clients, Sam, or anyone else. I am, for practical reasons, "off the grid," which isn't ideal for a start-up consultancy.

If I plant tomatoes and basil in this soil, if I get a few chickens to scratch the dirt and eat bugs in the grass here, then I will go broke without my high-tech work. This location is roughly two hours from five state capitals. Within this radius sits Albany, New York to the west, Hartford, Connecticut to the south, Concord, New Hampshire and Boston, Massachusetts to the east. It is a longer and more difficult drive to get from here to Montpelier, Vermont than it is for me to get to Albany. I can drive to Manhattan in three or four hours depending on traffic. One could think that this house holds the center ground for all of the northeastern United States.

As I have discovered repeatedly, the first hour of any trip from this house goes through a cellular and communication dead zone. Returning here from Albany once, I parked at a McDonalds restaurant to connect to a client's network, knowing that those golden arches represented a gateway out of an electronic black hole on the map.

In an effort to market myself as either an independent consultant or a senior engineer with a high-tech firm, I would be required to be in-touch and in-touch nearly always.

I look at the dirt and hear a truck climb the hill. I hear a blue jay complain about something. I now recognize that I would rather hear a blue jay complain than nearly anyone human complain.

I inventory the activities I could do in lieu of my job. Yes, I would rather be in Springfield digging through paper documents than studying the IP version 6 protocol. I would rather be on a computer researching newspaper articles than studying the difference between this version and the last version of free-space ethernet communications. I find it hard to get excited by the power-over-ethernet standards. I could save significant money by dropping the cost of the apartment in Massachusetts and moving in here.

You and I have discussed this topic. For some couples, the process of proposing marriage becomes an event with a ring and a bended knee. For some couples, marriage becomes the obvious next step. For others, marriage can be discussed as a remote concept. Vermont passed a law permitting civil unions between two people. The *Don't-Ask-Don't-Tell* policy of the Department of Defense tells soldiers, sailors, airmen, and Marines to keep any evidence of their relationships a secret from their employer. Given you have a top secret clearance, we cannot file with the State of Vermont binding Lieutenant Sarah Ann Musgrave and Brighid Doran in a civil union. We do that and you resign or get court martialed. Then we are both poor in a big house.

You put my name on a local bank account so that I could pay bills and make needed repairs on this place. We established the cover story that I am the housekeeper and part of the normal contingency that any combat soldier would need to have while overseas.

"It's only natural," you said, "that I would create long term plans for the family property."

Sharing a bank account, and being your medical power of attorney, and being your legal heir, and holding your legal power of attorney does not a marriage make. In the circuit of gymnasiums and lines that makes up the Soldier Readiness Program, each soldier drafts and signs their own will prior to deployments. They sign the various powers of attorney. These documents are formally filed within the mechanism of the Department of Defense. A copy of these documents got sent to a Vermont attorney, and a copy remains locked in the gun safe at the house.

I now have the key for the safe and the instructions for getting into it. There are two keys. One I had already found. It sat in a kitchen drawer with cotton tea-towels. I did not know what the key opened, but I had a guess. The other key and the combination were hidden in a big dictionary in the living room. The instructions and key had been tucked into the page with the definition for the word *safe*.

Riding a train from Landstuhl to Paris, two adult women discussed the logistics of not-marrying and the logistics of death and the wishes of a young first lieutenant who spends part of her week in the streets of Iraq, gathering intelligence for the U.S. Army during the third year of a long war.

Walking the streets of Paris, I saw the impact of the crowds on you. Instead of reveling in the Louvre and gawking at Notre Dame like normal tourists, I felt your sore feet. I felt your twitching. I grew to hate how you startled at each unexpected noise and movement. The war wounded you, my Sarah, in ways that doctors do not measure.

In a small jeweler's boutique, we picked matching gold rings. Mine fit me perfectly. You stopped at a gift shop to buy a length of stout, black ribbon. You tied your ring around your neck. Each evening as the sun set, you placed the ring on your own finger. You slept with it on, then removed it at dawn. As you dressed in your uniform that last day, you secured the ring on a section of 550 parachute cord. You then tied this permanently on your neck, with a loop too small to fall off, yet long enough to fall below the level of your t-shirt. There and yet out-of-sight.

The United States fights two wars in two countries with no end likely. Your time at home will be limited for years. When home, you will be assigned to a unit that will train for its next deployment. Every few years, you will be promoted and will be required to attend new schools.

I walk the fields, envisioning a section of lavender and a section of garlic, while acknowledging that I cannot have either. I cannot earn my money retreating to the top of a Vermont hill. I can write my articles here. I can study for exams here and take them in Springfield, Mass. My training and mentoring through my employer informs me that clients need lunches and dinner on my expense account. Clients need attention. Working from this hilltop while sending my messages over a satellite link will impair my ability to make money, to pay my own bills.

I take off my shoes and socks to walk on this soil with my bare feet, your way. The cool soil holds moisture and feels springy under my feet. The phrase, "I want to be here," repeats as a mantra over and over as I explore the yard and barn. I measure this world in the smallest of units: the blades of grass, the clovers, the sorrel.

The mantra, "I want to be here," ends with the arrival of the first mosquito.

17 | Food

SAM'S JOURNAL, JULY 2006

Brie,

We know I've ignored the old rules. Let's not inventory what I am not supposed to be doing. What I am supposed to be doing is: loving my favorite secret (you), surviving this tour, and doing my daily duty to Uncle. As a secret keeper and a harvester of secrets, I should not be journaling at all. I don't know where to go with my thoughts. I can't just hold them. I can't bury them. So, I write them. I am sorry you have to watch me and my spirit devolve. I should find a few four-leaf clovers and describe a rainbow and not an Iraqi sandstorm.

These weeks have been wicked. The workload exceeds any we've had this year. There is no routine. I plan a day for one mission, and by midnight have accomplished two more missions. And, not by choice.

I am tired. I am exhausted. I made a stupid mistake and didn't understand Brian's instructions last night at 0100. It has been so constant. Our team of fifteen soldiers is split and scattered. Five sent to another site. Several on mid-tour leave. Leaving us with three soldiers to deal with all the problems. Brian was traveling this week. One day, what few people were left were spread out at three sites. The Army, in its odd wisdom, has decided that radios are a risk. We have no communications while trying to work as one team on one problem. I am running and driving back and forth constantly through the only traffic jam, one caused by construction. When word comes to me that other problems are appearing, the major joins me to troubleshoot and fix those problems. Fourteen hours of running and moving in the sunlight without a break. The previous day included a Blackhawk ride then checking progress at the other site an hour away. The following day (yesterday) started at 0600 and ended, as I have noted, at 0100.

The dining hall is closed for repairs. I have gone now twenty-two hours on crackers, one muffin, and one serving of cereal. I have a headache, I am hungry, and I need a shower. There are a dozen Iraqi men outside my door with three cranes and four huge trucks removing blast walls and installing newer, taller, "better" blast walls. One can't sleep well with Iraqis yelling, the ground shaking, and cranes and chains swinging overhead. When I went to shower, there were male electricians in there.

On this Sunday morning, I can't eat, can't sleep, can't shower. I can find a muffin in my backpack and another bottle of water.

18 | Returning from the Sunset

BRIGHID, JULY 2006

I claim the dining room. It takes me a day to de-Aunt-ify the room, a bold decision to convert the formal dining room into an office for myself. Through the transitive property, I do love and respect Sam's aunts, "The Aunts," as we call them. Yes, I actually throw things away, although I keep the dozens of candle tapers. I peel the long rotten plastic wrapper. I toss silly paper beer coasters that the two ladies appeared to have collected during their travels. Maybe I should have kept them or found a place to sell them on an auction site. Ugh, I should have. I am clearing their history to make room for my own history. I assure you that they are still here, everywhere.

I've got a century's worth of research and documents: birth certificates, marriage certificates, pension records, and a growing stack of newspaper articles.

I have chased my Henry from New York to Springfield. Follow his trail from Massachusetts to Florida then to Cuba, which preceded his death at home in 1900, a death likely caused by a blood clot and injuries sustained in Cuba. At the national archives near D.C., I found Henry as a private enlisted in the regular Army assigned to the Department of the South, then to a squad in Chattanooga. With this effort, I found formal and written military orders for his unit.

The lieutenant colonel I met at the Massachusetts National Guard museum warned me that following a young private in public archives will prove difficult. And it has.

I thought these patterns with my government were new, but I guess not. Let's go use force to solve a problem we don't understand, get confused, get stuck, then find a way to withdraw. I am a bit young for memories of Vietnam, but Harry, the assistant chief of Trowbridge Rescue, is a veteran, and I think I have other relatives who were there. It does seem that my family was happy to sign up for any adventure, especially if it involved thumping people on the head.

In the years following my Henry's work on civil rights in the 1870s, the U.S. federal government withdrew. The Posse Comitatus Act was passed in 1878, closing the door on the U.S. military being used, domestically, for law enforcement. By this time, Henry had shipped west, and we had defunded the Freedmen's Bureau and gave up efforts to enforce the civil rights of new citizens. We'd arrest people for killing citizens and burning lands and stealing property, then watch them get set free.

As I read your journals and listen to your frustrations there in Iraq, I get the same sense. We jump in with some intension, lose track, face obstacles we didn't plan for, and then, in the face of criticism (right or wrong), we revise policy. 9/11 and Osama bin Laden were the reason for war. This Saudi man, linked with the Saudi ruling family, is hiding in Afghanistan, so let's attack Iraq because they have weapons of mass destruction? We declared the war over, saw the banner and a president standing in front of it. And yet, there you are, in Iraq, years later. We sent Private Henry McDonald to the south to protect the rights of Americans, then shipped him west of the Mississippi, giving tacit approval for local southern governments to steal, plunder, and lynch Americans.

Yay for the home team.

Anyway, there's Henry riding off into the sunset as cowboys do at the end of the movie. The lonely, forgotten hero (or lonely, forgotten band of heroes, whichever). Nearly all western movies take place between 1870 and 1901. We've created mythology and legends based on thirty years of history.

Henry landed in the west with a horse, a rifle, and a blue uniform.

His obit reads that he was "one of the guards for surveyors on the Union Pacific railroad," and in another passage, it states, "He was first stationed in the South during the reconstruction days and was frequently called into service to aid in quelling disturbances. He was also in service in the West and had heard the dreaded Indian yell." My research has confirmed this, yet the evidence fades as he travels west.

The bronze plaque that once hung in the Springfield City Guard armory read like this:

Navy - U. S. S. Hartford, 1865-1867
Army - Co C 2d U. S. Infantry 1869-1874
Militia - Co B 2d Regiment MVM 1876-1899
U. S. Volunteer - Co. B 2d Mass Infantry Spanish
American War 1898
Injured at San Juan Hill July 6, 1898
Died May 25, 1900

I can put check marks next to the early Army service, the militia service, and his time in Cuba. The items without check marks are his service on the U. S. S. Hartford and early adventures in Springfield, Massachusetts.

Given I am not returning to the archives for the U.S. Navy and the Hartford, I cheated by using *Wikipedia* and other online services. It clearly states that during the years in question, the Hartford was in the Pacific. The ship was built in Boston and named for Hartford, Connecticut, just a few miles south of Springfield Mass. It remains possible that seaman's apprentice Henry McDonald joined the ship in New York after repairs. The ship then sailed as the flagship of the Asiatic Squadron in the Pacific. In August 1868, she returned to New York and decommissioned. The dates basically align.

Whether the evidence exists or not, I'll take another stab at that in the years to come. It is a solid possibility that Henry, born and raised in New York, would have done this. His father was dirt poor, selling scrap metal from a pushcart on the streets of Manhattan. The youngest and least significant member of the crew may or may not be found in naval archives.

Henry established Springfield, Massachusetts as his home after his adventures in the south and west. *I should be able to find him,* I think.

I buy an online subscription to a newspaper archive and start searching. Within two days, I find over one hundred references to Henry. He clearly had an in at the *Springfield Republican*. They LOVED him. On July 7th, 1907, his home came up for sale. The notice in the paper read:

RESIDENCE
Of the late MAJ Henry McDonald

Park Avenue

A fine home, delightfully situated commanding beautiful view of River and Valley. Nearly new colonial house, 12 commodious rooms, every convenience, hardwood finish. A style and character about this property that will commend it at once to all in search of a high-class home for the price of the ordinary. Extra large lot.

Tel. 49-5 Edw. J. Murphy

When the Springfield City Guard, Company B of the MVM, presented Henry with the uniform of a lieutenant, the paper wrote about it on February 13th, 1880, the first mention of him in the paper. Seven years later, there are four articles in Chicago papers about Henry and the City Guard. In October 1887, someone hosted an international shooting competition. Apparently, the Prince of Wales attended.

Massachusetts Marksmen

The Massachusetts Volunteer Rifle Team, twenty men and officers arrived in camp yesterday morning. The members of the team are [...] This team won the naval and military championship of America at Creedmoor. They also won the interstate championship defeating New York and Pennsylvania. In the Hilton Trophy competition, they made the very best score ever made in this country or Europe with military rifles.

According to *Wikipedia*, Creedmoor was a seventy-acre rifle range that is now Queens Village, New York. The Hilton Trophy is still being awarded for competition marksmanship. The victors seem to be members of the National Guard or military reservist units.

In six days of reporting on the event, ignoring the issues of financial fraud on the part of the organizers, I see day after day that the Second Brigade Massachusetts dominated the competition as teams and individuals.

When promoted to captain in the city guard, the *Springfield Republican* stated that Henry won the state's officers' rifle competition in 1887. In this article, the editors state that, "for the last 13 months of his service [in the U.S. Army, he] was attached to Custer's famous 7th Cavalry." I really want to call bullshit on that, but if true, then maybe he really did make it to Yellowstone and fought battles against Native American tribes. Hard to feel pride for that, but I suppose that is the duty of a soldier. You'd know, huh? The good news is, the Battle of Little Bighorn happened two years after then-Sergeant Henry McDonald left the service of the regular Army.

In May,1891, when my Henry served Springfield as a deputy sheriff, he made the news again (given the sheer number of articles, I shouldn't be surprised). The headline reads "Another Prisoner Tries to Escape."

> The prisoner, Walker, managed to free the handcuffs from a fellow prisoner and "was practically free at the end of the big bus waiting on State Street. Walker stepped forward as if to enter the wagon, then with a sudden twist started across the street. He got on the sidewalk before the move was seen and would have probably trotted away at leisure had it not been for Deputy Sheriff McDonald, who was bringing up the rear of the procession. The officer drew his revolver and fired. The ball zipped just past the flying criminal and entered the fence just east of the Springfield House at the height of four feet; Walker thought it was time to run when another shot passed just in front of him and also embedded itself in the fence; Walker then broke into a wild gallop, when a third shot passed so close to the escaping horse thief's leg that he thought he was struck for sure. He crouched down in terror, although the bullet again struck the wooden fence just a few inches west of the town hall building. Deputy Sheriff McDonald and Miller were soon leading him back to captivity.

I think my guy was a funny blend of duty and showman; of substance and politics. A guy with the confidence not to shoot a runaway prisoner, but skilled enough to say, "Stop," rather loudly.

He's the guy that got his police officers on bicycles and installed telegraph devices around the city to coordinate police patrols. In closing my entry to you, my love, I want to tell you that I found a photo of the first ambulance in the City of Springfield, Massachusetts. It looks a bit too much like a horse-drawn hearse. But there it is, on a tree-lined street in the snow, with two Springfield police officers next to it. I had to show it to my friend Alex Flynn as soon as I found it.

Imagine that…110 years after Henry buys an ambulance for the police, I join the local rescue squad.

Hey, I boxed some of the aunts' stuff in the dining room and kitchen. It is dry in the attic. I hope that is okay.

Touching my ring as I sign off.

1-4-3.

19 | Oh Shit

SAM'S JOURNAL, AUGUST 2006

Brie, there are three documents open on my computer. I am still trying to follow the *Times* Rule. You'll figure it out, *ya Helw*. Two from CNN and my journal entries from February open. I re-read them both. There has been a steady linear progression from winter through spring to fall. The tone of my entries included awe and hope. The foci of my entries were about Israel and Iran. I even mentioned Hezbollah.

Events don't just happen. Events connect, ideas thread, binding the warp of phenomena, weaving a complex tapestry. Months ago, many hands spun the actions, movements, thoughts, and deaths of tomorrow. Arguably, years ago, hands were at work spinning these fibers. I can't argue that there is a master weaver at the treadle, no, I refute that. Yet, the story being revealed to us all can/must be fully visible. That vision ought to be understood by all.

I am not serving quietly here in the Middle East, alone or without a mission. I am a witness. I am your witness. I must witness. I wish to say: the vision is clear today. It was hinted at six months ago and the story will only grow deeper and more sanguine by the week.

It was six months ago that my general said, "Folks, the fuse is lit." Since then, we have lost Basra, Fallujah, and Baghdad. I don't mean that in a figurative way. I mean that during the course of the war, my comrades, the soldiers I am with every day, drove the streets of Baghdad in unarmored vehicles and shopped in stores. We've lost the streets. We've lost the people. We are losing control over the air with missiles and ground-to-air fire that is hitting our helicopters. A few months ago, a female British officer I know traveled in Basra alone in a non-tactical vehicle with a small side-arm and no armor. She would shop and go to restaurants. Today, it requires a team of heavily armed and armored soldiers to sprint from site to site.

Folks, there are open wars in half of the countries here. In fact, you can paint a checkerboard with red and black squares. The wars alternate their way across Southwest Asia and the Middle East. Honestly, start with Sri Lanka and move west. You can draw a line where it goes: war, no war, war, no war, war, no war. Sri Lanka, Nepal, Afghanistan, Iraq, Lebanon. But the countries in between are players in all neighboring wars. Iran has their hands in THREE wars. They are fighting in Afghanistan (their largest northern border). They are fighting in Iraq (their largest southern border). And they are funding, arming, training, and manning Hezbollah. Syria has fighters in Iraq and Lebanon. The U.S. and U.K. are involved in THREE wars as well. We are funding, arming, and training Israelis.

You never miss an excuse to open a map. Do you see what I see?

Now for today's headlines:

> LONDON, England (CNN)—The U.K.'s outgoing ambassador to Baghdad has warned government ministers that a civil war in Iraq is more likely than a successful transition to democracy, according to a news report.
>
> William Patey also predicted the division of Iraq along ethnic lines, in a confidential memo addressed to the Prime Minister, Foreign Secretary, Defense Secretary, and senior military leaders.
>
> Patey's warning was contained in his final diplomatic cable, leaked to the BBC, before leaving office last week, the BBC reported.
>
> "The prospect of a low intensity civil war and a de facto division of Iraq is probably more likely at this stage than a successful and substantial transition to a stable democracy," Patey wrote.
>
> "Even the lowered expectation of President Bush for Iraq—a government that can sustain itself, defend itself, and govern itself and is an ally in the war on terror—must remain in doubt." Patey also said that, although the situation was "not hopeless," he believed Iraq would remain "messy and difficult" for five to ten years.

TEHRAN, Iran (AP)—Iranian President Mahmoud Ahmadinejad said Thursday that the solution to the Middle East crisis was to destroy Israel, state media reported.

In a speech during an emergency meeting of Muslim leaders in Malaysia, Ahmadinejad also called for an immediate cease-fire to end the fighting between Israel and the Iranian-backed group, Hezbollah.

You don't need to be an analyst with the State Department, my Imzadi—don't think of applying, you'd hate it—but if you did join, you could help. We require smart people to think our way out of this situation.

For all practical (and legal) purposes, Iran has declared war on Israel. Not only that, but the Iranian president has also called on all Islamic countries to wage open war against Israel. There has been a long, open statement from leaders here to force the removal of the U.K. and the U.S. from Saudi soil and traditional homelands of Islam. There is a one-hundred-year-old Pan-Arabic movement. Once funded by the Nazis, and often resisted by the Brits. And by Americans. Please note that the leaders of the Islamic nations met this week in the world's largest Islamic state: Malaysia. They weren't in Rome with the Europeans and the U.S.

The violence and hostilities in this area are closer to the beginning than the end.

Keep this information in your mind as you read the news:

1) Iraq and Iran fought an eight-year war which resulted in the deaths of one million people.
2) Kurds in the north of Iraq were the victims of genocide under Saddam.
3) Turkey is violently afraid of an independent Kurdish state. They would enter a fight to subdue their own Kurds. Their fear is that the Kurds would rebel in Turkey to create a united Kurdistan.
4) Al Qaeda has struck at the Saudi royal family and has a stated aim to remove them from power

and, with them, remove the U.S. and U.K. from Saudi Arabia. The holy city of Mecca is located in Saudi Arabia.

5) There has been a Pan-Arabic movement for one hundred years. Remember my entry about the flags and how they are all derivatives from each other, using the same visual themes and colors?
6) The Islamic leaders met in Malaysia and there was no press coverage of the meetings.

Shall I be the first? Democracy isn't possible in this environment. Turkey, Iran, Syria, and Jordan do not want democracy. Syria and Iran want an Islamic republic. Turkey doesn't want the Kurds to have a strong voice. Democracies cannot be born in this environment. There is nothing that unifies the Iraqi populous and there are three nations on three borders working aggressively to divide the nation.

No banners, no protest, and no amount of yelling from the steps of the Capitol are going to bring peace to this place.

I do not have a solution. I see only destruction and war. With good luck, there will be no genocide, only wars. With bad luck, there will be genocide: Kurds, Jews, Christians. These wars are fused. These wars are one. They are united on the map. They are united by culture, by religion, by history. Study the map.

The land over which all of these wars are fought birthed the most beautiful carpets ever. At times, we have called them Oriental, at other times, Persian. We still do, don't we? We've never really called them Iraqi rugs or Iranian carpets. There is something here that people will fight over: the Fertile Crescent between the Tigris and Euphrates River, the home of major Islamic holy sites and mosques.

Are we fighting against a unified Arabic state that would be founded on ancient Islamic values and laws?

What would the impact of this Arabic state be on the world?

What would happen to Jerusalem and Israel on this map?

We must, absolutely must, understand why we are here.

We cannot view this as three wars, three dots on a map, three points of color in one tapestry.

This is but one. There is but one loom. The treadle only reveals color in a flash. We must see it all for what it is, for what it shall be, for what it could be. We must understand the risks, and all of the risks.

The decision to fight or not to fight belongs to each of you. I would venture to say that no greater decision will be made by our nation during the first half of the twenty-first century than the decisions made in this war. Look upon this map, this history, and these decisions. This is our map, this shall be our history, and these decisions shall be our decisions.

Value and trust doubt. One of the great differences between me and Captain Brian (beyond the more obvious age, background, lifestyle stuff) is that when Brian studies coincidences, he is more likely to see a force of will at work. Whereas I tend toward understanding on a smaller scale; for example, my understanding of coincidences is tied to my understanding of six-year-olds playing *futbol*. Everyone on the pitch runs to where the round black and white ball is. So often, the focus is the ball and not the pitch. Where Brian might see a conspiracy, I see ineptitude. Masterful manipulation and fantastic sleight of hand in his mind are but testimonies to the vanity and hubris of a few when evaluated in my brain. This difference between is my trust of doubt. In science, the rules that apply to the quanta world are entirely different than those that apply to the astrological, and neither apply perfectly to my nearly-Newtonian world.

20 | QRF

SAM'S JOURNAL, SEPTEMBER 2006

The Anatomy of a Quick-Reaction Mission

The team that we have here is a mixed lot. The major is on his fifth technical "specialty" in his officer career. And given that he is an O-4, he seems to retrain for each rank. In nearly eighteen years in the Army, he started as a private, like me. Now with two graduate degrees, he has changed jobs less than every three years. He has been a logistics guy, a supply guy, a missile guy. The jobs that follow each other have nothing to do with the previous one. His last combat mission had him in Afghanistan in October 2001, immediately after 9/11. He was in the first unit into Afghanistan. At that point, he was with a Special Forces' unit. And now, he is a military intelligence officer.

And Brian and I are as different as two folks can be in the same uniform.

Our new soldiers have been pulled from units through the division and told to become a single team. Most of the new kids feel more strongly attached to their original units than our unit. We have some good soldiers, soldiers who take a mission and roll. And we have soldiers who just don't work.

This isn't the Devil's Brigade, the Dirty Dozen, or such where the team is pulled from prisoners and misfits. This is just the reality of a worn, tired unit. In the Army where they tell people that they haven't lowered their standards, they now accept 42-year-olds to boot camp.

This is the classic Army story. Fates put people together. Then the missions come. They either learn to respond well, or they fail. Even when responding month after month, I am surprised to see the sense of camaraderie fail to coalesce for some of our individuals into the professional team it ought to be. I see the fissures. Brian may. I don't know if the others above us do.

Phase One: Notification

The story of notification in our field starts with vague reports of something wrong, somewhere. The division has large-format video monitors that are used to display the status of the battlefield in the Tactical Operations Center.

That's when I go. Most of the time, I lead the initial effort with a response force. During these months, the problems have varied. During our travel to the site, we guess about the scenario we are walking into. We'll parry ideas like toy swords. Let's start here...Let's start there...Let's start at the most logical problem. It is always a guess. Some guesses are just so very good. Typically, before we leave, we formulate a hypothesis. We call a platoon and give them a "warno," a warning order telling them to standby for an emergency callout. We grab our little go-team, our quick response force, and go.

Phase Two: Roll Out

From the initial investigation, the instructions go to the units that will be involved. This again is my specialty. Somehow, I do this crazy thing where I come up with several simultaneous plans. Then I execute on all of them with different teams.

"Hey, LT." That's me. The platoon sergeant comes to me on a fast walk. "Ma'am, I don't think we need...We'll be able to...about a half click from here."

Phase Three: The First Call In

"Brian, I have one soldier assigned to us from the 18th CSB and I have two soldiers assigned to me from the 440th SIG BN at Corps. I need..."

Phase Four: The Rhythm

Even with the options evaluated and a plan firmly developed and communicated, that plan is rarely the best of all possible options. Instead, it is constrained by resources, environment, equipment, time, and all sorts of issues that one may not have to deal with in The

World. But here, they are very real.

At the site, where mortars keep killing our comms, our soldiers have to work in 120 Fahrenheit (50 Celsius) heat while wearing thirty kilos of body armor and a Kevlar helmet.

Regardless of the situation, once we've started, the soldiers start joking and we discover a gentle rhythm. I put a plastic rod in a dirt hole, calling it the command post. While flowing with sweat, we wash our hands with bottles of sun-heated water and air dry them.

During some crazy hour of the night, we quit. Dehydrated, with a salt-stained jersey, filthy uniform pants, and a gritty face, I hit the shower, then sleep without a thought for the next day. We were once told we'd get the following day to recover from these emergencies. That doesn't mean much now. We all know that a knock can come to the door any day, any hour, regardless.

Final Phase: The Days After

Corps hears of our team's successes and our success rate. They decide they have found a functioning team. Now we get deployed by them as well. Fuck. We're barely holding it together.

Our lieutenant colonel calls me and Brian into his office. "Your Operation 84 was bold and successful." FUCK.

We don't want any more recognition. We've got enough paper Certificates of Appreciation to wrap holiday presents and enough coins from grateful commanders. The coins are cool. The stories can never be told.

21 | The Call

BRIGHID, SEPTEMBER 2006

"Is this Brighid Doran?" The voice sounds overtly formal.

"Yes." I hold my breath.

"My name is Ann Jackson. I am a member of the family support group for Lieutenant Musgrave's unit."

"Yes, Ma'am." I had recognized the Texas area code and her name appeared on the digital display. Facts pile on facts. My mouth is dry. My knuckles are turning white while I hold the 1980s-style trimline phone.

"I regret to inform you that Sarah Musgrave has been injured during combat operations. She is receiving the best possible medical care. She is alive."

"What happened?" But I am not confident that I actually finish that sentence.

"I don't know, yet. My husband in an officer in the same unit."

I slide to the floor, gripping the phone. The woman on the other end speaks in a trained and measured tone. She lets the silence go for a minute, during which the first tear wells on my lower lid and a lump develops in my throat.

"Where is she?"

"She is in a CASH in Baghdad. They will likely transport her to Balad, then on to Landstuhl."

"Landstuhl, Germany?" I ask stupidly, as if I don't know the place.

"Yes."

"Can I see her there?"

"Yes, of course you can."

"Is she safe? Is she well?" I mean, we all know the question I want to ask, right? I want to know if she will die. What the fuck do I do if she dies?

"She's been injured. She's had at least one surgery. My notes say that her leg is the worst injury."

She can hear my stuttered breathing.

"Take your time," she says professionally.

I sniffle.

"I'm alright. I made it through the 2003 deployment. I guess this is the call I have dreaded for nearly a year." I scream FUCK in my head. I breathe and sniffle again. I attempt to relax my hands.

"Time to get practical," I say. "What is your name? I missed it."

"My name is Ann Jackson. My husband is Darius Jackson. He is a military intelligence officer."

"Thank you, Ann. You have a difficult job. Sam is a military intelligence officer, too."

"Who is Sam?"

"Sam, that's our name for Sarah Ann Musgrave. Her initials."

"Nice. You've been friends a long time?"

"Yeah, we met in college."

"I am glad she has a friend like you." Ann is a kind person and likely ad-libbing between the lines of her script.

"Okay, so I need to get to Germany. We were there this summer for her mid-tour break." Shit, stop babbling. Don't offer information that the Army isn't asking for.

"We can help with that."

"Great. How soon do you think it will take the Army to transport her to Landstuhl?" I hear my own tone change. It is like hearing the tones drop for a 911 call in Trowbridge. I wipe tears with my left hand.

"I can't say. Typically, between one and five days. Depends on the care she needs."

"I've been to Ramstein and Landstuhl. I can't get past the gate without Sam escorting me."

"That's what we're here for."

"What should I do?"

"Gather the paperwork, your passport, cash, pack a small bag, and book a flight."

"I can do that."

"Good. You sound like a strong woman." At that, another lump appears in my still-dry throat. "I don't know about that."

I think about my autumn. My Vermont EMT exam is scheduled for October. I've got a boss who gets frustrated with my disappearing acts. I am allowed vacation and days off, but he hates it when I actually ask for them. He's one of these asses who says, "You can sleep when you are dead." He's the guy that told me, "I need to babysit tonight." But when I learned he meant minding his own children without his wife, I stuffed that boss in special box for assholes and misogynists.

I think Ann is telling me I need to be a strong woman. I ought to listen to her about that.

"Logistics. Okay, I pack. I get Sam's paperwork. She has it all stacked neatly in the safe. I am her medical power of attorney and I hold her power of attorney for legal and financial affairs. I have my passport. I know Landstuhl a little bit. So, I get a hotel, there. What's next?"

"At the gate, tell them the name and rank of Sarah. Tell them you are family."

"But I am not family." A flash of anger ripples down my body. I instantly feel my cheeks heat. Fuck, the Army won't let us be a family and now this woman is telling me to tell the Army that we are a family. I mean, if I say, "I am family" to the Army, then Sam's out. She's gone. Her career is over.

"But I am not family. I can't say that," I repeat. I crack.

"Listen, this is a lot for anyone to hear. Nobody wants this phone call. Family is a code word. Understand? The Army knows how to treat and process family, right?"

"But we're not family." I touch the ring on my finger. I should remember to tie it up on my neck, like Sam. I feel the need to protect her career, even if it means locking myself out of her hospital room.

"I understand. But you are her person. You are the one she designated. Does Sarah have living parents? Or siblings?"

"No. She was raised by her aunts and they died when she was in high school."

"You are it. You have her paperwork. I think I called you at her home in Vermont, right?"

"Yes, right. I am house sitting for her." Keep telling the lie.

"You are friends. And you are the person she designated on all her

Army forms. I can see that on my computer screen. Your name is the only name on these documents. That's our definition of *family*."

Clearly, this woman knows, huh? She is coaching me to tell a new lie.

"So, when you get to the gatehouse and when you get to the hospital, just tell them that you are family. Have your stack of documents and your passport at hand. You'll be amazed at how easily and quickly it goes. The Army wants to unite soldiers and their family quickly."

She is clearly telling me to trust her.

"When you get through, they will make you a pass, maybe even a short-term ID. From that point on, you'll be free to come and go from the base as you need."

"Okay. I get it." And maybe I do.

I lift myself from the floor. I have so much to do.

"Ann, can I get your contact information just in case?"

She gives me an email address and three phone numbers.

"And your husband's name?"

"Captain Darius Jackson."

"You've been amazing. I don't know how you do a job like yours."

"It's a privilege and duty."

"Well, I thank you."

My mind travels in a hundred directions at once. Alex Flynn, Trowbridge Rescue, my stupid job, my asshole boss, flights to Germany, drive to Boston, packing, finding my international electrical adapters, getting a mobile phone that works in Germany.

Family is definitely the right code word. I am the family of an injured soldier. It is a magic carpet ride, a special lane, the express train through chaos. Everyone in this special lane shares the same hurt, the same hopes, and the same fears. No shits are given about the legality or status of my connection. I hold the paperwork that matches the Army's paperwork. Sam's peppered my name in every blank field on every document. The key fits the escutcheon. The doors open. I am presented with my own paperwork, orders, and ID, of a sort.

I look exactly like every other family member in the hospital. We are all dazed and denying the tears that press outward. We nod at each other. Or we walk past each other without a glance. They are in their bubble of hell. I am in my bubble of hell and hope. Except, my Sam is still in Balad, Iraq, undergoing another surgery.

Nothing to do but wait.

"Shwartzer tee bitte." I order tea in German.

I think about opening my laptop at the café while I sip my black tea. Then I don't open the laptop. I sit in silence. I don't even fidget. I stare into nothing.

I walk to the base and to the hospital. It is slow, but I have no reason to rush. The hospital staff have my pre-paid mobile number and my hotel's number.

"Surgery went well. She is stable again," I hear from the medical staff.

I leave my hotel room and walk up the hill to the castle. I pat my pocket, confirming my phone is with me. Stupidly, I check every one hundred meters. I check my phone more frequently than I sip water, climbing that hill.

Technically, this is still day three since Ann's phone call, except I've been asleep when the phone by the bed rings. It is a sliver before midnight.

"Miss Doran?"

"Yes, sir."

"Lieutenant Sarah Musgrave is on a medevac flight from Iraq. They have already taken off. They are all safely in the air. We expect to have Lieutenant Musgrave in a room by dawn. You are welcome to come by anytime around breakfast, if you'd like."

"Thank you, sir."

"You're very welcome. She's in good hands. We'll take care of her and of you. *Que desconses.*"

"Gracias mil. Buenas noches."

"Buena." And the line goes dead.

I can breathe.

I have the desk call a cab for me. The taxi drops me at the gate.

At the gate, I show my passport and paperwork and my genuine fake ID. "Has the flight from Balad come in yet?"

"I don't know, Ma'am," answers the German soldier at the gate. "Are you expecting someone?"

"Yes, at the hospital."

"Would you like me to call transport?"

"Really? Yeah." Although I hadn't minded the walks in the past, the sense of eagerness demands that I move quickly.

At the threshold of Sam's door, I look in. The room is hospital-room dark. I can see the EKG monitor. I read her heart rate, her respiratory rate, her pulse-ox level. I evaluate the stand of IVs and their associated pumps. I look down at the bed. The bed sheets and blanket are artificially propped, or tented, over her leg. As bad as that can be, the machines confirm life.

Her face has cuts. Some Steri strips and a few stitches.

Her IV arm is wrapped with dressing on the upper arm. From my EMT training, I assume that they put the IV in her good arm. They tend not to put IVs below injuries, for obvious reasons. That means that her other arm is in worse shape.

I enter the room, closing the door behind me.

I drag the chair on the floor. My Sarah's eyes opens. Her amazing, brown eyes.

I pull the curtain around us, hiding us both from the window. I kiss her. And I cry.

I can't believe I am fucking crying. She's fine. She's alive. And I am crying.

The rest is just work.

—THE END—

During the final production of Captain Henry, the Next Generation Short Story Awards recognized I.M. Aiken's *Kahlil's Wall* as winner of the inspirational category for 2026. We include this bonus story because it provides more insight into the character of Sarah Ann Musgrave, during her fictional tour of Iraq with the U.S. Army.

If you enjoy this story, more can be found on I.M. Aiken's Substack in a series called *Trowbridge Dispatch*. The Next Generation Short Story Awards can be found at ShortStoryAwards.com.

Kahlil's Wall

BY I.M. AIKEN (SARAHBELLE SELIG, EDITOR)

I walk barefoot on soft New England soil. I wander my hills. I enjoy the moisture of the night's dew between my toes. I know I don't get any of Frost's words right, but he doesn't mind. I can swing birch trees, pause in a forest, and pick a path at the same time in my private version of his work.

I am in Tikrit, Iraq while writing this. My barefoot explorations of home arrive only after I close my eyes. We're a tiny military intelligence unit in a busy, confusing war. We're here on purpose. The bosses of bosses of bosses sent us here into the Sunni Triangle.

By now you know that I carry a copy of the Declaration of Independence and the Constitution with me. I keep the booklet tucked into my battle-rattle with two thousand calories of food, water, and the normal stuff one may need on a battlefield. My copy serves several purposes. Most obviously, the document serves as a talisman. I swore an oath to this document, why not make sure I know it? Two, it has secrets in it, literally. I underline passages such as, "We hold these truths to be self-evident, that all Men are created equal." This serves me as a password. I take the first letter of each word in a phrase, then make a mess: *Whtt2bse,all=*.

The other secret is the Longfellow poem that Brie stuck in there. That's a double secret, isn't it, given Brie found a way into my pocket a half-planet away. We all know why that's a problem, don't we? I am a female soldier on a battlefield with poetry in my pocket and in my head. That's the third purpose. This stapled document we got for free in Colonial Williamsburg transports me home.

Yes, I occasionally recite Frost's work in my head. Frost lived in towns that surround Trowbridge. Shaftsbury, Vermont lays to our west-northwest (from home, anyway) and Amherst, Massachusetts due south. Frost is buried forty-five minutes away. The most famous guys from here in Tikrit are Saddam Hussein, Chemical Ali (Saddam's cousin and architect of a massacre of Kurds), and— digging into history, now—Saladin. Saladin was a famous guy during the Crusades. A millennium of enemies were born in this town 140 kilometers northwest of Baghdad.

The soil here can be like concrete, and while it is green around the Tigris, we are surrounded by forest-free, trail-free, moisture-free desert, and heat like Vermont never sees. Regardless of my frequent deployments to Iraq since 2003, regardless of my rank, the longevity of the war means that I never really know who our enemy is today—whichever day today even is. I don't intend humor. The classic soldier's answer to enemy identification is the *ratta-tat-tat* of weapons. The guy firing at me is enemy. The guy next to me is friend. I am an intelligence officer and the best I can do is shrug.

My squad's mission is to rebuild an office, something that, in 2006, we now call a "fusion center." Today, my unit is the boss unit and the host to everyone else in the fusion center. The rest of the alphabet soup of other governmental and defense agencies will roll in with the confidence, volume, and kinetic energy of an army assault. My point is that they (the others) lack subtlety. I'll reserve that struggle for another day. I will play the role of Officer in Charge. These boys will expect me to play hostess and nursemaid. I'll save that fuss for another day, too.

My sergeant interviewed local laborers to help us. Ideally, we wanted Iraqis who support America and our vision for an Iraqi future. At the very least, men who will not kill us and maybe not pass on everything they see, hear, and read to the bad guys. Years of war against Iran. Then a war with America. Then peace? Then another war with America. Then an internal civil war while still at war with America. No one can draw a line on a map that describes "the front."

We started on Sunday, still a week or so before the Dog Star rises, the annual harbinger of summer's hottest days. We make plans for a pre-dawn start. We are not a "we." The army team involves members of two reserve units who have now met but never trained together. We've stitched ourselves into a platoon of fifteen with a platoon lieutenant and a platoon sergeant. We have four third-country nationals in dark blue jump suits and high-vis vests, a group of laborers universally identified as "TCN." These guys come from the poorest areas of southern Asia and live in shipping containers provided by an army contractor we would never call "Prime Prisons Incorporated." And we have our eight local Iraqi men. Languages on site: Arabic, English, Spanish, Bengali, Tamil, Urdu, and who knows what else.

Let's ignore day one. That's the day we learned we need six liters of cool water per worker. "Coolings," a universal word augmented by the gesture of an empty plastic water bottle run against the face. "Coolings," with an empty held out, is the phrase for, "I need water please." I allocated three uniformed soldiers to the continuous transport of water and ice.

We can ignore day two as well.

And day three.

Day four, we started at 0430 in the dark with many starting their travels as soon as *fajr* prayers have been said. Nobody stole wheelbarrows, or mortar. We had the coolings truck making circles. Whither it went, so followed a stream of ice melt and leakage from broken bottles, drawing a dark line in the fine Iraqi dust. On day four, we included mealtime at the local D-Fac (civilian: dining facility) into our routine. We entered the D-Fac as a single unit (Iraqi, TCN, and uniformed Americans), sat together, ate in thirty minutes, then returned to the site. Rise in the cool dark, work under lights, eat after sunup. Rest on a full belly, drink, pray, undertake necessary ablutions, then work again. Eat, drink, pray, work.

On day five, teams shared duties. South Asian guys mixed mortar and passed it to Iraqis. American soldiers laid bricks. The LT established an armory and appointed armorers to guard weapons. I served as boss, big boss.

We were building walls from Iraqi brick. Humans have been building walls for tens of thousands of years. There's no real trick to it. Follow a straight line on the ground and build vertically to the height of the ceiling. The Iraqi guys brought wooden boxes to serve as windows. One box is one window. Take the box out and lay the frame with glass. Done: window invented.

On day one, I wore my battle gear.

On day two, I dropped my battle gear and wore a pistol on my thigh and a combat helmet on my head.

On day five, I was in a baggy shirt with my head wrapped in an American-style blue bandana. Please recognize that "bandana" is a name and fabric we already borrowed from Hindi. I wore my pistol at the small of my back like a plain-clothed cop. I was the only worker on the wall with a weapon. From hand to hand, we passed bricks. From hand to hand, we passed ratty plywood boards loaded with mortar (yes, mortar boards, if you will).

Inshallah was the closest thing to vulgarity used by the team. Passing the liquid mortar was met with greetings of *inshallah* ("God willing") and variations of *shokran*, or, from others, a more Hindi version: *shukria*.

As boss, I tried to confirm everyone had coolings and found shade now and again. One of my buck sergeants, Sergeant Brown, took up that responsibility. She shepherded the crews. She got sunscreen on the lighter-skinned folks. She sent our folks off with soldiers to fetch water as a treat. A ride in an open truck, breeze, a few minutes without lifting bricks. You also get to pick up bags of ice and flats of cool, bottled water. Yes, a treat.

At the end of day five, with our new walls at various heights from thigh to shoulder, one of the Iraqi men came to me. He formally offered to shake my hand and greeted me in Arabic—"*As-salamu alaykum, rayiysat ʿunthaa*"—addressing me as boss. I returned the greeting in Arabic using his name, Kahlil. Then in English, he said, "You work hard. We see you work hard."

In Arabic, I said, "You work hard too. All of the team works hard."

"Good team."

He stepped out of his shoes and took his place as the mud-mixer. Yeah, we don't look a bit like an American worksite. The men mix mortar with their bare feet, kicking in Iraqi dust when too wet, adding water from a barrel when too dry. They take turns mixing mud. The careful eye would notice that the youngest get the afternoon mixing duties when the mixing water is as hot as the day. Through the afternoon, the guys use coolings to wash their feet after their turn as mixer.

Even the soldiers are calling bottled water coolings, using the same South Asian pronunciation. Please don't interpret that as mocking or disrespect. We are hearing the early stages of a patois being developed by a crew. Instructions flow in Arabic, Urdu, and awkward English. Our bricks are universally called "*toob*," Arabic for adobe.

The soldiers and Iraqis were the first to start trying jokes on each other, just little gags such as faking that a *toob* is falling or a little squirt of water. They tested each other for humor and boundaries. The third-country nationals were slower at playing along, but the bolder ones did.

At the close of day five, I paid every Iraqi in clean, crisp twenty-dollar bills. I also slipped the TCN guys a few twenties, too, some off-book accounting that will be disguised as material costs or additional labor costs.

On day six, Friday, we rested for the sabbath.

On Saturday, Kahlil greeted me again at the start of the day. We exchanged formalities in Arabic. Then in English, he said: "Good crew, hey boss?" And I answered, "Very good crew." This time, each crew member greeted me with a handshake and words. Then we stripped down to our work clothing. Soldiers secured their rifles in our makeshift armory and removed layers of armor and clothing. The mortar-mixers dropped their shoes. Towel-and fabric-wrapped heads and necks against the sweat and heat. We worked until breakfast. We also stopped to pray: *dhuhr* and *asr*. Sometimes *asr*, the afternoon prayer, fell after our workday completed.

We did not build a great wall. We built a functional set of walls on the foundation of a building brought down during any one of the recent wars. We weaved our work into the existing, standing walls. By the time we brought in an American construction contractor to hoist the roof with modern diesel equipment, our old-world magic had broken. These guys with their big yellow machines and flatbed trucks yelled in English and fussed about the lack of level and plumb on our new wall. Our brand new, thousand-year-old wall.

My job now involved presenting myself formally in uniform and with military authority. I could no longer be a laborer in my own crew, bossed by Iraqis and young sergeants. But we weren't done, not yet. I had one more duty before shifting focus back to the modern army.

I asked Kahlil for guidance on how to say thank you to the crew. I gave him three hundred dollars in American twenties. Before *dhuhr*, or midday prayers, we got word that a Toyota van was being held at the gate. The driver of the coolings truck drove me to the gate, where I met Fatima and her sister and Kahlil's brother as the male escort. They drove an entire feast including a live goat to our military gate.

While we worked, the ladies prepared the goat and bread and chopped vegetables and herbs. Then, prior to *asr* prayers, they laid out the meal on a wool carpet placed neatly in the shade of our new wall.

We placed our tools in our boxes. The prayers were offered, then the formalities of the meal started. Our host offered welcoming words in broken English and familiar Arabic phrases. Then I stood in my army tunic with rank showing. A proper cap replaced my do-rag. I offered my thanks to all: the cooks, the goat, and the heavens. I unfolded a page upon which I had printed a copy of Frost's "Mending Wall."

I read aloud and slowly. I let my voice crack. My efforts were answered with respectful silence.

I read Frost's words in English, then Arabic. At the line, "Stay where you are until our backs are turned!" most responded *Inshallah*, and all chuckled in shared memories of *toobs* that tumbled, crumbled, and slid from position.

"We wear our fingers rough while handling them." As understanding passed from person to person, fingers were held up and wiggled.

"In each hand, like an old-stone warrior armed." Yes, sorry Mister Frost, I adjusted the phrase. In response to this line, each person made a fist and showed strength.

"He says again, good walls make good friends." Again, I shifted the language for easier translation and better comprehension. Frost won't mind, will he? Could he have imagined that almost one hundred years after he scribbled a poem in New England, a military officer would be reading it during a war in Tikrit, Iraq as a gesture of peace?

I bowed my head in respect and touched my heart.

Shokran, shokran jazeelan.

They all answered with respectful silence. Then, as done in prayer, the men formally turned to their left and right to acknowledge and greet each neighbor.

"This poet, he writes of men, not walls," Kahlil said.

"I always thought so. He wrote of us, I believe. No?" I answered in English and Arabic.

"Yes, he wrote of us. Yes."

www.ingramcontent.com/pod-product-compliance
Lightning Source LLC
LaVergne TN
LVHW102334150826
845780LV00024B/145